WHEN THE HEATHER BLOOMS

WHEN THE HEATHER BLOOMS

Gwen Kirkwood

severn
House

This first world edition published 2008
in Great Britain and the USA by
SEVERN HOUSE PUBLISHERS LTD
9–15 High Street, Sutton, Surrey, England, SM1 1DF.

British Library Cataloguing in Publication Data

Kirkwood, Gwen
  When the heather blooms
  1. Country life - Scotland - Fiction 2. Scotland - Social
  life and customs - Fiction 3. Domestic fiction
  I. Title
  823.9'14[F]

ISBN-13: 978-0-7278-6644-8   (cased)

All Severn House titles are printed on acid-free paper.

Typeset by Palimpsest Book Production Ltd.,
Grangemouth, Stirlingshire, Scotland.
Printed and bound in Great Britain by
MPG Books Ltd., Bodmin, Cornwall.

Sweet land of the bay and wild-winding deeps
Where loveliness slumbers at even,
While far in the depth of the blue water sleeps
A calm little motionless heaven!
Thou land of the valley, the moor, and the hill,
Of the storm and the proud rolling wave–
Yes, thou art the land of fair liberty still,
And the land of my forefathers' grave!

Extract from *Caledonia* by James Hogg

One

A ndrew Pringle leaned his arm on the open window of the cattle lorry while he waited for the mail van to negotiate the last bend of Langmune's farm road.

'Morning, Kevin,' he called as the van drew abreast. 'Bringing us the usual bills, are you?'

'They're not all bills,' Kevin replied. 'There's one frae Edinburgh.' Over the roof of the van Andrew raised quizzical dark brows and his mouth twitched as he met the laughter in his wife's eyes. The country postmen knew everybody's business.

Victoria had helped Andrew load up three heifers for the November sale at Lockerbie market. She shared his pride in the stock they reared and she gave a good luck wave before she turned to take the bundle of letters from Kevin.

'That's a new lorry, eh?' he remarked.

'Yes, it's more convenient having our own transport now that we have a regular supply of heifers to sell. Andrew likes to get there early to get the cattle washed and brushed up ready for the ring.'

'Ye'll be hoping for a good trade today then?'

'We are.' Victoria smiled, eyeing the letters. 'We shall need it with this lot.' His gaze followed hers.

'The one frae Edinburgh is on top . . .' he offered, hoping she would open it. Victoria looked. She recognized the hand writing and her heartbeat quickened but she slid the letter to the bottom of the pile. Kevin sighed with disappointment. Victoria knew well enough what he wanted and she shook her head ruefully. At one time it had been Doris on the Darlonachie telephone exchange who knew everybody's affairs, but there was a central exchange in the town now.

In the kitchen she drew the letter from the bottom of the pile. In sixteen years she had not received more than a Christmas card from Catriona Sterling. Why did she have such a feeling of foreboding as she slit open the envelope? Memories of her twin brother, Mark, came flooding back. They had shared a bond which neither distance nor deceit could sever, and Catriona was the girl Mark had loved until war had claimed his life.

Victoria was happily married and blessed with three children but she knew there would always be an ache in her heart for her lost twin. His last request to her had been a plea that she should befriend his fiancée, Catriona MacNaught, but the girl had rejected Victoria's friendship. She had resented the bond the twins had shared, a bond that had been precious because they were orphans and had been separated for the first ten years of their lives.

Doctor Grantly and his wife, Anna, had treated Mark as a well-loved adopted nephew. They were proud when he qualified as a doctor and stricken with grief when he died fighting for his country. They had arranged a memorial service for him in Darlonachie village kirk. The whole village had attended but Catriona, his fiancée, was not there. Victoria had been stunned when she received a card the following Christmas with a brief message to say she had married Doctor Deane Sterling. She still remembered the shock and hurt she had felt. Last year, for the first time, Catriona had enclosed a snapshot of her three children – a tall, dark-haired boy and two younger fair-haired girls – but why was she writing a letter after all these years? Victoria scanned the single sheet. She gasped and read it again.

> *. . . I have no right to ask any favours from you but I have had time for contemplation and regret in recent months. I pray you can find it in your heart to forgive me and allow me to explain before it is too late.*
>
> *Rejecting your friendship was not my decision but it was weak and wrong of me to succumb to a stronger character than mine. I apologize with all my heart. I know Mark longed for us to be friends. I loved him dearly although we were so young. There are things I*

*need to explain. I need your help. If you cannot pardon
my conduct, for Mark's sake, I beg you to come to
Edinburgh and visit me here at the hospital. Time is
running out for me . . .*

As she folded the letter Victoria had an uncanny feeling that
Mark was standing beside her, urging her to go to Catriona
without delay. She wished Andrew had been at home, for
they shared all their problems and it would help to talk this
through with him. What could Catriona Sterling want of her?
Why was time running out? Catriona had been a year older
than herself and Mark but surely forty-one was too young
to be seriously ill? To die?

Victoria pushed her chair back. She would show Andrew
the letter as soon as he came home but in her heart she knew
she must go to Edinburgh. Her stomach fluttered as though
a thousand butterflies were trapped inside. She had never
travelled further than Dumfries or Carlisle, and even then
she had rarely been on her own. But she wouldn't be able
to put Catriona out of her mind until she had seen her, so
the sooner she went to Edinburgh the better. Mentally she
was already planning food to leave ready for Andrew and
Fraser. A smile lifted the corners of her mouth as she thought
of her eldest son. At eighteen he seemed to be permanently
ravenous, especially since he had started working on the
farm. It was a blessing the rationing had ended at last. Even
ten-year-old Lachie had a healthy appetite and could eat
almost as much as his father. First she must find out the
times of the trains from Lockerbie to Edinburgh and back
again. If she caught an early train she could ask Libby to
give her a lift to the station on her way to work.

Libby was the eldest of her three children. Two months
ago, on a beautiful day at the end of September, she and
Billy Lennox had been married in Darlonachie village kirk.
The two of them were happy, settling in at Darlonachie Home
Farm, less than a mile away down the glen from Langmune.
Libby was in charge of the laboratories at the local creamery.
Since the war, many married women had carried on working.
Libby seemed determined to prove she could be independent
and have a successful career, even though it meant being

away from Billy all day. Victoria had never spent a whole day away from Andrew and he didn't approve of Libby working away from the farm now she was married. There was tension between the two of them over this issue.

'Give them time,' Victoria had soothed. 'They're young to be married. Libby will give up working when the babies come along.'

'We were just as young when we married. It's not normal. I couldn't wait until midday to see you.' Victoria stood in the middle of the kitchen, remembering how he had nuzzled the softness of her neck and held her close, loving her with as much passion as if they were newly married themselves. She hoped with all her heart that their daughter would find as much happiness in her marriage as she and Andrew had done. The years had flown by. They loved each other as passionately as ever and she didn't feel old enough to have a married daughter.

Victoria brought her mind back to her proposed journey with an effort, wishing she didn't need to go, but she recalled Mark's earnest face and the promise she had made. Her thoughts returned to Catriona's letter, wishing she had been given more details. She didn't even know where to find the hospital. It was a relief when Andrew arrived home from the market late in the afternoon, looking pleased with himself.

'We got champion and top price for the Jenny heifer,' he announced with a wide grin, 'and the other two sold well.'

'I'm glad,' Victoria said, but Andrew sensed there was something on her mind. He had known her all her life and had always been sensitive to her slightest mood.

'What's wrong, Victoria?' She gave him the letter. He frowned as he read it.

'You feel you ought to go, I suppose. I'll come with you.'

'I thought that's what you would say.' Victoria smiled. 'But I think I should go alone. It sounds as though Catriona wants to talk. What do you think she means by "time is running out"?'

'I hope I'm wrong, but it sounds as though she is dying. I don't want you getting lost roaming around the city. Promise you'll take a taxi from the station, Victoria. Have you enough cash?'

'I'll dip into the egg money. You may need to draw from the bank to pay some of the wages at the weekend though.'

'Take plenty of money with you.'

'Dearest Andrew, don't worry about me. I don't want to go but I shall feel better when I hear what's troubling Catriona.'

'Guilty conscience, I should think,' Andrew said, 'considering the way she treated everyone after Mark died. She's lucky you're so forgiving.'

'I promised Mark, and her letter sounds desperate, don't you think?'

'Yes, I'm afraid so, though we could do without more bad news.'

'I know.' Victoria's thoughts moved to Joe and Polly Pringle, Andrew's parents, the kindest couple she had ever known. 'We have had enough sadness in the short time since Libby's wedding. It was such a happy day. Your father seemed to enjoy it as much as anyone.'

'I'm sure he did, Vicky dear,' Andrew sighed. 'At least it was a peaceful way to go. He just went to sleep that night as usual, Ma said.'

'Your mother has been very brave,' Victoria said. 'You know I wouldn't mind a bit if she decides to come and live here with us.'

'I know that, and so does Mother. She's always thought of you as her daughter, but for now she's clinging to her independence. We must let her decide.'

Victoria nodded. Polly and Joe Pringle had given her a home when she was thirteen years old, after the death of her great-grandmother. She had always loved them. They were the nearest she had to parents of her own. Her thoughts moved to the Grantlys. 'I wonder if I shall be able to tell Mrs Grantly I have seen Catriona before she moves away?'

'It depends what Catriona has to say,' Andrew cautioned, 'especially now Mrs Grantly is a widow and on her own. Catriona knew how much Doctor Grantly did for Mark and how they loved him, but she didn't consider them either, after he died. I agree you should go to Edinburgh, but only because I know your conscience would never be easy otherwise, especially if it does turn out that she is dying.'

'Yes.' Victoria shivered. 'I think that's what she means.'

'It will be a stressful day. Are you sure you want to go alone, Vicky?'

'I think I should.' She hugged him.

As soon as she heard Andrew creeping down the stairs for the milking the next morning, Victoria was wide awake. She was up and dressed in her best Hebe Sports grey suit and a crisp white blouse long before she needed to be. Her hat and gloves and bag lay on the bed and her shoes were polished and waiting for her to step into them. She made herself a packet of sandwiches. She paced the kitchen, went twice to the bathroom when she didn't need to, sat down and stood up, then called Lachie to get ready for school far too early.

It was a relief when Libby drew up in her little blue car and gave a toot-toot on the horn, more for her father's benefit than to let her mother know she had arrived. Victoria was out of the house and into the car almost before Andrew could get out of the byre to bid her goodbye.

'See her on to the train, Libby,' he instructed. 'Remember, you must take a taxi from the station, Victoria,' he called as he stood watching them disappear down the farm track.

Once she arrived in Edinburgh, the taxi driver seemed to sense Victoria's nervousness as she showed him the address of the hospice. He consulted with one of the other drivers on the best route to take. It seemed a long way to Victoria, perched on the edge of her seat, clutching the magazine and the packet of fruit she had purchased for Catriona. At last the taxi turned in between two large red-brick pillars on to a half moon drive, and drew to a halt before the wide double doors.

'Do you want me to wait, ma'am?' the taxi driver asked.

'No, thank you,' Victoria said, and told him what time she had to be back at the station that afternoon.

'I'll be here to get you in good time,' the man promised. 'If you're sure you want to stay so long?' His mate had said patients at this hospice were usually too ill for long visits and rarely came out alive.

'I've come a long way.'

'I'll give you a card. Ask a nurse to telephone and one of us will collect you.'

'Th-thank you, you're very kind,' Victoria murmured. Her stomach rumbled with nerves.

Once inside Victoria was directed to the second floor where she was asked to wait in a small room.

'Doctor Sterling left instructions that his wife is not to be pestered with visitors,' the nurse informed her. Victoria stared in dismay. 'She does seem brighter today and her son cycles over to see her before he goes home from school and she is always happy to see him. I'll ask her. What name shall I say?'

Victoria told her, and moments later the nurse returned with a beaming smile.

'I've never seen Mrs Sterling so eager to see anyone,' she declared, and led Victoria along a corridor to a single room. Victoria stood in silence for a few seconds and hoped she had not gaped with her mouth open. She barely recognized Catriona, who now looked like an aged skeleton of the girl Victoria once knew. Her skin looked greenish-yellow and it was drawn over the bones of her face, making her eyes seem enormous in their sockets, and her teeth too big for her small face.

'Victoria,' she whispered. 'Oh, Victoria. How can I thank you for coming . . . ?' Her eyes swam with tears. The sight of them cleansed Victoria's heart of grievances.

'I'll leave you with your visitor for ten minutes, shall I, Mrs Sterling?' the nurse asked.

'This is one visitor I would like to keep as long as she is able to stay, Nurse Kerr,' Catriona said. 'Please tell Sister Wilson we don't want to be disturbed, will you?'

'Well! That's a change!' Sister said when the nurse repeated Catriona's words. 'Doctor Sterling gave instructions. Who is she, Nurse?'

'Her name's Mrs Pringle; she must be a relation because she's just like the Sterlings' son.'

'Is she?' Curiosity got the better of Sister Wilson. As soon as the nurse had disappeared she went to peer in the small glass viewing panel. Victoria had taken off her jacket and drawn her chair up close to Catriona's bed. Sister saw her patient wipe away tears. There would be hell to pay from Doctor Sterling if she got upset. She glanced at her watch. He would be taking surgery but it wouldn't do any harm to let him know his wife had a visitor.

'I don't know where to begin,' Catriona said to Victoria. 'I wouldn't have blamed you for not coming after the way I have behaved. Deane, that's my husband, he thought it would be better if I severed all contact with Mark's family. He believed it would help me f-forget. He wanted me to put the p-past behind me. B-but there's some things you c-can n-never forget. I've had plenty of time to think and I know I should have followed my own instincts.'

'I see.' Victoria nodded. 'I suppose your husband didn't want you to be reminded of . . . of Mark.'

'It wasn't only that. Oh, Victoria, I must start at the beginning. Do you remember how Mark was adamant that he wouldn't get married until he could support a wife, even though my father wanted to help? Then when the war came he said he would never leave any woman as his mother – and yours – had been left when your father went to fight in the Great War and never returned.'

'I think the circumstances were rather different . . .'

'Not to Mark, they weren't. But I loved him so much, Victoria.' Catriona's eyes filled with tears again. 'I think I had a sixth sense that he would not come back. I-I couldn't bear the thought of never knowing what it was like to belong to him completely. You understand? S-so I arranged for us to be on our own together on his last might. My father was on duty at the local hospital. I taunted Mark, telling him he didn't love me or he would prove it, physically. I . . . I behaved like a . . . a whore, I suppose.'

'Oh no, Catriona, I'm sure that's not true.'

'I knew Mark loved me as I loved him, and in the end he gave in. I shall never, never regret that night, Victoria. I didn't care about a wedding ring then. All I wanted was to be with Mark, to be a part of him.'

'I can understand that,' Victoria said, knowing she would have felt the same with Andrew.

'Can you? Y-you don't despise me for what I did?'

'No. I know Mark loved you. I think you must have given him the happiest of memories to carry in his heart.'

'That's what he said himself!' Catriona exclaimed. 'It's how I felt too. As long as I live I shall never forget that one night we spent together.' Her eyes were brilliant with memories. Then the shadows returned. 'The next morning Mark was full of concern. He said he could never regret what we had done but as soon as he could get leave we must be married...' Her voice grew husky and her eyes took on a faraway look. 'There was all that business with Dunkirk... Y-you know the rest,' she said, her throat choked with tears.

'Yes,' Victoria said. 'Mark died with so many others. I'd had a feeling he would not return but it was still a dreadful shock when Doctor Grantly came to tell me.' She took Catriona's limp hand in hers. 'It must have been worse for you.'

'Doctor Grantly telephoned my father to ask him to break the news of Mark's death.' Catriona nodded. 'I fainted. I'd never fainted in my life.' She drew her free hand across her brow. 'Deane was in the next room. My father panicked and called him in. He—'

The door of the little room was thrust open suddenly. Both women stared in surprise.

'Deane! What are you doing here? Shouldn't you be taking surgery this morning?' Victoria met the cold blue gaze of the man who towered over them. He had a thatch of thick hair which had once been fair and was now almost steel grey.

'I must ask you to leave at once. You are upsetting my wife.'

'B-but, Deane, this is...'

'I know who she is. She is the image of... of Mark.' His words were clipped. He stared at Victoria. 'I know what is best for my wife. I don't know how you found her or why you came, but I'm telling you it is time to leave.'

'No!' Catriona's hand tightened on Victoria's fingers as she would have risen from her chair. 'I asked Victoria to come, Deane. I needed to talk with her.'

'You have talked with her. It's time for you to rest, my dear.' The endearment held no warmth, Victoria thought.

'I shall soon be at rest for ever,' Catriona reminded him. 'Victoria and I still have things to discuss.'

Victoria was conscious of the sister hovering in the doorway. 'Catriona, I will leave you with your husband for a little while,' she said, 'but I will come back before I leave. I promise.' She stood up and faced Doctor Deane Sterling. She knew in that instant that she did not like him. She guessed he was a man used to having his own way. 'Doctor Sterling, I have travelled a long way to see Catriona today. Since you interrupted our conversation I shall return when you have gone. Is that what you wish me to do, Catriona?'

'Yes, oh yes.' There was desperation in her eyes.

'Then I shall return in about ten minutes.' Catriona nodded and gave a wan smile.

As Victoria closed the door behind her she heard Deane Sterling say, 'You haven't mentioned the boy, I trust?'

What boy? Victoria wondered. It didn't sound as though Doctor Sterling was referring to their son, so who did he mean?

Two

The sister seemed reluctant to leave Catriona's room but Victoria closed the door behind them and asked, 'Where could I get a cup of tea, please?'

'You should do as Doctor Sterling says and leave the hospital.'

'I will deal with this, Sister.' Another woman was bustling along the corridor. 'I believe you are off duty now.'

'Oh, Matron, I didn't know you were up here.' Sister Wilson was flustered.

'So I've gathered. It was not your place to inform Doctor Sterling that his wife had a visitor, especially one she has been anxious to see.'

'But she was upset and he . . .'

'We shall speak about this tomorrow. You may go now.' She waited until the other woman was descending the flight of stairs, then she turned to Victoria with a smile.

'Come with me, my dear. I believe you are from Dumfriesshire?'

'Yes, my name is Victoria Pringle. I have no wish to upset Mrs Sterling but she wrote to me, asking me to visit.'

'I know, and I am pleased you have come. I'm sure you realize Catriona is very ill but I think your visit may bring her peace of mind. I was a sister in the hospital where she trained. We lost touch for many years but we have had several conversations while she has been in our care. I know how much she needed to talk with you . . . Nurse,' she called. One of the younger nurses appeared from a room further along the corridor. 'Show Mrs Pringle where she can wash her hands, then take her into my sitting room, please. Bring a tray of tea then go down to the canteen and see if you can get some sandwiches.'

'Oh, please, don't bother. I brought a packet of sandwiches with me but I would be very grateful for some tea.' Victoria smiled at them. Matron nodded her head and returned her smile.

'I met your brother when he was a young doctor. Your smile reminded me of him. I trained with a nurse who moved to Dumfriesshire. She married a doctor. Anna Grantly is her married name.'

'You knew Mrs Grantly? How strange. The Grantlys were wonderful to Mark, my brother. We all miss Doctor Grantly, and we shall miss his wife too when she moves away.'

'Anna is a widow now?'

'Yes, she is moving to live nearer her married daughter.'

'I see. If you will excuse me I will deal with Doctor Sterling while you enjoy a cup of tea. I shall come and tell you when Catriona is ready to see you.'

'Thank you.' Victoria nodded and followed the nurse.

Deane Sterling was reluctant to leave his wife's room but he had duties of his own and Matron was firm in her insistence that Catriona was her patient.

'You look exhausted, my dear,' Matron said when they were alone. 'Do you wish me to send Mrs Pringle away for today?'

'Oh no! We were getting on so well when Deane interrupted.' She sighed and rubbed her brow. 'He tires me so. I know he means well, but he is so . . . so . . .'

'Dictatorial,' Matron supplied with a wry smile.

'Yes, that's it.'

'Have you told him I know about your son?'

'No, and he will never forgive me if I tell Victoria, but I owe it to her and to Peter. She is kind and sensible and she loved Mark. I wish she could have met Peter but she has booked a taxi to take her back to the station. He will still be in school when she leaves.'

'I could telephone the school and ask the headmaster if Peter can be allowed out an hour earlier. I know Doctor Sterling doesn't agree but I'm sure it would be better if his teachers understood you are gravely ill, my dear.'

'Could you do that?' Catriona asked. 'Do you think they would agree? I don't want Peter to think I am worse though . . .'

'Just leave it to me, Catriona. I'll see what I can do. Now I will ask the staff nurse to set up another drip before I bring Mrs Pringle back in to see you.'

'You're so understanding.' Catriona sighed.

'That's what friends are for, and we all need friends at a time like this.'

A little while later Matron led Victoria back to Catriona's room. 'You will not be disturbed again,' she said. 'Ring the bell if you need anything.'

'Where were we?' Catriona murmured. 'It was too bad of Deane to interrupt like that, and Sister Wilson is an interfering busybody.'

'You were telling me about your father breaking the news of Mark's death, and how you fainted,' Victoria prompted.

'Yes I was. Did I say my father called Deane in? No, I didn't finish that bit.' She grimaced. 'Deane guessed what was wrong with me but he didn't mention it to my father.' Her tone was bitter as she added, 'He saw his chance and he seized it.'

'What do you mean, Catriona?' Victoria was puzzled.

'Later Deane told me he had wanted to marry me from the first time he came to our house. I was just starting my nursing training and he was ten years older than me so he felt he had to wait. He hadn't bargained for me falling in love with Mark, but when he saw us together he knew. Then, when my father told him Mark had been killed in action he . . . he persuaded me that it would be better if we married as soon as possible, "in the circumstances". You see, he realized I had fainted because I was expecting Mark's child and—'

Victoria gasped aloud. 'You were having Mark's baby?'

'Yes. I didn't care about not being married or the baby or anything else. Mark was dead and I wanted to die too.'

'I can understand that,' Victoria murmured and clasped Catriona's hand.

'I should have known you would.' Catriona's voice shook. 'I should have come to you. Deane took charge of everything. He reckoned I owed it to my father to avoid gossip. The following months were a nightmare. They're still a blur.' She shuddered. 'Deane said if we were married straight away

people would think the baby was his, even if it was premature.' She gave a harsh laugh. 'Later I realized he didn't
care about my father's patients and their gossip, or my
feelings. He wanted to make me his wife but I . . . I couldn't.
Even after Peter was born I couldn't bear Deane to touch
me. It . . . it was like a betrayal to Mark. That's the way I
felt. I think I wavered on the edge of a breakdown for the
first two years but having Mark's son to love kept me sane.
I admit Deane was patient then. Peter was about three years
old before . . . before it was a proper marriage. Deane knew
I didn't love him. I told him from the beginning I could
never love anyone as I loved Mark. That's why he didn't
want me to keep in touch with you, or with the Grantlys.
He wanted me to put the past behind us.'

'Oh, Catriona.' Victoria's voice shook. 'If only we had
known. So . . . your son? He is not your husband's child?'

'Peter? Oh no, he's not Deane's son. Mark always said if
he ever had a son he would call him Peter after Doctor
Grantly because he had been like a father to him. I had my
way over that. I christened him Peter Mark, but Sterling is
the surname on his birth certificate. Deane did treat him as
his own son at first, but when he had a child of his own
there was a subtle change. It was more noticeable when we
had another daughter. I think Deane had hoped for a boy.'

'I see,' Victoria said. 'How do they get on now, Peter and
your husband?' Catriona was silent for so long Victoria
thought she was not going to answer. She gnawed at her
lower lip.

'We all thought Peter would be a doctor,' Catriona burst
out. 'I was as much to blame as anyone. My father was a
doctor; Mark was a doctor, and so is Deane. I had been a
nurse. I loved it. It never occurred to me that Peter wouldn't
want the same sort of profession.'

'He must be, what? Sixteen years old? Surely he's too
young to know what he wants?' Victoria said.

'He's adamant that he will not be a doctor. He was doing
well at school but when Deane started talking about where
he should go to university he announced that he didn't want
to study medicine. He says he intends to leave school at
the end of the summer term. He and Deane argue all the

time now . . .' Catriona's eyes filled with tears and she
reached for a tissue. 'He's so unhappy,' she sobbed. 'I-I
can't bear it. He knows I'm dying. Who will stick up for
him then? I have tried to reason with Deane. If a man
doesn't want to be a doctor, is it wise to make him? If his
heart is not in it how could he be a good doctor? Deane
says he'll make him see sense. He's determined to make
him a doctor. He says he bears his name and he should be
proud of it.'

'What does Peter want to do?' Victoria's voice was troubled.

'He thinks he would like to live in the country. He always
wanted pets and Deane would never agree to have animals
in the house. Yet Peter wants to work with animals. Deane
says it's just romantic nonsense. He gets so furious, and then
Peter becomes stubborn; he takes off on his bicycle for the
whole day on Saturdays and during the holidays.'

'I see.' Victoria was thinking of her own dreams of making
Libby have a career as a teacher. She had been disappointed
when she had insisted on going to agricultural college instead,
but Libby had done well and she enjoyed her work, and her
training would be useful. 'We don't always know what is best
for them, even though they are our children,' she said to
Catriona. She told her about Libby. Then it dawned on her.
'Libby and Peter are cousins! And Fraser and Lachie . . .'

'Yes, I know.' Catriona said.

'Perhaps a love of the countryside is in their blood. My
father, Mark's father, he was a countryman, before he went
away to war. I love the countryside. I'd hate to live in a city.'

'Just as I would have hated to live in the country.' Catriona
smiled.

'Perhaps Peter could come down to stay with us during
the holidays? It might help him decide whether he really
likes the country or if it's just a dream. He may decide he
wants to be a doctor after all.'

'Ye-es,' Catriona said cautiously. 'Maybe Deane would agree
to him coming to stay with you if he thought it would rid
him of his romantic ideas. I know he will grieve when I'm
gone. I would like to think he had someone of his own to
care about him. That's why I needed to talk to you, Victoria.
I know it is a lot to ask, but if you would write to him

sometimes, remind him he does have an aunt and cousins, perhaps?'

'Of course – and I'm sure if he would like to—' Victoria broke off as the door opened and a dark-haired boy peeped into the room, a smile lighting his face as his eyes met Catriona's. He came right in then. Victoria stared at him. He was a slighter version of Fraser, her son. She looked again and saw he was gazing at her, his brown eyes wide and questioning.

'This is your Aunt Victoria, Peter,' Catriona said. 'Your father's twin sister.'

'My real father.' It was not a question. He came to her and held out a hand. 'Aunt Victoria,' he repeated, savouring the name. His smile grew wider. 'I am truly glad to meet you.' Victoria stood up and, before she had time to consider, she enveloped him in a warm embrace. Her eyes shone with tears as she met Catriona's gaze over his shoulder. 'You're so like my own son, Fraser, and so very like Mark was when he was a boy.'

'Am I?' he asked eagerly.

'You are. You must come down to Dumfriesshire and meet your cousins.' Victoria watched as the light died from his thin face. His gaze moved to his mother.

'I am sure it can be arranged, Peter,' she assured him. 'It will soon be Christmas and I would like you to spend this holiday at home, but perhaps you could go to visit during your Easter holidays?'

'You think he would agree?' he asked.

'Victoria has suggested a way of putting it to him. There is something else before you go to catch your train, Victoria. Mark took out a life insurance policy before he went off to war. He had named me as his beneficiary. I hope you don't mind? You were his next of kin, after all.'

'Of course I don't mind. You were the one he loved and you were his wife in every way that counts.'

'Thank you for that,' Catriona said and reached for her hand. 'I put the money in a trust account. It's for Peter, but when I'm not here Deane will have control. I had expected Peter would need it for his education. If I can I would like to change it into your name. It is not a huge sum but you would understand if Peter needed it for something worthwhile.'

'He may still need it for his education even if he's not a doctor,' Victoria said. She gave Peter a teasing smile. 'Even farmers need some education these days, you know, so be sure and do as well as you can while you are at school. It will not be wasted. My daughter and her husband both went to an agricultural college. Now, it's time I went if I am to catch the train home.'

'But you will not mind if I contact my solicitor and . . . and explain?'

'I wouldn't want to come between Peter and Deane,' Victoria said, 'but I promise I shall do my best to see that Peter is happy in whatever he chooses to do.' She bent and kissed Catriona's pale cheek. She saw her chin tremble and knew she was holding on to her tears with an effort. 'Come and show me the way out, will you, Peter? Please?' She knew Catriona needed time to regain control. It also gave her an opportunity to write down her address and telephone number. She had a feeling Peter was going to need a friend in the weeks and months ahead. She hoped Andrew would help her give Mark's son whatever support he might need.

Victoria felt drained and her head was thumping by the time the train drew into Lockerbie that November evening. She knew it was the strain of travelling. She was not familiar with railway stations and had been terrified of getting on the wrong train at Edinburgh and ending up in some far-flung place she had never heard of. Meeting Catriona after so long, and then to find her so ill, had been distressing. Then there was the discovery of a nephew she had known nothing about. She was anxious about his future with Deane Sterling. Officially Peter was the doctor's son, so he would have authority over him when his mother died. Victoria's thoughts were in turmoil and she almost fell into Andrew's arms when she got off the train at Lockerbie.

The November days were short and cold and a damp mist had swirled in as darkness fell. All Victoria craved was a hot cup of tea and an early night. It was a relief to tumble into bed and snuggle into Andrew's familiar embrace. On the way home from the station she had given him a sketchy report of the day's events. Now she answered his questions about Peter and about Doctor Deane Sterling. His arms tightened.

'Don't worry, Vicky. If the laddie has half the character of you and Mark he will be a survivor. His life could never be as hard as yours was.'

'No, but I had your mother and father and I knew they loved me and wanted me. I'm almost certain Deane Sterling doesn't love Peter, and I'm not even sure he will want him unless he agrees to become a doctor. He expects to be in control.'

'Well we know it's not possible to control a youngster who has the courage to make his – or her – own decisions. We'll invite Peter to stay with us at Easter. He will get to know us, and our way of life. It will give him new horizons and time and space to think. If he wants to return here during the summer holidays we shall make him welcome. We must take one step at a time.'

'Oh, Andrew, it is a relief to know you feel like that about Mark's son.'

'It's no different to the way you help my brothers. Willie and Josh have always come to you for help when they need it. Remember how Willie and Mary were filled with despair when Mimi had polio. You and Libby helped them face up to things. Wee Mimi may have a limp for life but at least she's alive and, thanks to yours and Libby's help and Doctor Ritchie's exercises, she can almost manage without her calliper now. She's a happy wee soul these days but she has real grit. Peter will have different needs but we'll help him if we can.'

'Mimi is blessed with such a sunny smile no one could help but love her and want to help,' Victoria said. 'You may not find Peter so easy to love if he is beset with teenage moods and the grief of losing his mother. They seem very close.'

'So long as I have you,' Andrew whispered against the soft hollow of her neck, 'I can deal with anything. I don't know how families coped during the war when they were separated for months, without news. Even just for a day the house didn't seem like home without you.'

'And I only went to Edinburgh, but it seemed a nerve-racking experience to me. Imagine how George must have felt being sent to France when he'd never been away from home before.' She shuddered.

Andrew drew her closer. He knew the surest way to set aside the day's anxieties was to love her until she thought of nothing else. Besides, he had missed her as though she'd been gone for a week. It made him realize how rarely they were apart. The mere thought of being without her awakened an overwhelming tenderness and he loved her with a passion that carried them into realms of ecstasy.

Lying awake afterwards with Victoria curled against him, so warm and soft, Andrew smiled to himself. He suspected Libby and Fraser considered their parents were far too old for making love, especially with such fervour. He was forty-four and Victoria was forty, which was just as well because he had been less careful than usual. There had to be some compensation to getting old – not that he ever felt old when he held Victoria in his arms, but at least they wouldn't now be presented with the surprise they'd had when Lachie was born ten years ago. Fraser had been eight and Libby ten and they had thought their family was complete. Fortunately there were only a few months between Lachie and his cousin, Mimi, who lived at High Bowie Farm at the head of the glen and the two had always been great companions.

At Christmas Victoria received a card with the usual greeting, 'from Catriona and family', but it was sixteen-year-old Peter who had written it. He had added a message.

> 'Matron says I must tell you Mother has found peace since your visit, but we must accept that she cannot be with us much longer.'

Two days into 1958, Catriona Sterling died. Again it was Peter who wrote to tell her, and he included the time and place for the funeral.

'That's the day after tomorrow,' Victoria said in consternation. 'I must go, for Peter's sake.'

'I agree.' Andrew nodded. 'But I'm coming with you this

time. I hate the thought of you going alone. The weather is changing. There could be snow.'

Victoria telephoned Home Farm to tell Libby. She was surprised at her daughter's response.

'I'd like to come to the funeral with you, Mum,' she said. 'I'll phone you back.' A few minutes later she telephoned Langmune. 'Mum, Billy says he will drive us all to the funeral if you think it would be all right for us to come with you?'

'Of course it would be all right, and it will be much easier by car because it's on the outskirts of Edinburgh.'

'I'd like to meet my new cousin, and Billy thinks we may be some support to him.' She shuddered. 'It must be terrible losing his mother, and Doctor Sterling sounds such a grim person.'

'Libby! Don't say that. The doctor has given him a home and brought him up all these years.'

'But you said yourself that he wants to dictate Peter's future, Mum.'

'No more than I tried to dictate yours,' Victoria said ruefully. 'I wanted you to be a teacher.'

'Well, I couldn't be happier.' Billy had come to stand close beside her and she squeezed his arm and smiled up at him. He grinned and whispered in her other ear.

Victoria could hear the lilt in her daughter's voice and the murmuring in the background. There was no doubting Libby's happiness. They had known and liked Billy all his life and they respected the man he had become once he had confronted his turbulent past. Even more surprising was the kindness and support he had given his half-sister, Charlotte Crainby, after her mother had squandered her birthright and committed suicide. Billy was the only relative she had now. Victoria was proud to know that Libby and Billy were prepared to show kindness to another unknown cousin.

Three

Deane Sterling stepped back from the head of the coffin and took each of his daughters by the hand. Peter had bravely held the cord at the foot as it lowered his mother into the earth but now he stood alone and the strain on the sixteen-year-old's emotions was apparent in the silent tears sliding down his pale cheeks. Andrew moved to his side, giving his shoulder a comforting squeeze. Victoria saw the muscle throbbing in his cheek, reminding her painfully of Mark. She moved to his other side, restraining herself from hugging him as she longed to do. He gave her a wan smile.

'I'm sorry,' he said. 'Father says it's unmanly to show emotion.'

'Easier said than done,' Billy muttered, joining the family group with Libby. 'I'm in the same boat as you, chum. I've never known my own father and we know Mother can't last long.' Peter looked at Billy with a spark of interest. Over his head Andrew's eyes registered surprised approval.

'Peter, this is our son-in-law, Billy Lennox,' Victoria said. 'And this is our daughter, Elizabeth, but we all call her Libby. You'll get to know both of them when you come down to stay with us. We all live in the same area.'

'Except Uncle Josh and Charlotte,' Libby said. 'Uncle Josh is Dad's younger brother. He's a lecturer in Glasgow. Billy's half-sister, Charlotte, is studying to be a teacher at the same college.'

'You have half-sisters too?' Peter asked.

'I have one half-sister. We had the same father.'

'Do you get on well together?'

'We do now, but one half of the family hated the other half for years.' Billy grimaced. 'I'll tell you about it someday.'

Before they left, Victoria managed to speak to Dr Sterling.

'We hope Peter will come to stay with us during the school holidays, and his sisters will be welcome too if . . .'

'I'm sure the girls would not enjoy being in the country,' Deane Sterling answered swiftly, almost with a note of alarm. 'But Catriona thought it would be good for Peter. He'll come to his senses when he sees the way you people live.'

Victoria's brows arched in surprise but the doctor had moved on before she could reply.

'You'll have to buy Mum a refrigerator just to show how civilized you are, Dad,' Libby teased on the way home when Victoria quoted Deane Sterling's remark.

'I might do just that, minx,' Andrew responded with a smile.

It was a crisp Sunday morning towards the end of February and Victoria and Andrew walked out of the kirk. Libby and Billy had stopped to talk to friends and Fraser and Lachie were teasing each other as usual.

'It's a beautiful morning,' Andrew remarked, breathing in the cold air. The sun shone on the frosted grass so that it sparkled like diamond fronds. 'Are we calling on Maggie, as usual?'

'I think we should go straight home today,' Victoria said. She felt hollow inside. She had never fainted in her life but she had felt very queasy whenever they stood to sing the hymns and the service had seemed to go on far too long.

'You seem out of sorts, Vicky,' Andrew remarked as they made their way to the car. 'I've thought you looked pale once or twice lately. Are you all right?'

'Ye-es, I think so, but I don't seem to have my usual energy.'

Victoria felt better as the day wore on but about ten days later she was overcome by a dizzy spell much worse than the others she'd experienced. She had to sit down in the middle of serving the breakfast. Andrew hovered until Fraser had gone back to work and Lachie had left for school.

'You must see Doctor Ritchie, Victoria,' he said. 'You may be anaemic or . . .'

'Or what?' Victoria demanded irritably. 'I'm sorry. I'm fine now I've had my breakfast. You know how I hate doctors and Doctor Ritchie seems so young.'

Andrew knew then she had been considering a visit to the doctor herself and his fears increased. 'Maybe he is young, but Doctor Grantly had a high regard for him.'

'I-I think it's just what women call "the change",' Victoria said.

'Aren't you a bit young for that?'

'I don't know much about it. I always thought it happened sort of naturally sometime after fifty.' She had considered mentioning it to Andrew's mother. Polly Pringle was the nearest she'd had to a mother of her own and they had always been close, but Polly had never been one for discussing women's problems or personal things. Andrew came up behind her and drew her against him, his arms encircling her. He leaned over her shoulder and kissed her cheek. It was as firm and smooth as any girl's.

'I couldn't bear it if anything happened to you, Victoria.'

'Nothing's going to happen to me. I'm as strong as a horse,' she insisted, but Andrew slid his hands over her stomach.

'Are you sure it couldn't be another baby?' he whispered. He couldn't hide a note of anxiety. Victoria turned to face him.

'So that's crossed your mind too?' she said, staring up into his tanned face. 'I didn't think it was likely at my age. B-but . . .' She frowned, hesitating. 'But if it's not the change then it must be . . . It-it's three months since I . . .'

'That's what I thought. You don't look forty and you've always been fit and healthy until the past few weeks.'

'Yes, I know. Gosh, Andrew! A baby?' She stared up at him, her brown eyes wide. Now that it was out in the open, and Andrew thought the same, she acknowledged her suspicions. She had been refusing to consider such a possibility. 'Imagine what Libby and Fraser will think if it is another baby. Whatever will they say?'

'What can they say? We're human, Vicky, and I do love you very much, even more than the day we married, if that's possible.' His voice was husky and his arms tightened around her. 'But I can't help worrying about you. Remember the trouble Mary had before Mimi was born.'

'I never had any trouble with the other three,' Victoria said.

'I know, but Lachie will soon be eleven, and . . .' He broke off, tracing the line of her jaw with a gentle finger. 'Will you see the doctor?'

'And I'm not so young this time, that's what you were going to say, isn't it?' She looked up at him, filled now with an odd mixture of elation and apprehension. 'Will you mind having disturbed nights again and nappies drying on the clothes horse?'

'So long as you're all right I shall not mind any of that. How can I when it was my fault? You will see the doctor soon?'

'Not unless I feel ill. I never had a doctor for any of the others, and I know Doctor Ritchie too well since Mimi had polio. He was so attentive, but he's too young . . .'

'Libby says he's getting married to June Appleby soon. They've had an invitation to the wedding, haven't they? He's getting a new surgery too. The people who bought Doctor Grantly's house want the use of all the rooms so the surgery has to be moved.'

'It will be a lot better in a separate building,' Victoria said, nodding her approval, 'but I still don't intend going there unless I have to.' She compressed her lips and Andrew grinned down at her.

'You always were stubborn when you made your mind up, even when you were ten years old.' He touched her cheek affectionately. 'But promise you'll take things easier?'

'I will,' she nodded. 'I never thought I'd be glad to get out my mending basket and Gran's old mushroom so I could sit darning socks.'

'I shall have to make more holes in my socks then,' Andrew chuckled.

'Don't you dare! There's plenty with Fraser and Lachlan. We'll have to make some plans though . . . We still have the cot, but I wish we hadn't let Lachie use the old pram to make himself a cart.'

'He and Mimi have had a lot of fun with it and we can afford the things a baby needs now. Libby and Fraser had to make do with hand-me-downs, and poor old Lachie had wartime rations.'

'Yes, but he's healthy enough. I just wish I didn't feel so awkward about telling Libby and Fraser.'

'I'll leave that to you,' Andrew answered, his mind moving on to other things. Ever since they were married he had promised he would restore the house at Langmune to the way it had been before fire destroyed the front half. Victoria deserved a decent home. Billy and Libby had a beautiful house at Darlonachie Home Farm, inherited from Sir William Crainby, Billy's grandfather, but Langmune had once looked just as lovely. He made mental calculations of the cost. Maybe they shouldn't have bought Throstlebrae Farm, but an opportunity like that would never arise again. It needed a lot of renovations but they would have to wait. Victoria must come first. She had always shared his dreams but this time the restoration of Langmune would be a surprise. He wouldn't tell her until he had made the arrangements.

As the eldest son, Fraser knew one of the farms would be his one day and meanwhile they could all be proud of Langmune when it was restored. Andrew frowned as a thought occurred to him. Fraser had never been jealous of Lachie in spite of the eight years between them, but would he resent having another young brother? He hoped not. Another baby around the house would keep him young. His spirits rose.

Victoria was relieved to hear him whistling a jaunty tune as he pulled on his wellingtons to go out to work. She still couldn't believe she was expecting a baby at her age but it was a relief to have her suspicions out in the open, and Andrew didn't seem to mind the prospect of another child. She knew his main concern was her own health and it was true she had never felt so tired before.

A fortnight later she was sitting at the kitchen table sipping a cup of hot milky coffee, wondering if she had the energy to bake scones for tea, when the door burst open bringing a rush of cold March wind.

'Libby!' Victoria exclaimed in surprise. 'I didn't expect to see you in the middle of a weekday afternoon.'

'I was working over the weekend so I'm having a half day today.' Libby grinned, looking rosy-cheeked and full of energy. 'I've promised to help June with her show of presents this evening.' Like everyone else she drifted towards the warmth of the Aga. 'Ah, I see you're nursing a sick lamb.'

She peered down into the cardboard box beside the cooker, drawing aside a piece of old blanket.

'It's a bitter wind out there. It got starved so your father brought it inside. I've been coaxing it to have some warm milk with a spot of brandy to revive it.'

'Any luck?'

'It took a little. I'll try again in a wee while.'

'You sound tired, Mum. Are you helping with the lambing as well as everything else?'

'Of course not,' Victoria snapped.

Libby raised her eyebrows. It was unlike her mother to be short. 'Can I join you for a cup of tea then?'

'It's Camp Coffee but there's some hot milk left in the pan if you fancy some?'

'Mmm, that will do me until I get home. I'll just warm it up a bit more. Meanwhile I'll get the flowers . . .' Even as she spoke she was across the kitchen and bounding up the stairs, calling as she went, 'I want them to decorate my hat for the wedding. I think I left them in the bottom of my wardr—'

Victoria closed her eyes. She could visualize Libby's face as she halted on the threshold of her old bedroom. She didn't know what had made her get the cot out and polish it up already. The blankets and the little embroidered quilt were all laid out on the bed. She hadn't expected anyone to go in there now that Libby had left home, but she had been so quick. She came down stairs, carrying a shoe box containing various sprays of flowers and ribbons, but her brows were knitted in a furious frown.

'Mother,' she growled, 'if you think Billy and I need . . .'

Victoria held up a hand, shaking her head. Libby looked as she had when she was a wee girl, frustrated and struggling with her temper. Suddenly Victoria knew what to say to this grown-up daughter.

'We've missed you so much, Libby dear, since you moved to Home Farm, and we – that is your father and I – thought we would try for another little girl. Not that she – or he, if it's a boy – could ever take your place in our hearts. You know that, don't you?' she said, smiling at Libby's startled brown eyes, at her lips parted in a silent O.

'You . . . you're . . . ? Oh, Mum!' Her eyes travelled over her mother's thickening waistline. 'Gosh, I can't believe it. I-I . . .' She was beaming now. 'I-I thought . . .'

'I was getting the cot polished for you and Billy? I'm sorry if it's a bit of a shock. We haven't told anyone else yet.'

'Then I'm the first to hear your news?' She beamed. 'When will it be? Do you feel OK? Will you still be able to cope with Peter's visit? We could have him to stay with us if you like. No wonder you seem tired. Will—'

'Steady on, Libby. I hadn't thought about Peter's visit but I'm sure I shall be fine. He must come. I can't let him down.'

'Has he written to you?'

'Oh yes, he's written every fortnight since his mother's funeral.'

'Has he? So regularly?'

'The first time I replied I didn't know what to say to a sixteen-year-old boy so I told him a few things about the animals. We'd just had a baby calf so I mentioned it. He still asks how it's getting on and he never forgets the things I've told him. He wants to know all the details, and about the ducklings that hatched without us knowing the duck was sitting.'

'It must seem like a different world to him.'

'I suppose it is. I couldn't disappoint him. Remember we bought Fraser a Kodak Brownie for Christmas? He took photographs of some of the animals and of your father and me and Lachlan outside the house.' She grimaced. 'Doctor Sterling will not think it's much of a house but that can't be helped. Peter seemed thrilled. He's made an album of pictures of Langmune. He would like a camera of his own to add to it.'

'It sounds as though he's hoping to make regular visits.' Libby chewed her lower lip. 'When is the baby due?'

'August.' She was not sure herself, but she didn't want to tell Libby that.

'Have you seen Doctor Ritchie?'

'No. Now don't you start. Your father is bad enough.' Victoria summoned a smile, but it was a bit strained. Andrew was worrying enough for two of them.

'I thought you were supposed to see your doctor, and . . . and things. I mean, everything is under this National Health scheme now, isn't it? You won't have to pay this time.'

'It's nothing to do with paying,' Victoria said. 'I never needed a doctor for you three. In fact I can't remember when I last saw a doctor.'

'I-I suppose it would be a bit embarrassing going to Steve for something like that.' She frowned. Billy wanted her to talk to the doctor on a personal matter but she had balked at the idea. 'It's embarrassing when we know him so well.'

'I agree, and to me he seems so young. But don't worry, I shall be fine. Aren't you going to make your coffee, and did you find the flowers you wanted?'

'Yes, yes I did. I thought I could trim my straw hat.' She turned to lift the pan of milk and make her coffee. 'Shall I make you another cup, Mum? There's plenty of milk left.'

'Yes, please.' Victoria nodded. She had a craving for milky Camp Coffee and she couldn't bear the tea she had always enjoyed. Libby brought the two cups and settled herself at the table.

'Well, this is a big surprise. I can't get over it.' She grinned. 'There's plenty of time for Billy and me at this rate.'

'Don't be so sure. I was expecting Fraser by the time I was your age and we already had you.'

'Are you still helping with the milking?'

'No, your father says the milk units are too heavy with all their attachments, and especially when they're full of milk. Modern gadgets aren't always an advantage.' She sighed. 'I used to enjoy milking when I was having you. It was soothing and restful to sit on my wee stool and listen to the milk strumming into the pail.'

'Yes, I suppose it is different now,' Libby nodded, 'but you have plenty to do with so many hens. The eggs are to be cleaned and packed, and you have the book-keeping and—' The lamb gave a loud bleat, making them both jump, then smile. 'At least he's still alive,' Libby said. 'Shall I try him with the bottle before I go?'

'I'll see to the lamb. You get away home to Billy. He sees little enough of you.'

'Oh, Mum, don't you start. I can't win. Aren't I proving

that I have a career that's just as good as the teaching you wanted me to do?' Victoria caught her breath but before she could say anything Libby carried on. 'Dad never misses an opportunity to tell me I should be at home with Billy. Even Granny was on at me the last time I saw her. Gosh!' Her eyes widened. 'Granny will not know about the baby either?'

'No, she does not, so don't go broadcasting it. I'll tell her when I'm ready.'

'Do you think she might be upset then?'

'I don't know. I shall always make time to care for her, if she needs me, even if it means employing a girl to help with the baby.'

'So far she hasn't wanted any help. She's as independent as ever and she still speaks her mind. She's always on at Uncle Josh for befriending Charlotte, even though they're at the same college.'

'I know,' Victoria sighed. 'I'm afraid your Granny Pringle will never forgive Henrietta Crainby for the spiteful way she treated me when I was a lassie working in the Castle kitchens. Nor can she forgive the way she sacked your grandfather in a fit of anger that had nothing to do with him, poor man. She took her vile temper out on him. She added insult to injury by putting him out of his cottage. Your grandparents had lived there all their married life. She didn't need it but she was furious because the army were taking over the Castle and the grounds. She was a nasty woman.'

'I know she must have been horrid to cheat her own daughter out of her inheritance, but Charlotte is not a bit like her mother. Henrietta Crainby was cruel to Billy too, and to his mother, but Aunt Maggie always makes Charlotte welcome at Ivy Cottage.'

'I know, but Granny Pringle is an old lady. It's not easy to forgive people like Mrs Crainby. She caused so much misery and heartache to everyone around her.'

'Yes, including Charlotte. She's sold off all the farms and paid her mother's debts. Even Granny must respect her for that, and now she's working hard to have a career so she can earn her living and stand on her own two feet. Uncle Josh admires her courage. He says it's not easy when she's older than all the other students, and after spending so long away from studying while she was recovering from tuberculosis.'

'Josh has always had a kindly nature. He'd help anyone in trouble.' Victoria smiled warmly.

'I think it's more than that but when I confronted Uncle Josh he said I was talking nonsense. He says Charlotte is just another student and he's far too old for her. Eleven years is not such a lot, though, is it?'

'That's Josh's business. You shouldn't interfere with people's relationships, Libby.'

'Mmm, well he's driving Charlotte down here for the Easter holidays. She'll be staying with us at Home Farm. If Granny Pringle would only meet her and get to know her . . .' Libby muttered in frustration. Her brown eyes widened as an idea occurred to her.

'You're planning something,' Victoria said, watching her. 'I can always tell, Libby.'

'I've been wondering how I could get them together.'

'They were both at your wedding.'

'But they didn't speak or try to get to know one another. Peter will be here for Easter. You'll have plenty to do, so it would be a good excuse for me to cook the dinner on Easter Sunday and have the whole family at Home Farm, instead of you having all of us here.'

'I'd appreciate the offer,' Victoria sighed. 'But Granny Pringle may refuse to join us if she knows Charlotte is staying with you. We can't leave her at home on her own.'

'We'll see,' Libby said, her eyes sparkling. She liked a challenge. 'Just let me know when you've broken your news to everybody.'

'I've no intention of broadcasting it.'

'No, but you'll have to tell Granny before she guesses, won't you?'

'Yes, I suppose so.' Victoria sighed again.

'And Aunt Mary and Uncle Willie. Mum . . .' Libby looked at her. 'You do seem tired and I've never heard you sigh so much. You are happy about the baby, aren't you?'

'Yes, of course we're very happy. It's just that I seem to be so short of energy. I was never like this with any of you, at least not until near the end when there was extra weight to carry around.'

'You will take care, won't you?' Libby said. 'And tell me if there's anything I can do to help. Maybe you should consult Doctor Ritchie.'

'Ach! Get away with you.' Victoria summoned a smile and waved her away.

It was two evenings before Doctor Steve Ritchie's wedding to June Appleby, a girl Libby knew well from her days in the Young Farmers' Club. A number of friends and neighbours had gathered for the Scottish custom of viewing the wedding presents. These had been admired and refreshments served and now most of the women had departed. Libby stayed behind to help June wash the cups and saucers while her mother packed away the remaining cakes and biscuits.

'Just one more show tomorrow afternoon and then we can all prepare for the wedding,' Mrs Appleby said before she bustled away to tidy up, leaving the girls to chat as they worked.

'Did you read about the fuss all his fans are making because Elvis has to do his National Service?'

'I can just imagine.' Libby grinned. 'But you can't make an exception just because he can sing, can you?'

'No,' June chuckled. 'Some of them were crying because he's to have his hair cut in the style of the American soldiers – a short back and sides!'

'I suppose he'll be lucky if that's the worst he ever has to suffer,' Libby said. 'Did you hear the anti-nuclear lobby are planning an Easter march from London to Aldermaston?'

'Yes. We shall be well clear of London by then though.'

'Ha-ha – so does that mean you're going down there for your honeymoon?' Libby teased.

June hesitated, blushing. 'I'm sure you can keep a secret, Libby. We're going to Paris and I'm so excited. I couldn't believe it when Steve told me what he was planning.'

'That's lovely, June. I'm sure you'll both enjoy it, and you deserve it. Who will cover for Steve while he's away?'

'He's made arrangements with the practices on either side of Darlonachie to take it in turns. The new surgery is finished now so it will be easier for them and Jessie Ross is reliable and efficient on reception, so I hope everything goes well. Steve worries so much about his patients. He has so many more since the free health service started. Did I tell you he's getting an assistant when we return?'

'Another doctor?'

'Yes. One of the applicants is a lady doctor. She's well qualified, Steve says, but he's not sure how his patients would react to a woman. You know how country folks are set in their ways, especially the farmers.' She grinned.

'Don't I just!' Libby said. 'But you tell him we need a lady doctor as much as they need a man. I mean, it's the women who have babies and now that family planning is becoming an accepted thing for women . . .' She broke off, blushing.

'Ye-es,' June said, noting her flushed cheeks. 'I hadn't thought of that. Why do we always consider the male point of view first, I wonder? I'll mention it to Steve.'

'Er . . . yes, but do you need to tell him it was my idea?'

'I suppose not. But he values your opinions, you know, Libby. After all, it was you who got the two of us together and he still talks about the way you've helped Mimi cope after the polio.'

'Och, but that's different.'

'Is it?' June looked at her. 'Are you expecting a baby, Libby? Is that what's worrying you?'

'No! I-I mean no, it's not that.'

'I can keep a secret you know, even from Steve, if I have to. There is something bothering you, isn't there?'

'Y-yes, I believe you can keep a secret. It's Mum. I think she ought to see a doctor but I can understand it would be embarrassing for her to see Steve when we all know him so well.'

'Is your mother ill? Is it women's troubles?'

'She . . . she's expecting another baby,' Libby said, and watched June's eyes widen in surprise. 'Please don't tell anyone – anyone except Steve, that is. I'm the only one who knows yet.'

'I won't, I promise. That's wonderful. I mean, I thought for a moment if it was women's trouble it might be the dreaded cancer or something like that, but a baby . . .'

'I hadn't thought about it like that.' Libby shuddered. 'As you say, a baby is relatively harmless, compared with some things. I mean, you know you'll be back to normal in nine months. Even so, Mum does seem tired and Dad wants her to see Steve.'

'I'll mention it to him. I think his instinct is to choose the lady doctor and it may help him decide. He says she's in her forties and she's a widow with two daughters aged twelve and fifteen so she wants to move back to Scotland to be nearer her parents.'

The wedding of Darlonachie's young doctor went off splendidly, with a large crowd from the surrounding area waiting outside the little kirk to see the bride and groom.

During the dance that followed the reception Doctor Ritchie claimed Libby for a waltz. He looked happy and relaxed, so she was surprised he still thought about work on his wedding day.

'June told me about your mother, Libby.' He had bent close to her ear so that she could hear him over the music. 'Things have changed since Lachlan was born. We have the National Health scheme, with health visitors in most districts. Many of them are trained midwives. Shall I ask the local nurse to call on her?'

'Oh! I-I don't know.' Libby stumbled and trod on his toe in her confusion. 'I don't think so. If I get a chance I'll mention it, but Mum would be angry if she thought I'd discussed her, even with you.'

'That's all right, I understand. June told me you think we should take on a lady doctor.' He grinned. 'So I'm taking your advice. Whatever we do there will be some patients who are not pleased. It was the same when I joined Doctor Grantly. Perhaps your mother will feel easier with Doctor Burns – that's her name.'

'I think Mum considers birth – and death too I suppose – as events which should happen naturally.'

'They are, but there's a lot we can do to maintain better health for both mothers and babies. Do persuade her to have a medical check if you can. She's not as young as she was ten years ago.'

Libby nodded but she knew she wouldn't make suggestions to her mother. Perhaps she could ask Billy's mother to talk to her though. Aunt Maggie and her mother had been good friends for years and she had implicit faith in Doctor Ritchie.

'What were you and the new bridegroom whispering about?' Billy asked as soon as the dance finished. Libby looked at him, recognizing the brooding tone, the spark in his blue eyes. She had seen a lot of Doctor Steve Ritchie when she was helping Mimi with her exercises after the polio. She knew Billy had been jealous and resentful of their camaraderie then, but he was the man she had married. He must know she loved him, yet beneath the confident exterior there still lurked the uncertainties of the boy who had never known his father, the teenager who had been filled with insecurities when his family's skeletons had become public knowledge with vile interpretations published in many of the newspapers. They had shaken the self-esteem of a young man setting out into the world. Libby understood the demons that had haunted Billy but he had earned respect and made good friends during his time in Yorkshire and she had believed their marriage would sweep away the lingering uncertainties.

Billy had been impatient to make her his wife. He wanted the reassurance of marriage, of knowing she belonged to him, but her boss had been furious when he heard their plans. She frowned, remembering Mr Whittaker's grim expression. There had been no congratulations or good wishes.

'You haven't been here five minutes,' he had growled. 'There were several applicants I could have chosen for your job. You never wore a ring or mentioned you were engaged, let alone planning to marry so soon. You've just left college. I don't know why you bothered going, wasting your parents' money and taking a place from some other poor bugger.'

Confronted with her boss's disapproval she had been assailed by guilt and doubts and it hadn't helped that he had gone on and on.

'You knew it was a whole new laboratory set-up that you were to organize and two assistants to train. It was part of our agreement. You promised . . .'

'And I *shall* train them,' she had said, but he had banged out of the door in anger. That evening Billy had sensed that her joy had diminished. She'd told him about Mr Whittaker's outburst.

'I did promise him. Perhaps we have been too hasty and wrapped up in ourselves,' she had said. 'And I wanted to prove to Mother I could have a career and be independent even if I was not a teacher as she had hoped.'

'Would she have expected you to put a teaching career before marriage?'

'Mother and Father want all of us to be happy, but I wanted to prove I could have a worthwhile career. Do you think we should wait a while, Billy?'

'No! No, no, a thousand times no!'

Even now Libby's cheeks felt hot, but she had to smile as she recalled his reaction, the way he had picked her up and kissed her with mounting desire. 'I can't wait a year to make you my wife.' She had returned his kisses with equal fervour and she had known then that she wanted Billy more than anything in the world.

'I don't want to wait,' she'd whispered, 'but in my heart I know Mr Whittaker was justified in being angry. I was so pleased and proud when he offered me the job, and it is a challenge I enjoy.'

'You could promise to stay on for a year after we're married. Lots of married women keep on working, since the war. That would give you time to train the other girls and keep on the right side of old Whittaker. We don't want to offend the old boy. The milk from Home Farm and Langmune goes to his creamery. We don't want him rejecting it.'

'I don't think he'd be that spiteful. Wouldn't you mind me being away all day? How would you manage?'

'Of course I would miss you,' Billy had said, hugging her, 'but it would be better than waiting a year to make you my wife. So long as I have you beside me at night I'm willing to compromise through the day, for a year anyway. Julie Dunlop will be glad to carry on helping in the house, if you don't mind having someone else in your kitchen.'

Mr Whittaker had been placated by this decision and their wedding had gone ahead. Libby had no regrets. She loved

Billy, but life had not been as smooth as they had expected. Recently Libby had begun to feel it was impossible to please everybody.

'Shall we dance?' Billy said now, bringing her attention back to their surroundings.

'What's troubling you?' she asked.

'I want to go home and take you to bed and make passionate love all night.' His answer was swift and full of desire. Libby knew it was the truth but she heard the underlying anger and frustration that had become part of their love-making recently. It was vital she should not become pregnant, and Billy bitterly resented being responsible.

'June and Steve will be leaving soon and then we can go home. It would look bad if we left before the bride and groom.'

'I suppose so,' he agreed grudgingly. 'We may as well make the best of it.' Billy was a good dancer and he drew her close, his breath stirring the tendrils of hair on her forehead. 'I do love you, Libby. I know it's crazy but I hate to see you close to any other man, even your good Doctor Ritchie.'

'He's not *my* good doctor. As a matter of fact he was asking about Mother. He wants me to persuade her to see a health visitor and have a check-up. It's not my place to tell my own mother what to do. Anyway, he's getting a woman doctor as his assistant.'

'Is he now? That's interesting. Maybe you'll agree to see her then?'

'Maybe.' Libby flushed. Why did they have to keep returning to the one subject she hated discussing?

Four

'Peter must be eager to come to visit us,' Andrew grinned as he and Victoria waited at the little Lockerbie station, 'if the school holidays only started yesterday.'

'If his letters are anything to go by he can't wait to see everything. I hope he'll not be disappointed.'

'I suppose the farm will be a novelty. Even the village will be different after living in the city.'

'Yes, I think he'll be surprised how friendly people are, especially those who knew Mark and notice the resemblance. I do wish Doctor Grantly had lived to meet him.' She sighed. 'Catriona would never expect things to turn out like this, of course.'

'No, she would not.' Andrew's mouth tightened. 'It's a good thing she had the sense to get in touch. She almost left it too late. Here comes the train now.'

Peter was one of the first to alight and he almost ran to greet them. Victoria opened her arms and hugged him but he didn't seem to mind – unlike Fraser, who kept saying he had grown out of hugs. But he knew he was loved; he didn't need reassurance. As they drove home to Darlonachie, Peter gazed from side to side, trying to take in everything at once.

'I hope you've brought your old clothes,' Andrew chuckled. 'Whatever else you do, you'll get dirty.'

'I've got a pair of Fraser's wellington boots for you,' Victoria told him, 'and a couple of pairs of his old bib and brace overalls, although I do believe you're almost as tall as he is for all you're only sixteen.'

'I'm seventeen now. I was seventeen in February.'

'Of course.' Victoria was silent for a moment. 'I didn't know when your birthday was, Peter, or I would have sent you a wee present.'

'We never have birthday presents, but Cathy made me a card. She loves to draw.'

'I see. Lachie and Mimi have started their school holidays today. They can't wait to meet you.'

'Mimi is Lachlan's cousin? But she's not my cousin, is that right?'

'It is,' Andrew nodded. 'Mimi is my brother's bairn. They live across the glen from Langmune, higher up than we are. It's a sheep farm. Their ewes lamb later than ours so they're busy lambing now. You'll find there's dozens of different kinds of farming, Peter. Willie, my brother, always preferred sheep to cows.'

'Shall I be able to see them too?' he asked.

'Aye, you will that. Willie likes company. He and our brother George were inseparable when they were boys. George was killed during the war, like your father. Willie enjoys having young folk around him and Mary will make you welcome if you feed the pet lambs. They'll have one or two around.'

'Don't let Mimi and Lachlan play too many tricks on you, Peter,' Victoria warned. 'They're a pair of rascals. They'll pester you to join in their games. You'll have to be firm.'

'Mimi had polio when she was five or six,' Andrew said. 'She has a bit of a limp. Sometimes she has difficulty keeping up with Lachlan and he's not always very considerate.'

'Mimi never seems to worry though,' Victoria said. 'She always has a smile and she's the hardiest bairn I ever knew. She faces up to life with more courage than many a grown-up. Libby thinks the world of her.'

'I'm looking forward to meeting them all,' Peter said, his dark eyes shining in anticipation, 'and I can't wait to see the animals and all the things you've described, Aunt Victoria. Even Father admits you write good letters. Dinah isn't a bit interested but Cathy is always impatient to hear what you have to tell us, and she insists on reading them again herself in case I've missed any bits out.' He grinned and Victoria could tell by his tone that he was fond of his younger sister. She already knew there was some constraint between him and Dinah. Even Catriona had said her elder daughter was like Deane Sterling. She wanted to be a doctor like him too.

If they all read her letters it was a good job she had not mentioned the baby in any of them. She hadn't realized Doctor Sterling would censor them. She guessed he would disapprove of her having a baby at her age, and after a ten-year gap. He wouldn't have allowed such things to happen in his well-ordered life, but she couldn't imagine him ever being spontaneous or loving Catriona as Andrew loved her.

'Here we are,' Andrew said, drawing the car to a halt. Peter scrambled out and looked around, his brown eyes alight with interest.

'The house is exactly as you described it, Aunt Victoria. How strange.' He turned to look up at Andrew. 'You must have been very brave to go in there to rescue someone when it was on fire,' he said. 'I would have been scared of it falling on top of me.' Andrew looked at Victoria with raised brows.

'Have you been telling tales of my youth?'

'You were brave, and we're proud of you.'

'I expect you'd do just the same, laddie, if someone you knew was in danger,' Andrew said to Peter. 'Speaking of danger, don't let Lachie or Mimi persuade you to go near the old quarry. It's on the neighbouring farm but it's near the Langmune boundary. The edges are crumbling. If you fell in you'd be killed before you reached the bottom – even if you weren't, you'd drown. Mr and Mrs Adamson bought Quarrybrae Farm last year and Lachie has become good friends with their son, Tom. We have warned him he must never go near the quarry.'

'Right. I shall remember that, sir.'

'Oh, don't call me "sir", lad. It makes me feel like a school master.' Andrew grinned. 'Is that how I sounded?'

'Not when you grin like that, it isn't,' Victoria smiled. 'Call him Uncle Andrew, Peter. He is your uncle after all. He's not telling you what a naughty lad he was himself when he was young. The first time he ever came to Langmune he had climbed on to a ledge in the quarry to rescue a collie dog. It belonged to the farmer who lived here then, Mr Rennie.'

'Fate took a hand in my life that day,' Andrew reminisced. 'I was given my first job. I worked at Langmune for Fraser Rennie and I've been here ever since.'

'I hope fate gives me a helping hand then,' Peter said. 'My stepfather never gives up. He's convinced I shall be glad to get back to Edinburgh and he's expecting me to stay on at school another year and study to be a doctor.'

'He may be right, laddie,' Andrew said. 'A doctor is a worthwhile profession, but whatever the future holds I hope you'll enjoy staying with us during your Easter holidays. Always remember we're your family too and you'll be more than welcome to come whatever you decide to do.'

'Thank you, Uncle Andrew.' Peter beamed.

'You look just like your father,' Andrew remarked, 'when he first came to Darlonachie. He had a lively interest in everything.'

'I shall take you round our childhood haunts, Peter,' Victoria promised, 'although many of them have changed since the war. The Castle is too big and dilapidated to maintain. It's to be pulled down any day now, and the gardens are wild and neglected. They used to be beautiful.'

'You will be careful if you go roaming over there, won't you, Victoria?' Andrew's eyes moved to the gentle swell of her stomach.

'Of course I shall.' Victoria's cheeks flushed. She wondered what a seventeen-year-old boy would think to her having a baby. He probably regarded her as an old woman. She remembered how often she had cycled that distance without a thought, and Andrew had done it every morning and evening. 'Maybe we'll drive down to the village and out the Castle road. We can walk from there. I'll show you where Mark stayed with the Grantlys too, but there's new people living there now.'

Lachlan came running round the corner of the house and almost bumped into them. Mimi was a few yards behind him.

'Hello, Mimi.' Victoria returned her young niece's beaming smile. 'I didn't know you were coming over today. Had your mum forgotten we were meeting Peter off the train? Come and say hello to him.'

Mimi stepped forward, smiling shyly, holding out her hand. Peter took it and grinned down at her.

'I'm very pleased to meet you, Mimi. I have a sister a wee bit bigger than you.'

'You won't be pleased you've met her when you find out what a pest she is,' Lachlan teased, giving his closest ally a poke in the ribs.

'And this cheeky wretch is Lachlan,' Andrew said, 'and he's the real pest around here. Don't stand any nonsense from him, Peter.'

''Lo, Peter.' Lachlan grinned but he didn't offer to shake hands. 'Uncle Willie's here,' he announced. 'Mimi came over with him.'

'He gave me a piggy back over the burn on the big stepping stones,' Mimi said. 'I told Daddy about your new lamp, Uncle Andrew. The one you used for the wee lambs when they were shivering. He wondered if we could borrow it,' she added as Willie came round the corner, deep in conversation with Fraser. More introductions were made. Fraser and Peter stared at each other in surprise, each seeing familiar dark brown eyes and even darker brows and hair, the same stubborn jaw and high cheek bones. They were both tall and slim. It was Mimi who remarked, 'They look like brothers.'

'They do indeed,' Willie said, holding out his work-roughened hand and clasping Peter's in a firm grip. 'Welcome to Darlonachie, laddie. I hear you want to know all about farming and the countryside. You're welcome to come over to High Bowie if you feel like it. Lachlan and Mimi will show you where we live.'

'Thank you. Uncle Andrew says you have lambs. I'd like to see them,' Peter said, overwhelmed by the warmth that radiated from the little group. It was all so different to his family. Even when his mother was alive there hadn't been much laughter or teasing, and things were even more constrained now.

'I don't know about you lot, but I'm ready for my tea, and I'm sure Peter must be too,' Victoria declared. 'Come inside, all of you. Mimi, be an angel and help me set the table, will you?'

'Oh goody. Have you got any strawberry jam left, Aunt Victoria?' She turned to Peter, her blue eyes sparkling. 'It's the best strawberry jam in the whole world.' Then her small face became serious. 'Our Grandpa has died though. There won't be anybody to grow the strawberries this year.' Over

her head Willie, Andrew and Victoria looked at each other.
None of them had considered how much Joe Pringle's
gardening skills were going to be missed, but Mimi was
right.

'We shall have to look after Grandfather's garden
ourselves,' Fraser said. 'Do you like gardening, Peter? You
can come down to Gran's cottage and help me if you like.
Grandpa often showed me what to do. He said Dad and
Uncle Willie could only grow potatoes.' He grinned at them.
'He said I'd have to tend his garden or there'd be no vegetables. He was always passing on his secrets.'

'Mmm, it's strange that, Fraser.' Andrew nodded at his
elder son. 'I'd forgotten what a lot of time you spent following
my father around when you were younger. You've always
liked growing things more than looking after the cows. You
must take after him. Libby was the one who knew all the
animals by name. I thought she'd find it too tough but she
enjoyed working with the cattle. I don't know why she doesn't
give up that job of hers and help Billy.'

'Now, Dad,' Fraser warned. 'You said Doctor Sterling
wanted to run Peter's life, but you're as bad.'

'I am not.' Andrew frowned. He looked at Victoria. 'Am I?'

'I suppose it is the same sort of thing, dear,' Victoria said.
'I wonder why we always think we know what's best for the
next generation?'

'Well, I can give you two reasons why Libby is sticking
in at her job at the creamery,' Willie said bluntly, 'and if she
was my lassie I'd be proud of her.'

'And what are they, Willie, these reasons?' Andrew asked
with a faint note of irritation. All the young folk seemed to
confide in Willie, or maybe he just paid more attention.

'Well, for one thing Victoria wanted her to have a career.
She thought being a teacher was the best thing she could do
for herself.'

'I'm afraid I did,' Victoria admitted, glancing at Peter.

'Aye, well she's proving she's got herself a responsible
job, and she could have made a career if she needed one.
The other thing is she promised that crotchety manager she
would stay until the new laboratory was up and running effi-
ciently, and until she's trained someone to take her place.

You'd know that if you listened instead of lecturing, big brother.' Willie's grin took the sting out of his words. 'Libby's not the kind to let anybody down if she can help it. Maybe she and Billy should have waited a while before they got married but they're in love. Anyway, I reckon Billy needed Libby to be his wife. His needs are different to ours on account o' the past. We needed Victoria and Mary to work beside us because we were short o' money and labour was scarce during the war.'

'Unpaid slaves, that's what we are,' Victoria chuckled.

'Now I suppose I've put my foot in it,' Willie sighed, 'but that's my spiel over.' It was true Willie usually spent his time observing and considering, rather than talking.

'Aye, you'd better shut up and eat up.' Andrew grinned. 'Here, have a scone.'

'Bet you didn't know you were coming to such a crazy house,' Fraser said as an aside to Peter.

'It's wonderful. It makes me realize how serious we are in our house since Mother died, and even before that. My stepfather doesn't have much humour, I suppose.'

That first day at Langmune set the tone of Peter's Easter holiday and he offered a silent prayer to his mother for introducing him to the family he had not known existed. She had almost left it too late. He thanked God she had acted in time, even though it had meant friction and going against his stepfather.

Libby was home early and she hummed as she prepared Billy's favourite steak and kidney pie for dinner. She felt like dancing and skipping. Everything had been so much simpler than she had expected; Doctor Burns had been so gentle and understanding. She did a pirouette around the table as she laid out the cutlery and glasses and added two candles in their heavy silver candlesticks. When everything was ready she skipped upstairs to have a bath. She added some of the scented bath essence that one of her college friends had sent for Christmas. It was wonderful to lay back and relax.

She must have languished longer than she had realized. She heard Billy calling up the stairs and sat up with a great swoosh, reaching for her bathrobe.

'You're home early, Libby. Something smells delicious.' She hurried to the top of the stairs, her cheeks flushed and eyes shining. She had pinned her glossy hair on top of her head but tendrils had escaped and curled around her face. 'What are you doing having a bath at this time of day?'

'Come up and I'll tell you.'

'That's a bit risky,' Billy chuckled, taking the stairs two at a time and imprisoning her in his arms as soon as he reached the top step. His eyes darkened with desire as he caught the scent of her skin and felt the softness of her body beneath her robe. 'You're still damp,' he said, moving his mouth down the graceful curve of her neck.

'You come and get in the bath too.' Libby was already unfastening the buttons of his shirt and pushing aside the braces he always wore for work.

'Eh, what's this then?' His eyes sparked with passion.

'I want to bath you like a baby,' Libby laughed, drawing him into the bathroom, already easing down his corduroy trousers, allowing her hands to linger as she felt him harden. 'In you go.' She pushed him towards the scented water.

'In there? Do you know what you're doing to me, Libby?' He sank into the water and looked up at her. Her robe had fallen open as she bent over him. Libby was shy about her body, about him seeing her, always insisting he turn out the light, yet here she was half naked and driving him to distraction. 'Have you been drinking?' he asked, pulling himself up a little. She pushed him back, laughing with delight.

'Of course I haven't been drinking, but I do feel intoxicated.' She laughed and rubbed the sponge over his face, making him gasp, then over his chest, moving down and further down until he groaned at her detailed washing. 'Shall I do your back now?' she asked, her eyes holding his gaze as her hands roused him still more.

'No!' He leapt out of the bath, splashing water everywhere, but Libby didn't care as he hugged her against him, pushing aside her gown so that they were skin to skin, pressed together. 'I don't know what's got into you, wife o' mine, but whatever it is I like it.' His mouth nuzzled the softness of her breasts.

'Would you like your dinner now?' Libby asked innocently.

'Dinner!' he growled. 'I thought I was hungry but it's you I want to devour.' He lifted her in his arms and carried her to their bedroom, where they fell on to the bed together, unwilling to part, even for a moment. Libby felt liberated for the first time in her life and her response was everything Billy could desire but he sighed as he drew away to reach for the drawer where he kept the hated condoms. 'Passion killers', he called them.

Libby held his arm. 'There's no need for them anymore.'

'What?' His eyes widened as he stared down into her flushed face and shining eyes. 'You've been to the doctor? You . . . you . . . I don't . . .'

'Love me, Billy, just love me. Now.'

Much later they ate their dinner by the light of the candles. Outside the birds sang their last songs of the day as the calm of the April evening descended. Through the window the sun set in a glory of vermilion and gold, aquamarine and orange as the purple shadows of evening enveloped the world at the close of the day.

Libby felt loved and cherished beyond her wildest imaginings as Billy came to stand behind her, his arms sliding under her arms, drawing her close.

'I love you so much, Libby.'

The following evening Libby drove to her grandmother's cottage on her way home from work. She had warned Billy she would be a little late.

'Charlotte will be coming to stay tomorrow and I want to persuade Granny Pringle to come here for Easter Sunday lunch. I so much want her to meet Charlotte. I want them to like each other, or at least accept each other.' She smiled at Billy and stretched her arms wide. 'I want everyone in the world to be as happy as we are.'

'That's impossible.' Billy grinned, seizing her and whirling her around until she was dizzy. He gave her a lingering kiss. 'If you don't leave now I shall imprison you here for the rest of the day.' Then more seriously he added, 'I'll come with you to your granny's this evening, if you think it would help? After all, Charlotte is my half-sister.'

'When Granny makes up her mind nothing helps,' Libby said, pouting her lower lip. 'But I intend to have a good try.

I don't want her to spoil Easter for any of us, including Uncle Josh. I know he believes he's too old for Charlotte, but she does like him and she trusts him. She will be finished at college in a few weeks' time so she will not be his student then. If he does love her I think he ought to have his chance of happiness too.'

'Oh, I couldn't agree more,' Billy agreed, 'but he will never marry Charlotte if it means hurting his mother. We both know your Granny has plenty of reasons to hate the Crainbys.'

'Only Henrietta Crainby,' Libby said. 'She liked everyone else. She says everyone respected Sir William and he was Charlotte's grandfather as well as yours.'

'Maybe, but that bitch of a woman was Charlotte's mother, however much we all wish she wasn't. Anyway, if anyone can win your granny round, it's you, my wee charmer, and I hope you succeed. I like your Uncle Josh. He's genuine and sincere and I know how rare that is.' There was a familiar trace of bitterness in Billy's tone. Libby stepped close again and gave him an extra hug and another goodbye kiss.

All day she had felt buoyed up with happiness, sure she would be able to persuade her grandmother to meet Charlotte on Easter Sunday. When she parked her little car outside Granny Pringle's cottage and saw her peering out of the window with a frown on her brow all her doubts returned and her heart sank. She wanted her first big family gathering to be a happy affair, with everyone present.

Five

Polly Pringle had aged since her husband's death but she was pulling open the cottage door before Libby was out of the car. She looked anxious until she saw Libby's radiant face.

'Well, bairn, you're looking well and there's no need to ask if you and Billy are all right.' She gave Libby a warm hug and drew her indoors.

'Oh, Granny, we're so happy.'

'Mmm, I can see that. Blooming, ye are. When I recognized your car I thought you might have come to have a wee grumble about your mother's news . . .' It was almost a question.

'Mother's . . . ? Oh, you mean the baby. I suppose I have come about that in a roundabout sort of way but so long as Mum and Dad are happy, I'm happy too. But I do want to ask you a big favour, Granny. I need your help.'

'My help? Whatever for, lassie?'

'Mum's looking tired whenever I see her, and you know she has Cousin Peter staying over the school holidays?'

'Aye, I do. He was down here this morning with Fraser. They could be brothers to look at them. They're going to put the garden in for me. I was worrying about it. It's far too big now Joe's gone, so it's a relief to have them do it, even if they don't make as good a job as your grandpa would have done. So? What's the favour, lassie?'

'I offered to make a dinner for all the family on Easter Sunday, to save Mum. I have to be at work tomorrow morning though and I wondered if you would make one of your big trifles?'

'I'm sure ye dinna need me to make a trifle. You've been learning to cook ever since Lachie was born – ten years now.'

'I know, but there'll be such a lot to do and Aunt Mary and Uncle Willie are coming too, and Mimi of course. I . . . er . . .'

'Och, come on, lassie. Spit it out. It isna like you to beat about the bush, Libby, and I ken fine what ye're wanting, and the trifle is naething but an excuse.'

'Wh-what do you mean, Granny?' Libby's cheeks coloured. Polly's eyes had a wicked twinkle.

'All this is about getting me to Home Farm to meet that lassie, isn't it?'

'I-I don't know what you mean. I do want you to make one of your special trifles.'

'You havena mentioned that Charlotte Crainby will be at Home Farm,' Polly said drily. 'But ye needna worry, lassie, I'll be there.'

'You will? Oh, Granny, thank you.' Libby threw her arms around the old lady.

'Och, there's no need to throttle me, lassie,' she grumbled, but her blue eyes were beaming at Libby. 'You were all ganging up on me so I had to give in and I suppose the lassie could never be as bad as her mother; no woman on earth could be that bad.'

'I think you'll like Charlotte when you get to know her,' Libby said.

'Aye, so Josh has been telling me.' She met Libby's startled eyes and nodded. ''Tis so. I don't think he realizes he's smitten wi' the lassie yet, and her eleven years younger than him, and one o' his students too. He's just like his father though, when he's made his mind up. The last time he was down from Glasgow he told me he would be bringing Charlotte to stay with you at Easter and he expected me to meet her and be civil.'

'Uncle Josh said that?'

'Indeed he did. Very firm he was about it too.' She began to laugh. 'Neither o' ye need have worried though. I'd made my mind up to take your grandpa's advice. He had a wee talk with the lassie at your wedding. One o' the last things he said to me before we went to sleep that night was that she seemed a pleasant lassie and he wouldna mind if Josh got a wife like that. He said he didna want to see him staying a bachelor all his days, or missing his chance o' happiness on our account. Joe was aye a good judge o' character. Mind you.' She wagged a finger at Libby. 'Don't you go telling Josh I've told ye that.' Her eyes sparkled, reminding Libby of Mimi and she wondered what her grandmother had been like when she was a girl. 'It willna do him any harm to be a bit nervous and sweat a wee bit.'

'Oh, Granny, you're as bad a tease as Lachlan under that sober expression you put on.'

'Aye, weel, I need to keep you all in order sometimes. And don't worry about the trifle, lassie. I have a tin o' fruit and a jelly. I'll soon whip up a sponge and I'll make it in my big cut-glass bowl. Perhaps you'll get the cream though? We'll put it on the top when I get it to your house. What else are ye making?'

'I've got a big roast of beef and I'll make Yorkshire puddings if I can get the oven hot enough. Charlotte will prepare the vegetables. She's not very good at cooking yet. She's never had a chance to try but she's a great help with preparing. She's bought the *Glasgow Cookery Book* to learn the basics. When you get to know her you'll be able to give her lots of tips.'

'We'll see about that,' Polly said cautiously. 'I'll bring some horseradish sauce.'

Libby sang all the way home. It had been so much easier than she had expected and she was glad Uncle Josh had been firm about Charlotte. It showed he cared, even if he didn't love her.

In spite of her show of philosophical acceptance in front of Libby, Polly had grave doubts about meeting Charlotte Crainby. It was hard to think the girl was becoming accepted in the family when her mother had been such a vile woman.

For her part, Charlotte's stomach was a knot of nerves at the prospect of meeting Josh's mother. She knew how spiteful and nasty her own mother had been to the Pringle family and she didn't blame the old woman for harbouring resentment.

Libby had left Charlotte to pour the batter into the roasting tins to make the Yorkshire puddings while she whipped cream and checked the dining table and the rest of the food. Neither of them heard Josh's little car arrive. The fat was so hot when Charlotte drew the first tin from the Aga that it was turning the air blue.

'Libby!' she wailed. 'Come back! I think I've burned the tin. What shall I do?'

'There, there, lassie, ye havena burned anything,' Polly soothed, coming into the kitchen. She set a huge trifle on the table, peeling off her coat without a pause. 'Get the batter in as fast as ye can and put the tin back into the oven before it cools.'

'Oh!' Charlotte gasped in shock at the sight of Josh's mother, still in her hat, reaching for a large apron hanging behind the kitchen door.

'That's the style. Ye're doing fine. Bring out the other tin while ye're at it and set it on the hot plate. The secret of a good Yorkshire pudding is to have the fat hot and get it back into a hot oven as fast as ye can.'

Between them they got the two meat tins back into the Aga before the oven began to cool.

'Th-thank you,' Charlotte stammered.

'That's all right, lassie. We all have to learn and Libby is lucky to have such a fine cooker. I always have a job stoking up my fire to get the oven hot enough for Yorkshire puddings. Josh loves them.'

'Oh!' Libby halted in the doorway. 'You've met.'

'Aye, so we have.'

'Aren't you going to take your hat off, Granny?' Libby began to smile. 'And what are you doing putting on a pinafore? You're not supposed to be working.'

'Mrs Pringle helped me get the batter into the meat tins for the Yorkshire puds,' Charlotte said. 'I-I thought they were going to burn.'

'Oh, I see.' Libby's bright brown eyes moved from one to the other. She sighed. 'Well if you both want to help me make the dinner, that's fine. Mum can sit in the room and rest. I've whipped up the cream, Granny. Will you put it on top of the trifle? Perhaps you'd slice the carrots for me, please, Charlotte?'

'She's a right sergeant-major, dishing out orders, isn't she?' Polly said.

Charlotte chewed her lip and looked at Josh's mother, who was already spooning cream on to the trifle. Polly winked and gave her a crooked smile which was so like Josh's that Charlotte wanted to hug her. She was not the frightening woman she had expected. She was small and cuddly and lovely with her sparkling blue eyes and round cheeks.

Charlotte was not the only one who had been nervous about the family gathering. Peter was used to the stiff formality of the dinner parties which his parents had held for colleagues of his stepfather. He was dreading a large gathering and long drawn-out conversations excluding anyone under thirty. He soon discovered he had nothing to worry about. Billy welcomed him and showed him round the ground-floor rooms, including his grandfather's library, of which he was justifiably proud.

'It's a beautiful house,' Peter said. 'The rooms are so spacious and each one has a beautiful view – to the flower borders or to the hills, or down to the farm.'

'According to Mother, Langmune house looked like this before the fire, except it didn't have a library or a conservatory. My father had those built on when Grandfather moved in here.'

Peter was looking round the shelves of books which covered three walls from floor to ceiling. 'You have a fine collection,' he said in genuine admiration.

'You're welcome to borrow them, any time you like. Libby and her mother are avid readers. I read about farming and nature and local history, but I haven't had much time since I took over the farm.'

'I love reading,' Peter said, 'but I'm discovering what a lot I have to learn about farming and country life. If you can recommend any books to teach me some of the basics, I'd be grateful.'

'I can give you a couple right now on general agriculture.' Billy reached for his own copy of *Elements of Agriculture* and his Watson & Moore. 'Things are changing fast since the war though, so you need to keep an open mind. After we've had dinner I'll show you round Home Farm if you like. Fraser wants to see the bulk milk tank.

That is one change I think will come in the next few years.'

Peter didn't like to admit he hadn't a clue what Billy was talking about, but he nodded. 'I'd love to see the farm, but I don't think I shall ever get used to the size of the cows. Fraser thinks I should go to High Bowie and learn about sheep from his Uncle Willie.'

'He's a grand fellow. You'll like him,' Billy said. 'He listens but he only offers advice when asked.'

'Mmm. Not like my stepfather then.' Peter grimaced. 'He doesn't advise, he commands.'

'Libby has some useful books on bacteriology which should impress him,' Billy grinned. 'I take it he's still determined to make you into a doctor?'

'He is sure I shall hate being in the country with all the animal smells. He has no idea I have spent a lot of my spare time at the zoo for the last couple of years.'

'You go to the zoo?'

'Yes, most Saturdays and during the holidays when I can sneak away. I saved up to buy a decent bicycle. I know most of the keepers now and they let me help them. Sometimes it's chopping up fruit and vegetables for their feed; sometimes it's helping clean out the lions and tigers, but they're always shut away for safety while we work. If the vet comes to attend any of the animals he always takes me round with him if I'm there. He knew my mother when they were young.'

'I see,' Billy mused. 'So you are serious about wanting to live and work in the country then? It's not just a whim as your stepfather believes?'

'No, it's not a whim, but I know my stepfather will make things difficult if he can,' Peter said. 'He'll not give me his blessing to do what I want with my life.'

'We'll all help if we can,' Billy said, 'and I know Libby's parents will support you if you can convince them farming is what you want, but it will cost money for you to go to college or university.'

'That's all right,' Peter assured him. 'My own father was insured. Mother put the money in the bank for me, thinking I would need it to study medicine. Before she died she said I should use it for my education, whatever I decided to do.'

'In that case you need to concentrate on the practical experience first,' Billy advised.

'Come along, you two,' Libby called. 'Dinner is ready.'

It was a happy meal. Sitting next to Josh, Charlotte felt she had never been happier in her life. Mrs Pringle seemed to treat her with the same mixture of asperity and humour as she treated her grandchildren. Mimi, sitting on her other side, chatted non-stop except when she was eating. She did not allow her weakened hand to hold her back, any more than her limp prevented her from following the men out to the farmyard when the meal was over. Charlotte was happy to help Libby clear away, leaving Maggie, Victoria and Polly to relax.

'I shall never be able to make a meal like that for so many people,' Charlotte said as she joined Libby in the kitchen with a pile of dirty plates. 'Everything was delicious.'

'What will you do when you finish at college?' Libby asked.

'I must get my parchment. I've applied to teach in a large school in Glasgow. Josh thinks I shall find it hard to cope with a class of boisterous children but I think it will be a challenge. Besides, I want to help them and I would hate to be in a school where the children had snooty parents who want to interfere every time their child needs to be chastised.'

'Mmm, I can see there must be disadvantages to both kinds. You will still see Uncle Josh then, if you stay in Glasgow?'

'I shall keep the same flat.' Charlotte flushed. 'I shall not see your uncle at the college though, but he has promised to help if I run into any difficulties.'

'He will too, knowing Uncle Josh, but I'll bet he'll be round at your door at the end of your very first day, to see how you've got on.'

Charlotte's cheeks grew even pinker. Had Libby guessed how she felt about Josh?

During the following week Peter spent most of his time at High Bowie watching Willie with his ewes and lambs and helping Mary feed the three pets. Lachlan usually accompanied him and he and Mimi tagged along behind except when Willie took him to the heather-clad moor at the highest part of the farm. He loved the views. He felt he could spend the whole day in the peace and beauty. Mimi found the steep, rough ground too difficult, though she never grumbled, and Peter's heart warmed to the bright-eyed, cheery little girl. He thought of his half-sister, Dinah, and her trivial complaints, but he thought that Mimi and Cathy might get along well together.

On the Friday before he was due to return to Edinburgh, Victoria drove him down to Darlonachie and showed him the house where his father had lived with the Grantlys. They called in on Maggie.

'This cottage will be yours now, Peter. Before he died Luke Crainby transferred the Langmune land into my name and he gifted Ivy Cottage to your father. I suppose he thought Mark would come back to Darlonachie as Doctor Grantly's partner. Maggie pays a rent and I've started putting it into an account for you. It's not a large amount because the cottage is small. Before we knew about you I didn't want to take any rent from her because she moved out of Home Farm to let Libby take over when they married. Billy and his mother insisted on paying a rent and I'm glad now. Even small amounts add up and you'll be glad of it for books and fees when you go to university.'

They called in at the butcher's and the grocer's and stopped to speak to some of the people they met in the village. Peter couldn't believe how friendly they were towards him. One or two said he was like Fraser and Mr Ross, the grocer, said he remembered his father coming round with the doctor and that he was the image of him. Victoria insisted on making a brief visit to Mr Nelson, who had been her teacher and Mark's. He was an old man now and his eyesight was failing but he always welcomed a visit. She had brought him some fresh eggs.

'Why! For a moment I thought I was seeing a ghost,' he exclaimed as he peered at Peter. 'How like Mark you are.'

'Peter is Mark's son, Mr Nelson. We didn't know until recently.' She gave a rueful smile. 'It seems to be my lot to discover my closest family when they're already half-grown, but I'm so glad to have found Peter. He is staying with us for the Easter holidays and he may come back in the summer.'

'Oh I shall, there's no doubt about it. So long as you'll have me,' he added with a note of uncertainty.

'You can be sure of a welcome at Langmune whenever you want to come, Peter.'

Mr Nelson asked about his education and Peter was happy to tell him.

'Just like Mark then.' The old man nodded with satisfaction. 'He always excelled at maths and wanted to know everything about science and nature. Are you going to be a doctor too, young man? It's a very worthy calling.'

'No, sir. I want to be a farmer.'

'A farmer!' Mr Nelson looked from him to Victoria and back again. 'But . . .'

'Mr Nelson thinks that will be a waste of a good brain, Peter.' Victoria smiled, her eyes twinkling as they met the old man's gaze.

'Aye, well lassie, you and Andrew were the best of scholars but you two had little choice but to find work and earn a living. It's different for young folks since the war. You should persuade your nephew to pursue a good career, Victoria.'

'At the end of the day it has to be his decision, but I shall do my best to support him whatever he decides to do.'

They took their leave and drove out of the village and past the end of the wood towards Darlonachie Castle and the cottages. Victoria parked the car and they wandered together through the overgrown gardens and round the castle and the outbuildings. She told Peter about the old days when Sir William was alive and her great-grandmother was the cook. She described the gardens and immaculate grounds, the various cottages and the people who had lived there.

'I'm glad to have one last look before they start demolishing the castle,' she said.

'I heard Charlotte telling Uncle Andrew they are starting at the beginning of May. She said if he wanted some of the oak doors he should help himself.'

'Oh, he would never do that! It would be like stealing.'
Victoria was aghast.

'That's what he told her but he did say he would like to
buy some. He offered to store some for when Charlotte gets
a house of her own.'

'Yes, it would be lovely to think we had preserved a bit
of the past and I'm sure Charlotte must feel sad to see the
end of Darlonachie Estate, although she never had anyone
to tell her about her Crainby ancestors and her mother had
no respect or appreciation of their heritage. Come on, we'll
climb up the little hill through the woods and I'll show where
your father and I used to spend our time together.'

The path was overgrown and the sight of it saddened
Victoria but the little shelter they had called their cave was
just as it had always been. The old tree trunk where they
used to sit was a little rotten and one end was growing orange
fungi, but Victoria was pleased to take a seat. This baby was
taking more out of her than the others had done.

'I've often heard people say you should never return to
childhood haunts,' she said when she regained her breath, 'and
I must admit things do seem rather sad and forlorn . . .'

'Oh, but I'm glad you've come this once to show me, Aunt
Victoria,' Peter said. 'I've longed to know all about my father.
The few times when Mother mentioned him, my stepfather
glowered at her. I think he wanted to pretend he had never
existed.'

'I expect he was jealous.'

'Jealous of a dead man? How pathetic is that?'

'Your mother and father loved each other very much, even
though they were quite young. I don't think your mother
ever stopped loving him and I suppose Doctor Sterling knew
that. To be fair, Peter, perhaps you had a better chance in
life as a member of his household than you would have done
with just you and your mother.'

'That's what he keeps telling me,' Peter said. 'But the
house and the surgery belonged to Grandfather. He moved
in and took over everything. I expect Grandfather grew too
old to argue with him.'

'Maybe. Peter . . .' Victoria hesitated, her eyes gazing out
over the fields and glens. She could see Langmune like a

child's farm in the distance. She remembered when Andrew had first pointed it out to her. Peter was looking at her, waiting. She frowned. 'I want you always to remember, whatever happens, whatever you need, so long as Andrew and I are alive, you can come to us and we shall do our best to help in whatever way you need us, but . . .'

'But you don't think I should be a farmer,' Peter said, his voice bleak with disappointment.

'I didn't say that. I want you to consider and I don't want you to choose a path just because it's the opposite of what your stepfather wants for you. It is your life, but Mr Nelson is right. You do have the intelligence to make a good career for yourself. Farming is a hard life. Andrew and I have been lucky. We could never have been where we are now without the generosity of Mr Rennie and Luke Crainby. Andrew would still have been working for someone else.'

'I don't think he would,' Peter said. 'I think he would have found a way, even if it took all his life.'

Victoria's eyebrows shot up and she eyed him keenly. 'How like your father you are. You may be right. Andrew planned to keep a few pigs in a large garden and look after them in his spare time.'

'And Uncle Willie got started on his own, even if it is worrying him having money borrowed from his bank. I shall never tell my stepfather that. He thinks it's a sin to borrow money but he didn't mind using Mother's inheritance to extend the surgery and buy a car. When I stand beside Mimi's father at the very top of High Bowie I feel like a god. It's a wonderful feeling. Anyway I don't mind getting my hands dirty and I enjoy looking after animals. They're more helpless than people. You have to guess what they need. Do you understand, Aunt Victoria? I think there's something in here.' He tapped his chest with his clenched fist. 'Something that tells me I want to work in the open air, and care for things.'

'You could be a vet,' Victoria suggested.

'We'll see.' Peter looked at her and smiled and his brown eyes twinkled. 'I shall tell my stepfather you did your best to discourage me from farming. That will please him and he might agree to me coming back during the summer holidays.'

Victoria missed having Peter around when he returned to Edinburgh for what he hoped would be his last term at school. He had taken two of Billy's and one of Libby's college books home with him but he had done little in the way of his own studies for his final exams. He said he worked hard when he was at school and he didn't see any point in getting brain fatigue. Fraser grinned and agreed with him but Victoria was convinced Doctor Sterling would blame her if his results were poor.

Every day Billy or Libby called in at Ivy Cottage to see Maggie, on the pretext of taking fresh milk or eggs, but they were both concerned at her increasing lack of energy and difficulty in breathing. Doctor Ritchie and Doctor Burns both kept an eye on her but they could not give her a new heart and increasing her medication made little improvement. She was always cheerful and pleased to see them and Victoria made a point of calling once or twice a week. She called one evening towards the end of May and Maggie seemed improved. They reminisced happily and Maggie smiled as she told Victoria of her first meeting with Luke Crainby and how he tried so hard to behave as a gentleman.

'The attraction between us was too strong,' she said with a happy smile. 'It was like a magnet, a force that would not be denied. I have no regrets.' She went on to talk of her childhood and her parents. It was later than usual by the time Victoria left that evening and forever afterwards she was glad she had insisted on seeing Maggie into bed. It was Billy who called the following morning and found the door still locked and Tibbie the cat jumping at the window, needing to get out. Billy reached above the door for the spare key and let himself in, his heart sinking, dreading what he might find. At first he thought his mother was still sleeping, a faint smile on her lips as though having a pleasant dream, but he soon realized she would have no more dreams. The first thing he did was telephone Libby at work. Libby was his rock in times of trouble. It did not take Doctor Ritchie long to come to the cottage and confirm what Billy already knew, but Libby was there before he left.

'You must have driven like the wind,' Steve Ritchie chided, but in fact Libby's thoughts had been to reach Billy's side and she had little recollection of anything except grabbing her coat and handbag and telling her two assistants what had happened.

Billy decided the funeral should be private but Charlotte and Josh both came down from Glasgow for the day and travelled back together in the evening. Billy appreciated their support. He was more distressed than he had anticipated, considering they had known Maggie's health was so fragile. Libby telephoned Mr Whittaker, her boss, and told him she needed to be off for the rest of the week.

'I understand you need to be with your husband at a time like this, Libby, but we shall have to have a serious talk when you come back to work.'

'Oh?' Libby was already tense and she felt she couldn't cope with any more trouble. One of her assistants was Mr Whittaker's niece. She was a cheery girl but she was a complete scatterbrain. Libby knew she would never make a laboratory technician. If her uncle had not been the creamery manager Libby would have told him so but it was Mr Whittaker who had given her the job. 'What sort of meeting?' she asked when he didn't continue.

'Things have got a bit out of hand while you've been off,' he said. 'In fact they're in a hell of mess up in the lab. I don't think we'll be able to manage without you at the end of the summer.'

'B-but I promised Billy I'd give up work then,' Libby said in consternation.

'I know, I know. As I said, we'll have a talk when you come back. I see now I shall need to make changes. Why didn't you tell me Dolly is such a bird-brained madcap?'

'A-a what?' Libby gasped, then she gave a sigh of relief. 'She's got a lovely nature, Mr Whittaker, but I didn't know how to tell you she's no use at lab work.'

'Aye, well I know now, and so do a lot of the farmers who are spitting nails down the phone at me. She's sent out some queer results. She must think half the cows give double cream, while the other half gives nothing but water.'

'Oh dear.'

'You can say that again. I've told them all you'll sort them out when you come back to work.'

Libby set the phone down with a sigh. She longed to stay at home with Billy. He was taking his mother's death badly. But at least Mr Whittaker now knew the difficulties she was having with Dolly and with any luck he would find a replacement.

Six

L ibby still kept in touch with two of her college friends
but she owed both of them a letter so she decided it
was time to catch up with her correspondence while she
was at home. They had both met Billy's mother at the
wedding, so she told them of her death. They also knew
about her problems with her scatterbrained trainee so she
told them of her relief now a solution was in sight. She was
astonished when Alma wrote back by return. She expressed
her sympathy to Billy but from the rest of her letter it was
clear she was increasingly unhappy about her own work.
She asked whether Mr Whittaker might consider her as a
replacement and if Libby would put in a word for her
with Mr Whittaker when she resigned at the end of the
summer.

Over at Langmune, Victoria missed Maggie's company
and the chats they had shared but she had Peter's letters to
look forward to. He wrote humorous descriptions which even
Fraser enjoyed now they had met. He said he was working
hard at his Higher Grade exams but he hoped to return to
Langmune as soon as they were over at the end of June.
When a second letter arrived in the same week, however,
Victoria was concerned.

'Peter and his stepfather have had a serious quarrel,' she
told Andrew when he came in for lunch. 'Doctor Sterling
has delivered an ultimatum. He says Peter can come here
for the summer but he must return for sixth year and to
continue his studies to become a doctor. If he refuses he will
not get a penny of the insurance money.'

'It's not his money!'

'Catriona didn't see her solicitor before she died so Doctor
Sterling still has control. Peter was relying on the money to

help pay his college fees. I feel so sorry for him. He wants to know if he can still come to Langmune.'

Victoria passed the letter to Andrew, her lips compressed.

'I have to get away from here. I have to think and make my own decisions, even if it means I never go to agricultural college.'

'Telephone the laddie tonight,' Andrew said. 'Tell him he is welcome to come and stay for as long as he likes, but we must make him see that Doctor Sterling may be right over this. It's getting more difficult than ever to get a start in farming. Of course he may get a degree in agriculture and go round farms inspecting or advising. There's a lot of that creeping in with all the rules and regulations and grants for projects the government wants us to carry out. They still want more production.'

'I did try to tell him that at Easter but he said he felt a yearning in his heart for the countryside. I suspect he's a bit of a romantic. He said it was wonderful to stand on the highest point of High Bowie and survey the world, yet any farmer would tell him what a hard farm High Bowie is, and what hard work it is to make a living.'

'We would say that,' Andrew agreed, 'but I don't think Willie would change it for anything else. He always said he'd never milk cows seven days a week to earn his living. It's always Mary who milks the house cows if you notice.'

'Mmm, I suppose you're right. Willie enjoyed Peter's company at Easter. He said he'd never had a young fellow who asked so many questions. He reckons he's like a sponge the way he absorbs things, and he has a keen eye.'

'Perhaps we should treat him as we did Libby and set him to work like the rest of the men. If he finds it too hard he'll know farming is not for him.'

Victoria chewed her lip thoughtfully.

'It may seem hard,' Andrew conceded, seeing her doubtful expression, 'but Peter has to learn what the life is really like. If he does decide it's what he wants he could work for a couple of years and pay his own college fees. The practical experience will be as much benefit to him as college. He's starting from scratch. Libby and Fraser grew up knowing what's involved. They sense when an animal is sick. It's amazing how much Mimi and Lachlan know already but Peter has everything to learn.'

'I agree the experience will be good for him, and saving the money. There's the cottage too. We must look for another tenant. Three pounds a week for rent will add up.'

'I'm sure things will work out, Vicky, one way or another,' Andrew said gently. He knew she felt great affection for her only nephew already.

'I suppose so but I'd like to give Doctor Sterling a piece of my mind,' she said angrily. 'Catriona specifically said Peter should do what he wanted with his life and the money was there to help him.'

'You mustn't get upset,' Andrew cautioned. 'It's not good for you. Doctor Burns said you were to take life calmly. Has she booked you in at Cresswell yet?'

'Don't change the subject, Andrew. I don't want to think about going to the maternity hospital. Going to the clinic was bad enough, waiting in line like the cows waiting to be milked. I hated it. You know the names of all the cows and they're all individuals. I felt like a number rather than a person and two of the younger nurses were giggling like school girls until a senior nurse glared at them. I detest it and I'm not going back and I wish I hadn't let Doctor Burns persuade me I should go to the hospital to have this baby.'

'Hush, Victoria, don't get upset,' Andrew urged, drawing her into his arms and stroking her hair. He'd intended to take her mind off Doctor Sterling and he'd only ended up upsetting her. She was easily upset these days but the baby was due in about eight weeks. Having Peter to stay would make extra work and it worried him a bit but he knew Victoria would never hear of postponing his visit.

When Andrew met Peter off the train at Lockerbie station he was glad he had not suggested the boy should stay in Edinburgh. He was thinner and his young face looked haggard. There were dark rings under his eyes, which should not be on the face of a young man like Peter.

'I'm glad to see you, laddie,' he greeted him warmly and saw the dark eyes light up for a moment. 'You look as though you've been working hard at your exams. You're thinner than you were at Easter.'

'I did work hard for my exams, and I think I shall have done reasonably well in most of them.' He sighed heavily. 'But if I have it will only make my stepfather more determined to rule my life. Dinah wants to be a doctor and Cathy thinks she wants to nurse. Why can't he be satisfied with that?'

For a moment Andrew thought the boy might burst into tears. 'I expect he wants what's best for you, laddie,' he said gently. 'Come on, here's the car. Victoria will have the tea ready.'

Victoria was shocked by Peter's appearance. She couldn't resist giving him a welcoming hug. She was surprised when he hugged her back, almost as though he needed reassurance of some kind.

'Take your case to your room, Peter, and then we'll have tea. You'll need to eat plenty because supper will be a bit later tonight. Libby and Billy are coming up to see you. Mimi wanted to come too but Mary said she had to wait until tomorrow. I expect she'll be here first thing if Willie will see her over the burn.'

'Th-thank you,' Peter said huskily. 'Y-you don't know what it means to be made so welcome.' He disappeared quickly up the stairs, unwilling to let them see the tears that had sprung to his eyes. Victoria and Andrew looked at each other.

'He looks exhausted,' Victoria said in a low voice.

'He's very tense. I suspect there have been more arguments.'

Fraser and Lachlan were washing their hands ready for tea when Peter returned to the kitchen.

'Hi, chum.' Fraser grinned, slapping him on the back. 'It's good to see you again. I hoped you'd be here before Saturday. We're having a farm walk and there's a Young Farmers' dance afterwards.'

'Aren't you supposed to be working on Saturday?' Andrew asked.

'I was. I've swapped with Jocky.'

'Hi, Peter,' Lachlan said as he joined them, still drying his hands, his grin spreading from ear to ear. 'Are you for a game of football after tea? I've been practising.'

'For goodness' sake, Lachie, give Peter chance to get here before you pester him,' Victoria chided, but Peter was pleased to see his cousins and grateful for their welcome.

Billy and Libby greeted him with the same warmth as the rest of the family but after the evening meal was cleared away the conversation turned serious.

'Are you just here for the summer holidays, Peter?' Billy asked with a smile. 'Or have you decided farming is the life for you?'

'I-I don't know,' Peter said unhappily. 'I know what I want, b-but this morning . . .' He gulped over the lump in his throat. 'Before I left, my stepfather told me there's no place for me under his roof unless I study medicine. He says he's supported me long enough and Dinah wants a worthwhile profession so she will make better use of the money Mother had set aside.' There was a stunned silence. They all stared at him.

'He wouldn't mean that,' Victoria said. 'I expect he's disappointed.'

'He does mean it. He says I can have until the end of the summer holidays to make up my mind. Unless I toe the line I've to collect the rest of my things and leave his house for good.'

'That's awful!' Libby gasped. 'He can't threaten Peter like that, can he, Mum?'

'I don't know, lassie.' Victoria's face was troubled. She looked Peter in the eye. 'I'm so glad your mother found the courage to go against his wishes and send for me before she died. I suppose you know he did his best to cut us out of her life after your father died.'

'That's all in the past,' Andrew intervened. 'You're here now, laddie, and we're pleased to have you. You have all summer to make up your mind. Victoria and I have discussed what we're prepared to do to help you. You'd better discuss our suggestion with Libby. We made sure she knew what hard work farming involved before she went to college. We wanted her to be sure too.'

Peter met Libby's eyes, his dark brows raised.

'It's true, Peter.' Libby nodded. 'Some of the work is hard, but I was prepared for that and I knew it was the life I wanted.'

'It's what I want too.'

'In that case I propose to set you to work, like Fraser and Jocky Conley and Jem Wright. You'll work alongside them and learn to do whatever jobs are needed. No shirking or taking a day off when you feel tired. Farming isn't like that. Animals still need fed, cows still need milked, even if you have been up half the night helping one of them to calve.'

'That's what Uncle Willie said about the lambs,' Peter said. 'Does that mean you'll let me do proper farm work, Uncle Andrew?'

'Aye, laddie. We'll probably give you more to do than you want, but when it comes to the end of the summer, you can tell us whether you want to carry on, or go back to Edinburgh and have a profession. There'll be no hard feelings whatever you decide. You'll still be welcome whenever you want to come for a holiday, won't he?'

'Of course he'll always be welcome,' Victoria said.

'But right now this is a business arrangement,' Andrew went on. 'You'll start work on Monday. We're busy with the hay so there's plenty to do. You'll need to learn to drive the tractors. We'll pay you a wage and deduct your board and lodging as it says in the government wages schedule.'

'You'll pay me? Even though I'm learning?' Peter asked incredulously.

'Of course we'll pay you. The agricultural rate for a man is seven pounds, eighteen shillings and five pence for a forty-seven-hour week. It will be a bit less for a seventeen-year-old, and as I said we'll deduct board and lodging. If you work for Willie or for Billy then they must pay you too. As I said, Peter, this is a business deal and it'll be hard work. When you've had enough it will be up to you to admit it. If you do decide it's the life you want by the end of the summer, we'll find you work for a couple of years. The experience will be good for you. I know Willie would be glad to employ you for a few weeks when he's lambing, and for the shearing, but he couldn't afford to employ a boy all year round. Maybe Billy will give you some work too when his men are on holiday?'

'I could certainly do that,' Billy nodded.

'The broader your experience the better it will be for you.

If you save your money for the next two years I reckon you'll be able to pay your own college fees if you can get one of the new grants. You'll be independent of everybody, including your stepfather.'

'I can't believe it! I just can't believe it!' Peter exclaimed, his dark eyes shining. He looked young and eager now; the weary look had vanished, along with the invisible burden that had seemed to weigh him down. 'I-I can't tell you how unhappy I've been these past few weeks.'

'Well, laddie, we'll do all we can, but you have to be honest with us if you change your mind. I've one thing to ask in return, and that applies to all of you.' He looked at Lachie and Fraser. 'And that's to consider your mother. You'll know we're expecting another wee bairn in August, Peter?'

'Ye-es.' Peter blushed. 'I didn't know when . . .'

'Och, never mind about me,' Victoria said, feeling embarrassed. 'There's the cottage to think about too. We must get another tenant. I shall be putting the rent aside for you, Peter. Billy, do you want any more of your mother's furniture out of Ivy Cottage before we let it?'

'I think we've taken out all the things we want to keep, haven't we, sweetheart?' He smiled at Libby.

'Yes we have, but, Mum, if you could hang on for a couple of weeks . . . You remember Alma? She's coming up for an interview at the creamery. I told Mr Whittaker she's looking for a job away from the city. I'm almost sure she'll get it. She's had the same training as I had from Miss Cuttle. She'd be ideal and I wouldn't feel I was letting Mr Whittaker down either.'

'Does that mean you're giving up working then?' Victoria asked.

'Yes, at the end of the summer. I've agreed to stay until my successor gets into the routine.'

'About time too,' Andrew said. 'Billy has been very patient.'

'Mmm? He's already handing over the calf sketching and the pedigrees, as well as the accounts,' Libby said darkly.

'And helping me with the relief milking when Arthur Williams and young Robbie Dunlop have their weekends off,' Billy said with a grin.

Peter made the most of his few days of freedom, joining

Lachie and Mimi, catching up on the changes since Easter, marvelling how fast some of the young animals had grown. He went over to High Bowie and walked to the highest peak with Willie, eager to gaze on the panorama which he remembered from his last visit. He listened to advice on what to look for in a good lamb ready for market and helped Willie catch some of them, feeling their rumps and the thickness of their fleeces and their supple skins.

'That laddie has a thirst for knowledge,' Willie said later that evening.

Mimi returned to Langmune with Peter. He hitched her up on his back to give her a piggy back across the burn. He noticed she had started wearing slacks now instead of her cotton skirts and ankle socks. He wondered if she was growing conscious of her lame leg and he felt a pang of sympathy for her. She was such a lively sprite. Her father had told him she tired easily so he never took her to the top of the rough, steep hill at High Bowie. Peter suspected it was a warning to him not to encourage her. He thought Mimi's parents were slightly over-protective but he was beginning to suspect their ten-year-old daughter would have enough determination to conquer Everest if she set her mind to it. He had seen the way she clenched her teeth and thrust out her little pointed chin when she was struggling to keep up with Lachlan, but she had such a sunny nature she seemed to make the world a brighter place, especially after the atmosphere he had left behind in the house in Edinburgh. He paused, forgetting he was in the middle of the burn with one foot on the large stepping stone and the other on the opposite bank.

Mimi squealed; her soft arms tightened around his neck and her fair curls brushed his cheek as she clung to him.

'Don't you dare drop me in the middle of the burn, Peter Sterling!'

'Such a thing had never entered my head.' He grinned. 'At least not until you put it there.' He pretended to drop her and her arms nearly throttled him. 'I was admiring the water. It's crystal clear as it comes tinkling over the stones.' He stepped out of the burn and set her down on the grassy bank.

'It's not always like this. You should see it when it floods.' She shuddered. 'It comes right up over the sides and you'd think it was boiling and it's red with soil washed from further up. It would sweep you away. Even Daddy and Uncle Andrew go down to the new bridge to cross when the water is high.'

'I'll remember,' Peter said, smiling down at her serious face. 'Today the burn is singing to us.' He bent to pick a flower. 'You don't know how lucky you are to have such beauty around you every day.'

Mimi looked up at him and then down at the grass and flowers around their feet. She frowned. 'Don't you have flowers in the city?'

'In gardens we do, but just look at that blue vetch climbing up the hedge. It's a heavenly blue, just like your eyes. Then there's the pink campion over there, and the scent of the honeysuckle is wonderful.' He breathed in and Mimi did the same.

'Mmm, it smells nice. I suppose we're so used to it we don't think about it.'

'What's the golden flower beside the water?'

'Golden? Mmm, I suppose they are gold. We have masses of them in the spring. They're nearly over now. It's a kingcup. Daddy calls it Luckan Gowan. Aunt Victoria knows the names of most of the flowers and the birds, and Libby and Billy have lots of books. I always go to Libby if I'm stuck with my lessons for school.'

'I'd like to know all about the flowers. I shall ask Libby if she has a good book I can borrow.'

'I do hope you like it here, Peter. Daddy says you may be able to get a job as a manager if you go to college and he says you'll learn a lot from Uncle Andrew.'

'Oh, I intend to stay, if Uncle Andrew will have me. It will take more than hard work to sicken me, and everybody is so friendly and happy.'

'Doctor Ritchie says people should be happy and count their blessings. I think he means I should forget my wonky old leg, but sometimes I can't forget when I can't keep up or run as fast as everybody else. He says I have other things to make up.'

'He's right about that,' Peter nodded. 'You have the sunniest smile I've ever seen.'

'Mmm, that's because I'm happy. I don't want to live

anywhere else, not ever.' She raised her small innocent face
to his. 'Mummy says I must work hard at school and then
I can go to college and be a teacher, or something like that,
but I don't think I'd like to stay inside all day when the sun
is shining, or when the lambs are being born.'

'You've a long time before you need to decide,' Peter
comforted her. 'When I was ten I never dreamed I'd want
to live in the country and look after animals. It was after I
went on a visit to the zoo with a friend from school. When
I got my bicycle I cycled there whenever I could get away.
Some of the keepers let me help.'

'But Daddy says you're clever at your lessons too. Lachlan
is too, but don't tell him I said so.' She grinned and looked
up at Peter, her blue eyes sparkling conspiratorially. 'He's
not sure whether he wants to be a farmer though and Uncle
Andrew bought Throstlebrae Farm so that he and Fraser can
have a farm each.'

'What would Lachie like to do then?'

'Och, he doesna know. Daddy says he'll end up being a
farmer when he comes to his senses.' She shrugged her thin
shoulders. 'Come on, it's tea time and Aunt Victoria might
have rhubarb pie. She's promised to show me how to make
it but Mummy says I've not to pester her until she gets the
new baby. Look, there's wild roses. Do you like them? They
have big scarlet hips later on. Libby says they glow like
rubies but I've never seen a ruby.'

'I like all the flowers, even the dandelions and buttercups
and daisies.'

'Sometimes we sing a song about them at Sunday School.
*"Daisies are our silver, buttercups our gold, These are all
the treasures we can have or hold"*,' she sang in her clear
melodious voice.

'That's lovely, Mimi!'

She flushed with pleasure and gave him a shy smile.

Seven

'I'm afraid we've thrown you in at the deep end, laddie.' Andrew smiled as he looked at the rivulets of sweat carving paths through the dust on Peter's face. He wiped his own brow with a dusty hand, leaving a dirty streak down his cheek. 'We can't miss a chance to get the hay in while the weather is good.'

'I love the scent of new-mown hay.' Peter breathed in deeply. 'It's worth the toil and it's satisfying to see the stack of bales getting higher.'

'Aye, it's a lot quicker now we have a baler instead of making it all into wee haycocks, and then into bigger ones as it dried. After that we'd to load it on to carts and get it into the sheds or into stacks. Things are easier than they used to be, but it's still hard work. Billy has made some of his grass into silage this year. He reckons it doesn't depend on the weather as much as hay. He's dug out a pit and lined it with concrete panels. We'll go down there one evening when we've finished the hay. I'd like to see what's going on and whether it's an improvement. Never think you know it all in farming, laddie. Things are always changing since the war. Learn all you can whenever you get the chance.'

'I doubt if I shall ever know half the things I need to be a farmer,' Peter sighed. 'I'd no idea there was so much to learn.'

'Och, next year at this time you'll be doing it as though you've done it all your life. Some things come instinctively, like when a cow will have her calf. Other things need practice, like you driving the tractor and trailer whenever you've a bit o' spare time. Practise the reversing. Ah, here comes Jocky with another load. We'd better get on. It'll be dark before we know it.'

Dark? Peter smiled, knowing his stepfather would think he was crazy to contemplate a life like this. It barely seemed to be dark at all with the long summer evenings and the birds heralding the dawn at four o'clock in the morning. During his first week he had fallen into bed exhausted and aching in every limb but already his muscles were hardening as his strength increased. He couldn't believe how hungry he was by midday. Now he understood why Fraser was always ravenous and yet he remained so lean.

As soon as the hay was in at Langmune, Andrew despatched Fraser with the tractor and baler to High Bowie to bale the hay which Willie had already cut and raked into rows for lifting. He insisted on paying Andrew for the use of his man and machine.

'You can go with Fraser if you like, Peter, unless you're sick of loading bales on to trailers and stacking them in heaps?'

'I'd be happy to go to High Bowie.' Peter grinned. 'I'm just getting my muscles.' He flexed his arm to see how big his muscles would bulge.

'Aye, ye're hardier than I expected.' Andrew smiled. 'You're doing all right.'

'Can I go to High Bowie?' Lachie pleaded.

'All right,' Andrew agreed. He looked at Victoria. 'It will do you good to have a rest from feeding everybody in this hot weather.' She nodded. She couldn't remember ever feeling so tired and ungainly. She longed for this birth to be over although she was dreading going to hospital, but Doctor Burns had been insistent.

'I think Lachie and Peter had better go across the burn,' Andrew said. 'It's not safe for all of you on the tractor.'

'Oh, but Dad . . .'

'You heard what I said,' Andrew warned. 'If you get away now you'll be at High Bowie by the time Fraser drives the tractor and baler round by the bridge and back up the track.'

'Come on then, Lachie.' Peter grinned at his young cousin. 'I'll give you a piggy back across the burn.'

'With those long legs I should think you could nearly stride across it, Peter,' Victoria smiled. 'Your father was tall but I think you're already taller than he was.'

'I'm five feet eleven, half an inch taller than Fraser.' He chuckled, a deep warm sound for a gangly youth. 'Jocky Conley measured us last week to solve an argument – a friendly debate,' he corrected, his smile widening. It was one of the things he enjoyed about staying at Langmune – even arguments were friendly and there was never the sombre atmosphere and grim expressions that had been so much a part of life in the Edinburgh house. He was not yet aware of it but he no longer thought of his stepfather's house as home.

At the beginning of August Libby's friend Alma moved into Ivy Cottage and started work at the creamery. Libby had promised Mr Whittaker she would stay on until the end of the month until Alma got into the routine. After that she would be free to lend a hand when her baby brother or sister was born. Although the techniques were familiar the routine of the country creamery was different to the large London creamery where Alma had worked. She would be responsible for the chemical and bacteriological testing, from reception of the raw milk to the end product for sale to the public.

'I never even saw the milk coming in, or the bottles of pasteurized milk going out,' Alma said. 'I was stuck with checking and testing the processing equipment all day, sterile rinses and strength of detergent solutions and all that stuff. That's why it was so boring, but this is a bigger responsibility than I realized. I'm grateful for your support, Libby.'

'Och, you'll soon get used to it, though it takes a wee while to know which farmers might give you problems and which creamery workers are a bit slap-dash.' She grinned. 'Janey will make a good lab assistant by the time we've finished training her. She's from a farm so she's aware of the tricks some of them try.'

Billy was going to Cheshire on August 12th to attend the sale of a well known pedigree herd. He asked Andrew if he and Fraser would like to go too.

'We-ell,' Andrew hesitated. 'Fraser and Jocky Conley are busy overhauling the binder, ready to start the harvest.'

'I could help Jocky,' Peter volunteered, 'if Fraser wants to go.'

'It would be good for you to see round another farm and another part of the country, Fraser,' Andrew said.

'Yes, they have a milking parlour and a bulk milk tank. I'm looking forward to seeing that as much as the cows,' Billy said.

'All right then.' Fraser nodded. 'So long as you don't expect me to be interested in the pedigrees. That was always Libby's interest. I'm a commercial man.'

'We shall need to be away very early. The sale starts at ten and we want a look at the cattle before they begin selling.'

'Are you meaning to buy?' Andrew asked.

'No, not this time.' Billy shook his head. 'Though there's some excellent breeding and it would have been a grand chance. It's a dispersal of the whole herd, not just a selection. The owner died of a heart attack. If I'd known I wouldn't have bought a combine but we can't afford any more expense this year.'

'You've got a combine?' Fraser's eyes widened. He was all for modern machinery and change. Sometimes he felt frustrated by his father's caution and it made him irritable. 'You lucky so and so,' he muttered. 'I keep telling Father what a lot of labour and hard graft it would save us. We're stuck with cutting and stooking sheaves and carting them in, not to mention all the threshing that's to be done in the winter. I expect we shall still be doing it next century.'

'Don't exaggerate, Fraser,' Andrew said. 'I've made a lot of changes in the last ten years, let alone fifty. I haven't even lived fifty years myself, damn it, but I've seen plenty of changes. A combine is a huge capital expense and it's only used about two weeks in the year. We'll wait and see how Billy gets on with his.'

'It's a second-hand one from Yorkshire,' Billy said. 'Mr Butler's neighbour has bought a bigger one but he grows a big acreage of wheat. Mick's father thought this was a good bargain for me.' He glanced at Fraser's set young face. 'I couldn't have afforded a new one either,' he admitted. 'Maybe you'll let me combine a couple of fields at Langmune if I get my harvest finished in good time. Anyway, I'll pick you both up at quarter to six on Tuesday morning.'

Lachie was cross at being left at home all day. Victoria

was feeling too out of sorts to humour him so when Mimi telephoned to ask if he could go with her and Willie to the blacksmith's she agreed, on condition he was back in time to bring the cows in from the field for milking in the afternoon. There would be only her and Peter for dinner and there was plenty of soup left and a meat and potato pie with onions and carrots. She sat down to ease her aching back. She had not slept well for several nights now and she had been up early to cook Fraser and Andrew a good breakfast before they set out for Cheshire. The house was quiet and Victoria dozed. She wakened with a start and with an excruciating pain which seemed to start in her back and spread right through her. Beads of perspiration coated her upper lip and her brow. She wiped them away with the back of her hand. As the pain receded she closed her eyes thankfully. But it returned. The baby couldn't be coming so early. It must be something she had eaten.

Eight

Victoria soon realized the baby was not only coming, it was coming faster than she could believe. She glanced up at the clock, ticking away the seconds. The steady swing of the pendulum held her mesmerized until another violent contraction shook her. It was midday and she had not even put the soup on to warm. She tried to stand. A rush of fluids told her the waters had broken. She must telephone . . .

'Whatever's the matter? Aunt Victoria, are you . . . ? Is it the baby?'

'Thank goodness you're here, Peter,' Victoria gasped. 'Can you telephone for Doctor Burns, please?'

'OK.' Minutes later he turned to her with a frown. 'The doctor is out on a call. They asked if you're sure it's the baby. I told them you're certain.' He saw Victoria was in serious pain now. 'Shall I telephone for an ambulance? Aren't you supposed to go to hospital?'

'I-I don't think there'll be time. Phone the midwife, please, Peter. Then bring some towels and a sheet from the airing cupboard—' She broke off as the pain made her gasp. 'Lay them on the floor in the wee sitting room. I d-don't think I can manage the st-stairs. Quickly.'

Peter ran up stairs first and prepared a space in the room as fast as he could before he telephoned the midwife. By the time he had contacted her Victoria had made her way through to the room. He hesitated, wondering whether he should go in.

'Peter!'

'I'm here, Aunt Victoria. What do you want me to do?'

'Boil a small pan of hot water and put in the white tape from my mending box and the scissors. Sterilize them. I-I . . .' She broke off as another spasm convulsed her. 'Bring a white towel and a blanket from the cot to wrap the baby in. It . . . it's coming.'

Peter flew up the stairs. He didn't panic. He had never done anything like this but he had been brought up in a household where emergencies were part of life. He had absolute faith his aunt would tell him what to do. Much later he marvelled that he had felt so calm.

'Shall I phone for Libby?'

'She's at work.'

'Aunt Mary?'

'N-no t-time . . .' She gave a convulsive groan and Peter realized the baby's head was crowning and seconds later it slithered out into the world. He knew babies had to cry to clear their lungs but this one was already howling its tiny purple head off as he knelt beside Victoria and wrapped it in the soft white towel as well as he could with the navel still attached. He felt an amazing feeling of satisfaction, but he was not so sure he could deal with the tape and scissors.

Victoria was instructing him what to do next when they heard the voice of the midwife calling. Peter ran to the door and greeted her with profound relief.

'Well!' the midwife gasped. 'Well, I never . . .' After the initial shock she dealt with the baby then carried her through to the kitchen and handed her to Peter, still howling. 'I'll bathe her in a few minutes. You hold her and keep her warm, young man. You've done very well. I'll deal with Mrs Pringle now.'

Minutes later Doctor Burns arrived. The baby had stopped crying and was lying peacefully in Peter's arms. She bustled through to the room.

'The ambulance is on its way. They'll soon have you and the baby in hospital.'

'Hospital?' Victoria echoed. 'I'm not going to hospital now. The baby is born.'

'I see.' Doctor Burns pursed her lips. 'I don't believe you ever meant to go to hospital.' Steve Ritchie had won his bet after all. He had been convinced Mrs Pringle would have her baby at home; she had been certain she had persuaded her hospital was the best place. 'You took a terrible risk leaving things so late before you called us. It's a good job there were no complications and Mrs White was able to reach you in time. You were very foolish.'

'But I didn't deliver the wee mite. That young man through in the kitchen had everything under control by the time I arrived,' Mrs White announced. 'He was as calm as though he delivered babies every day.'

'That's disgraceful!' Doctor Burns said.

Victoria closed her eyes. She felt near to tears and completely drained. 'It came on very suddenly,' she protested.

'I don't think you ever intended going to hospital.'

Peter could hear the doctor through the open door. Why did they try to dictate other people's lives? he wondered, thinking of his stepfather. He moved to the door.

'It's true,' he said. 'Uncle Andrew would never have gone away if he'd thought the baby might be born today. When I came in it was just starting. It came so fast.'

'Well, I think you would still be better in hospital, you and the baby,' Doctor Burns persisted.

'No,' Victoria insisted. 'Peter, will you make me a cup of tea, please, and then telephone Mary? She'll come over. And put the soup on for your dinner. You must be famished. There's a meat and potato pie in the bottom oven. I hope it's not burned.' She tried to stifle a yawn.

'I think Mrs Pringle has made up her mind, Doctor,' Mrs White said. 'I'll get them both cleaned up and I'll help her up to bed when she's had some tea and toast. What are you going to call your wee girl, m'dear?'

'I think I shall have to let Peter choose since he came to our rescue. I don't know what I'd have done without you, laddie.' She smiled at Peter as she accepted the cup of tea he had brought. Doctor Burns declined the offer of tea and went on her way but Mrs White sipped hers gratefully.

'It's not often Doctor Burns is so cross,' she remarked. 'She must have been called out during the night or had a bad morning. Never mind, all's well that ends well and we must be thankful you had such a grand young man to help.' A little while later she announced, 'She's a fine baby with a good pair of lungs and she weighs six pounds and six ounces.'

'How small she is!' Victoria exclaimed. 'All my other babies were nearer eight pounds.'

Andrew was amazed when he returned home that evening to find Libby, Mary, and his mother there and no sign of Victoria or Lachie. He had seen Peter was still in the stack yard working on the binder with Jocky Conley. Before he could even unlace his boots and pull them off Libby was telling him the news.

'You have another daughter, Dad,' she grinned. 'Mum's upstairs and we can't tear Lachie away from them.'

'What? The baby has been born already? Here? At home? I thought . . .' Andrew stood up, one boot on and one off. His ruddy face had drained of colour.

'Everything is fine, Andrew,' Mary soothed. 'I think the babe came very quickly and took everyone by surprise, but it's better that way now they're both all right,' she added, recalling her own long and difficult labour.

'B-but, there was no sign this morning when we left,' Andrew said in bewilderment, placing his boots side by side and padding in his stocking feet towards the stairs. He bounded up them two at a time and pushed open the door. Although it was August someone had kindled a small fire in the grate to make sure the baby didn't get a chill. He guessed that would be Mary. Victoria lay back against the pillows, her eyes closed, her mouth curved in a tender smile as she listened to Lachie singing to the baby as he rocked the crib. He moved forward on silent feet. All he could see of his new daughter was a white cocoon and a tiny fist beside her cheek.

'Dad!' Lachie exclaimed. 'You're home.' Victoria opened her eyes at his exclamation.

'Ah, Andrew.' She smiled up at him but he could see she was tired. 'I'm glad you're home.' He felt a lump in his throat as he bent to kiss her. Lachie crept away.

'They're kissing up there,' he announced in disgust and everyone laughed.

'I'd better get home to Billy now.' Libby smiled. 'Will you tell Mum I shall be back first thing in the morning, Granny? Mr Whittaker has agreed to me staying off the next two weeks so long as I go back and finish training Janey later. I think Julie Dunlop would come up and help Mum on the days I can't be here.'

'Don't worry, Libby, we'll all help,' Mary said. 'I shall get no peace until I bring Mimi over to see her new cousin.'

'Right, I'll get away home now then.' Libby picked up her car keys but she was surprised when Fraser accompanied her outside.

'You'll get a surprise too, when you get home,' he told her.

'Oh?' Her eyes widened. 'Billy didn't buy any heifers, did he? I know how good the breeding was but he knows we can't afford to buy any. He promised faithfully we wouldn't get into debt after what happened to Charlotte's mother.'

'Och, you'll have to wait and see,' Fraser grinned. 'Anyway I thought you were supposed to trust the person you marry?'

'I do trust Billy, but . . .' She glared at Fraser's teasing grin. 'You're winding me up. You'd better go and see your baby sister and Mum before she falls asleep. She was struggling to stay awake until you and Dad were home.'

When Fraser entered the bedroom he found his father stroking the cheek of the tiny bundle in the crib. His mother looked exhausted but happy. He wondered if he would ever love anyone like his parents loved each other. He went to stand beside his father, looking down at the sleeping baby.

'What are we going to call her, Mum?'

'I think Peter should choose, since he helped her into the world. He says we should choose her first name but he hopes we might call her Catriona as well.'

'We could always call her Trina. Or Tina, or –' Fraser grinned wickedly – 'or Cat?'

'Och, Fraser! You're always inventing nicknames. We must choose something you can't shorten. Have you a favourite name?'

'We could call her after you.'

'No, no. Wait until you get a wee girl then you can name her after her granny.' To Victoria's surprise Fraser's face coloured up and she eyed him, then added, 'But I hope that will not be for a long time. You need to enjoy your life while you're young.'

Fraser didn't meet her eyes as he mumbled, 'I'll leave you to sleep.' He made his way to the door and escaped his mother's steady gaze.

'I wonder if Fraser has his eye on a girl?' she said.

'I wouldn't be surprised.' Andrew smiled. 'I hear Jocky and Peter teasing him sometimes when they're working together.'

'I hope it's not serious; he's far too young. He's only eighteen.'

'Don't fret about Fraser,' Andrew said. 'Get some rest now and I'll be up soon.' He kissed her tenderly.

When Libby arrived back at Home Farm, Billy was eager to hear all about the baby and how Peter had coped. He didn't mention any surprises and she guessed Fraser had been teasing, winding her up as he used to do when they were at home together. She asked about Billy's day and he told her some of the local farmers had been at the sale and a couple of them had bought cows. They had both had enough excitement and they were tired and ready for bed.

It was just after three in the morning when Libby was wakened by the sound of a lorry in the farmyard. Billy had heard it too and he was soon out of bed and scrabbling into his trousers.

'The driver said they wouldn't get this far north before morning,' he muttered.

'What driver? Why is that lorry here? Billy?'

But he was running down the stairs. By the time Libby had pulled on some clothes and followed him, Billy was already in the yard, guiding a huge cattle lorry as it reversed up to one of the sheds.

So Billy had bought a pedigree animal, Libby thought, filled with a mixture of anxiety and excitement. No wonder he had distracted her with questions about Peter delivering the baby last night. He knew how keen she was to breed a pedigree herd but not if it landed him in debt. So many breeders got carried away and paid high prices in the belief they would get the money back when they had progeny to sell, but Libby knew animals could die and prove a dead loss, or if their progeny did not always breed true they could be worthless. It was a gamble, albeit an exciting one for those who enjoyed breeding.

She watched as the driver lowered the back door of the

lorry to form a ramp and opened the guide gates at the sides. She moved forward to help while the lorry driver coaxed a neat, well groomed young heifer down the ramp into the shed, but he didn't stop at one, or two. Her face paled as the fourth heifer trotted into the Home Farm cattle yard and sniffed around the clean deep straw, while the lorry driver asked Billy for directions to the next farm where he had to deliver a cow, and another farm with a delivery of two stirks. Then he climbed back up into his cab and Libby watched him draw away before she turned to Billy. He was smiling, leading her into the shed.

'Come and inspect the latest additions to Home Farm and the Prinnox herd.' They had agreed on a combination of their joint surnames for the name of their herd. They had dreamed of building it up together.

'Th-they look good heifers,' she said, her expression troubled, 'but we agreed, Billy. You know we have no spare capital . . .'

He came to her then and hugged her close. 'I know that. Your father asked which ones you had picked out of the catalogue for the best breeding. Of the six you had picked three of them were backed up by their confirmation.' He pointed out three of the four heifers. 'The other one I fancied for her looks and your father agreed, though she's not so good on paper.'

'B-but I don't understand. Are you saying these are to go to Langmune?'

'That's what I thought when your father bid for them, but when we went to arrange the transport he booked them to Home Farm. Then he said they were his gift to you now that you and I are farming in partnership and you're coming home so we can work together. He seems pleased about that. He says you were always keen on the cattle, even when you were young.'

'I was, but I didn't expect . . .' Her voice was husky and she chewed hard on her lower lip to stop it trembling. Billy hugged her closer.

'It's what he wanted. I was as surprised as you are. At first I thought Fraser was going to be jealous and angry. I know he has set his heart on having a combine harvester but your father had been saying earlier that he couldn't afford to buy one. On the drive home your father explained to him that he and Lachie would each inherit a farm one day and he couldn't give you anything like that, but you were still his child. He said four pedigree heifers were nothing in comparison to owning acres of land but he hoped they would be the nucleus for our own pedigree herd.'

'What did Fraser say to that? He's grown up with the idea that boys should inherit and girls don't matter. I don't think he means to be so selfish or chauvinistic. In some ways my parents think like that too.'

'I know.' Billy pulled her close into his arms. 'But they've given me all I could ever want from them.' He kissed her, searching her mouth with increasing passion. 'Come on, these girls are settling down after their journey. We'll inspect them in daylight. Let's get back to bed.' But sleep was not their first priority as they snuggled up in bed and his mouth claimed hers.

About a fortnight later, Libby invited all the family to Sunday lunch while both Charlotte and Uncle Josh were down from Glasgow, and before she returned to work. It was a gesture of appreciation for her father's generosity over the heifers, and to save her mother preparing a meal.

Neither Peter nor Victoria had mentioned the birth, but Willie remarked on the admirable way he had stayed calm and coped with it all.

'Has it made you change your mind about being a doctor, Peter? Your stepfather would have been proud of you, laddie. I'm sure Victoria will tell him how well you managed.' They were all surprised when Peter stopped eating and put his head in his hands.

'Don't tell him, don't ever tell him,' he groaned.

'Peter, whatever is the matter?' Victoria asked in dismay.

Peter knew his stepfather would offer nothing but disparaging remarks about a baby being born in such circumstances. Then he would say he'd always known he should be a doctor.

'Is something wrong, Peter?' Victoria persisted. She had noticed how subdued he had been during the last few days.

'You had a letter from Edinburgh. Was it from Doctor Sterling? Is that why you've been so quiet?'

'He's insisting I must return home by the end of next week, prepared to study medicine. He . . . he hasn't relented about anything. If . . . if I refuse he says he'll dispose of my belongings after next week, and . . . and I must never visit my sisters again.'

'That's terrible!' Mary exclaimed.

'He's a harsh man if he means that, but it's your life, laddie, and it's your choice. What do you want to do?' Andrew asked. 'Whatever you decide, we'll do our best to help. There'll always be a home for you with us, whether it's permanent or for holidays, but it's cruel to prevent you seeing your sisters. Surely he'll change his mind about that?'

Victoria threw him a grateful look, glad he had made such a spontaneous offer. She had grown to love Peter. Apart from being the son of her twin, he was kind and considerate.

'There's no doubt in my mind,' Peter said. 'I want to be a farmer.'

'He sounds thoroughly unreasonable to me.' Josh frowned. At his side, Charlotte looked sympathetic. She knew what it was like to have an unreasonable parent.

'If I don't study medicine I forfeit the insurance money. He'll use it for the girls' education.'

There was a stunned silence around the dinner table.

'He sounds awful,' Libby declared. 'We'll take you to collect your possessions, if that's what you want?'

'Yes,' Billy assured him swiftly. 'Libby and I will drive you there. We'll help you pack all your things and you can bring them here.'

Peter looked at them gratefully, but his gaze moved uncertainly to his aunt and uncle. 'It means I shall have nowhere else to go.' He looked at them, his dark eyes wide and anxious.

'Your home is with us, laddie. Have no doubts about that,' Andrew assured him. He glanced at Victoria cradling the baby in her arms. 'So long as you're sure you're making the right decision, we're happy to have you, even if we didn't owe you a debt we can never repay.'

'Andrew's right,' Victoria smiled, stroking the baby's cheek with a gentle finger. 'We are in your debt, Peter.'

'I didn't do anything. I just happened to be there,' Peter said. 'I have far more reason to be grateful to all of you. I feel as though I belong in a way I never belonged in my stepfather's house.'

'I know what you mean, Peter.' Charlotte nodded.

'You can have a room with us when the builders start work at Langmune. We have plenty of spare beds,' Libby said.

'He can have a room at our house as well, can't he, Mum?' Mimi piped up.

'Aye, any time,' Willie chuckled. 'There's plenty of beds and plenty of work on offer, Peter. The main thing is to make the right choice, make a success of your life, and be happy in what you're doing – isn't that right, Josh?'

'I couldn't agree more.' Josh nodded. 'Have you decided on the name for this famous baby yet?' he asked, changing the subject to give Peter time to control his emotions. 'No one has told me if you have.'

'She's Mollytrina,' Fraser said promptly and grinned at his mother.

'Don't you dare give her another of your nicknames, Fraser,' Victoria scolded. 'She's to be called Molly but we are christening her Molly Catriona,' she said firmly.

'That sounds lovely,' Charlotte smiled. Earlier she had been allowed to cuddle the tiny bundle and Josh had seen the wistful look on her face when she had handed the baby back to Victoria. She loved children but he knew she had made up her mind she would never have any of her own. She didn't talk much about her time in Switzerland but Libby had told him there were still as many as sixteen thousand people a year dying of tuberculosis and the doctors had told Charlotte she was fortunate not to be one of them. Charlotte had even told him once she wouldn't risk having a child who might inherit her mother's nature.

Peter felt his spirits begin to rise, surrounded as he was by offers of friendship and hospitality so generously offered. He felt warmth spreading through him as he looked at the faces around the table. He had sensed a long time ago that his stepfather didn't love him as he loved his daughters. Although he had given him his name, Peter knew there were times when he had resented him, especially when his mother had shown him tenderness. When she died he had felt as though an arrow of ice had pierced his soul. He knew there would be times in the future when he would feel the same loneliness but his new family had dispelled it for the present.

'I shall write to my stepfather tonight,' he decided. 'Can I tell him which day we are going to collect my things? I will write to Cathy too. She might pack some of my books, if they allow her. I must bring my bicycle, that's the most important thing. It's one of the things I treasure most.'

'We'll tie it on the back of the car,' Billy said. 'We'll take some ropes, and if that doesn't work we'll take it to the station and send it down by rail.'

Peter sighed with relief and Mimi squeezed his hand and beamed at him. She knew how much he cherished his bicycle. He had told her it meant freedom to get to the zoo or out of the city, or to visit his friends – anywhere away from the house and the surgery. But even Mimi didn't realize how hard he had saved to buy it, delivering newspapers and orders of butcher meat for their local butcher on Saturdays and sometimes after school. His mother had given him extra money two Christmases ago so that he could buy one with gears and lights.

The following week Billy, Libby and Peter set off for Edinburgh expecting it would take some time to pack all Peter's possessions and load them into the car, then deal with his bicycle. Libby had packed sandwiches and two flasks of tea as her mother had warned her Doctor Sterling might not be hospitable towards them. Despite Victoria's warning it was a shock to find Peter's possessions packed in boxes in the hall, ensuring their visit would be as short as possible.

'B-but how do I know everything is here?' Peter asked, white-faced and hurt. He could see that Cathy had been crying and he could guess the reason when she ran towards him, only to be yanked back by her father. 'I-I want to see my room, t-to make sure . . .'

'You have no room here,' Doctor Sterling snapped. 'You forfeited any claim to a place in this house when you disobeyed my wishes. Don't come mewling back to me, or to your sisters, when your new friends get sick of you.'

Libby gasped and Billy clenched his fists but Peter stared

at his stepfather, his face deathly white, and his eyes like twin pools of darkness.

'You hate me because I'm another man's son and my mother loved him. She always loved him, until the day she died,' he said in a low, vehement voice.

'Get out! Get out of my house!' Doctor Sterling took a step towards him, one arm raised.

'No, Daddy! No!' Cathy grabbed at him, sobs racking her thin body.

'Go into the kitchen, Cathy. Dinah, take her away and keep her there until he has gone.'

'Come on, Peter,' Libby said. 'We'll get this lot into the car.'

'B-but there were some things I . . .'

'Everything is there that you're removing from this house,' Doctor Sterling almost snarled. He watched in silence as they carried the boxes and stacked them in the boot.

'Now for your bicycle, Peter,' Billy said. 'I reckon we'll be able to tie it on the back.' None of them saw the malice on Doctor Sterling's face.

'It's in the garage. I'll bring it round,' Peter said. He thought he might be able to sneak in the back door and say goodbye to Cathy, with any luck.

'You've taken everything that belongs to you,' Doctor Sterling growled. 'Now get out and don't come back.'

Peter stared at him. 'I haven't got my bicycle. You've forgotten about that.'

'I've forgotten nothing.' Deane Sterling's lip curled. 'I know your mother must have helped you buy it behind my back. She ruined you, gave you too much freedom. Well, I've sold your precious bicycle.'

'You've *what*?' Anger flared in Peter's dark eyes and his fists clenched. Billy moved to his side. 'I saved up to buy that bike. You can't have sold it! You can't!'

'I have sold it. That's the end of it. Now see how you get on stuck out in the wilds.'

'If you've sold it you must owe him the money,' Billy said reasonably.

'Owe him? Owe him! I owe the brat nothing. I've given him a home all these years.'

'It was my grandfather's house, and his practice.'

'I gave you my name.'

'Well, don't think I'm proud of that!' Peter retorted. 'In fact I shall change it as soon as I can.'

'Come on, Peter, come away now,' Libby said, stepping forward and taking his arm. 'You'll be much happier with us. We're your own kith and kin. You'll always be part of our family now we have found you.' Her dark eyes met Doctor Sterling's and he was the first to look away. She hoped he was as ashamed as he deserved to be. He could be in no doubt of the contempt she and Billy felt for him.

As the car drew out of the drive they heard a child's cry. Peter looked through the back window and saw Cathy running after them, tears streaming down her face. In a moment Peter was out of the car and scooping her up in his arms.

'Send me the address of your best friend, Cathy. I'll write to you there,' he whispered, then with a fierce hug he thrust her away from him as Dinah grabbed her arm and dragged her back to the house.

Nine

'Doctor Sterling was even more mean and obnoxious than I thought possible,' Libby told Victoria and Andrew when they returned to Langmune later that day. 'It made me realize how lucky we are to have parents like you.'

'It doesn't surprise me,' Andrew said. 'The best thing we can do for Peter is to keep him busy so he has no time to brood. The harvest is ready and waiting for the binder; there'll be sheaves to stook soon, and the carts to load and bring home. He'll be too tired to think about Doctor Sterling.'

'Julie is a grand worker and very pleasant, Mum. Shall I ask her if she will help you until Molly is older?'

'Yes, please ask her to come up and see me.'

Julie Dunlop had worked for Maggie in the house at Home Farm since her husband was killed. When Billy married she had continued working there, but since Libby had finished working at the creamery she no longer needed help.

Julie's home was a tied cottage belonging to Billy. Her son had begun working at Home Farm the year his father died. Her daughter, Fiona, was sixteen and doing well at school. She didn't want to upset her by moving house so she was pleased to get part-time work nearby. Molly was a contented baby and between Lachie and Mimi she never lacked attention so things were settling into a routine when the builders arrived to start on the restoration of Langmune.

Peter moved to Home Farm to sleep until the alterations were complete. He was reminded of his stepfather's spite daily, however, because he needed his bicycle to get to work at Langmune early in the mornings.

'Mine is a bit shabby and it's a ladies' bicycle,' Victoria said, 'but you can use it if will do, Peter.'

'There's the bike Gran used to use as well,' Fraser remembered. 'We could do them both up when we have a couple of free weekends. Then Peter could sell them and buy a decent bicycle for himself.'

'That's a good idea.' Andrew nodded.

'B-but don't you want them?' Peter asked, looking at Victoria.

'It's ages since I used mine and Granny Pringle hasn't been on a bicycle for years. See what you and Fraser can do, laddie. We used to have a cycle shop in the village but it closed down. You'll have to go into Dumfries or Annan.'

'It will not be long before you can learn to drive the car,' Andrew said. He knew Peter spent every spare moment practising driving the tractor and learning to reverse the trailer and hitch on the implements but these things did not come as naturally to him as they did to Fraser. On the other hand he was proving an observant stockman.

'I shall never be able to afford a car to drive.' Peter grinned. 'Anyway I enjoy cycling, with the air rushing by and the challenge of peddling up a hill. It means I can get around and explore. You see more of the flowers and the country-side than speeding by in a car.'

'Aye, that's true enough.' Andrew nodded. 'Well, see what you can do with the two ladies' bicycles. You've earned quite a bit of overtime working at the harvest so you may as well get a decent bicycle.'

'Have I?' Peter was surprised. He hadn't expected extra money. Uncle Andrew was nobody's fool but he was a fair man and completely different to his stepfather.

Charlotte was spending the last fortnight of the holidays at Home Farm before she started work in the Glasgow school. Josh was staying with his mother so the two of them spent a good deal of time together, driving to the coast in Josh's little car, sometimes taking a picnic, walking and talking, happy and content in each other's company. On their last evening Polly invited them both for a meal. Charlotte was nervous but the evening passed pleasantly.

'Did you ever hear who bought Mr Glenys's wee farm, Charlotte?' Polly asked. 'I see he's still living in the house and renting the land.'

'No, I never heard who bought it. He couldn't afford to buy it so it was the last to be sold. The solicitor said it would be a struggle to get a decent offer while there was a sitting tenant. I've had no reason to be in contact with him since he concluded everything.' She shuddered. 'I was glad to put it behind me and to know I'd paid off my mother's debts. I have enough left to buy a small house for myself but I want to complete my year's probation first. I need to know where I can get a permanent post.'

'Aye, ye're quite wise, lassie. It's just that I noticed some of the repairs have been done to the house at Lintysmill. Mrs Glenys will be pleased, although they'll be due to retire in another year or so, I should think.'

'They are but I'm so glad they are able to stay on until then,' Charlotte said with feeling. She had hated the thought of turning people out of their home when they had lived on her father's estate all their lives.

'Aye, they're lucky the new owner isna needing the house himself.' Neither of the two women noticed that Josh made no contribution to this exchange. Polly was thinking it was difficult to remember the girl had been brought up in a castle. She seemed to have adapted well to her changed circumstances.

'I'll write down the two recipes we talked about,' Polly said. 'They're Josh's favourites and I'm sure ye'll make them well enough if ye follow the instructions.'

'That's a sure sign you've found favour with my mother,' Josh assured her with a grin as they left the cottage to walk back to Home Farm.

'Do you think she is expecting I shall entertain you at the flat, since she gave me your favourite recipes?' Charlotte asked.

'Maybe she is. Will you? Invite me for a meal, I mean?'

'Would you come if I did?' Charlotte asked.

'Of course I would.' Josh put his arm around her shoulders and gave her a squeeze. Charlotte did not move away and Polly, watching from the window, gave a satisfied little nod. She hoped to see Josh married before she died. It wasn't normal for a Pringle man to remain a bachelor all his life, and Joe and Libby were right, Charlotte Crainby seemed to be a decent, caring girl and she was not responsible for her mother's evil deeds. Now that Polly had come round to this way of thinking she wanted to give the pair of them a push and tell them to get on with things. She knew Josh was conscious of the difference in their ages, and of his humble background, but she was convinced neither of these things mattered to Charlotte and at thirty-seven it was time Josh got on with life. Charlotte seemed so unsure of herself, not at all like her Crainby ancestors. Polly decided Josh would be good for her.

Mimi and Lachie had both qualified for the Academy. Peter had settled into farming as though he had been brought up to it. He enjoyed every minute. He didn't mind the cold, dark mornings of winter, or the heavy work of mucking out the byres, but he was looking forward to spring and helping Willie with the lambing at High Bowie. He was developing a preference for sheep rather than cattle and this pleased Willie.

Charlotte found teaching a large class of eight-year-olds difficult and exhausting but Josh had become a regular visitor to her flat since she was no longer one of his students and she found his support invaluable. She trusted Josh as she had never trusted anyone before and she began to rely on him and look forward to his visits. Sometimes he drove her out of the city to a country inn for a meal.

'You'll feel as though you have been teaching all your life by the time Christmas comes,' he told her during the first difficult weeks.

'I don't think I could have continued without your encouragement,' she said as they drove down to Home Farm together at the start of the Christmas holidays.

The restoration of Langmune farmhouse was almost complete and Victoria insisted she would make Christmas dinner for all the family.

'We have so many nursemaids for Molly she's getting spoiled,' she laughed. 'And Julie Dunlop is a treasure around here. We shall celebrate Christmas and the completion of our house.' Victoria smiled. 'I never thought I should see Langmune restored to its former glory but it's beautiful now.

Andrew, I think Mr Rennie and Miss Traill would have approved.' She reached up to kiss his cheek. 'You're a good husband.'

'It's a good thing we made the doors as wide as the old castle doors or I'd never get my head through,' Andrew chuckled.

Peter received a Christmas card from Cathy which she had made herself, but he did not hear anything from Dinah, nor from his stepfather. He looked forward to getting Cathy's letters but he was becoming more interested in the progress of Mimi and Lachie than in his sister Dinah's achievements. Mimi was finding the Academy rather daunting with all the moving from room to room for different classes, carrying books and travelling on the bus. She was often exhausted at the end of the day. Lachie, on the other hand, thrived on the stimulation and the variety of subjects.

'Lachie is clever,' Mimi confided to Peter. 'He loves science and I can't keep up with him.'

'Don't worry, Mimi,' Peter said. He hated to see the shadows in her big blue eyes. 'I'll come over each weekend and explain things if you tell me what you're doing. I liked science when I was at school but I had to work hard at French.'

'Oh, that's like Lachie. I like French and I love my English teacher.'

Peter smiled down at her eager, expressive face and he was pleased to see the sparkle back in her eyes. It seemed a long time since he'd left school and yet it was no time at all. He kept his promise and each weekend he went over to High Bowie and helped Mimi get to grips with her science projects.

He had moved back into his new bedroom at Langmune and he now owned a decent bicycle, almost as good as the one his stepfather had sold. He loved being able to explore the surrounding countryside. Everything was new to him and sometimes he cycled for miles on his free weekend. One weekend, in search of shade, he was cycling along a track in a large wood when he came upon an elderly man who had taken a tumble from his horse. Peter suspected he was trespassing on private property but he couldn't leave the man lying there.

Peter crouched beside him, noting the beads of sweat on his brow.

'You must be in pain. Can I help you?'

'It was my damned horse. Shied at a blasted rabbit.' He was holding his thigh and trying to sit up. Peter helped him to a sitting position and dragged a small log nearer as a back rest. 'Think I've broken my leg,' the man wheezed.

'I'll fetch help,' Peter said. 'Can you tell me where we are? I've lost my bearings.'

The man eyed him quizzically in spite of his pain. 'You're not from this area, are you? What's your name?' Peter told him and explained that he was living at Langmune with his aunt and uncle, prior to going to college. The man nodded, interest and pain vying with each other on his ruddy face.

'If you take the right fork about twenty yards ahead and keep straight on it will bring you to Croston House. My name is Gerald. Ask for Mrs Phillips, the housekeeper. Explain what's happened and where to find me. She'll organize some help.'

Peter followed the man's instructions and gave the message to the housekeeper, but he returned to the man and waited with him until help arrived, answering his questions to try and take his mind off his injuries. Later he recounted his adventure during the meal at Langmune. Andrew's eyes opened wide and then he began to smile.

'It sounds as though you rescued Sir Gerald Croston. He owns the Croston Estate.'

'Oh my goodness!' Peter exclaimed. 'No wonder the housekeeper gave me a strange look when I told her I had found Mr Gerald. She said Mr Gerald was away abroad. I had difficulty convincing her that the man was injured and needed help. That's why I went back to stay with him.'

'The housekeeper would be thinking of Sir Gerald Croston's son. I believe he is called Gerald too.'

'I see.' Peter nodded but he thought no more about it.

Occasionally Fraser accompanied Peter on his rides. The two got on well together and they both enjoyed the Young Farmers' Club meetings. The other members often joked about Peter's low scores in the stock judging competitions but he never took offence.

He listened, asked questions and watched. His scores improved. Willie told him he was getting an eye for a good beast, at least as far as sheep were concerned. Libby coached him in the finer points of a good dairy cow until he could at least hold his own with Fraser, who was a reasonable judge if not the best. Peter had set himself to work for two years before going to college in order to earn enough money, but he was enjoying the work and he knew the practical experience would be valuable when he had to look for a permanent job away from Langmune. He told no one of his dream to have animals himself one day, however small his farm had to be.

Charlotte's probationary year in teaching drew to a close. She had applied for, and been appointed to, a job in Glasgow, starting in September 1959. It was near enough for her to travel from her flat and she hoped Josh's visits would continue, and maybe become more frequent. They often travelled down to Darlonachie together and she knew Polly had accepted her as Josh's friend, but she still sensed a restraint in him. She knew the reason but she didn't know how to put things right or move them on. They had reached a crossroads.

Libby was sure Charlotte loved Josh. Like her grandmother she was impatient for their relationship to progress. She had found true happiness with Billy. She knew beyond doubt that he loved her and that their love had helped him banish most of the shadows of his earlier life. Maybe Uncle Josh would do the same for Charlotte.

'Now that you're a qualified teacher, Charlotte,' Libby began hesitantly, 'do you think . . . I mean, you do still see a lot of Uncle Josh when you are both in Glasgow, don't you?'

'Yes, we do. He has been a real help and a true friend.' Charlotte nodded.

'A friend? Is that all he is?' She couldn't hide her disappointment. The two of them were preparing vegetables for lunch and Libby glanced sideways and saw the pink in Charlotte's cheeks, the wistful look in her eyes, and the way she chewed at her lower lip.

'You've seen how good Josh is with children, even with

wee Molly,' Charlotte said at last. 'He deserves a family of his own.'

'So? What's stopping him having a family – with you as their mama? You love children, Charlotte. I've seen the look on your face when you cuddle Molly, and I've seen how patient you are at playing games with Mimi and Lachie.'

'Josh knows I shall never have children. He knows I shall never marry,' Charlotte said in a rush.

'Never marry? Oh, Charlotte, you can't mean that.'

'I do, and your Uncle Josh knows that's how I feel. I-I keep expecting that he will find someone to be his wife and to give him children and then . . .'

'But he never looks at anyone else. What makes you say you will never marry?' Libby asked in bewilderment.

'Because – because I couldn't bear to treat Josh as my mother treated my father, and . . . and drive him into the arms of another woman. I-I would rather have the friendship we have now. I could never risk spoiling that.'

'But you do love Uncle Josh?'

'Love?' Charlotte echoed. 'How do I know what love is? I've never known love, not even from my own mother.' She was speaking quickly, a swift torrent of words which took Libby by surprise and kept her silent. 'How could I be sure that what I feel for Josh is love? How do I know I could endure all the . . . the painful intimacies a wife is supposed to endure to give a man pleasure and keep him loyal? What if I'm like my mother? She never allowed my father back into her bed after she had me. She told me so. Could he be blamed for finding his pleasure with Billy's mother?'

'No, no, Charlotte. Don't get upset,' Libby said as Charlotte stifled a sob. 'I've always thought Uncle Josh hadn't asked you to marry him because he thinks he is too old for you and . . . and because your background is so different to his. I-I mean, you were born in a castle and he was born in the gardener's cottage and he'll never forget that.'

'That's rubbish!' Charlotte stared at Libby. Then she gave a harsh laugh. 'Josh is far above me in every way.'

'Does he know you don't want to get married?'

'Yes. I told him.'

'Does he know why? How your mother has poisoned your mind against men?'

'Of course not!' Charlotte's eyes widened at the thought.

'I think you ought to tell him the reason. You owe him that after he has been such a true friend to you.'

'I couldn't! We . . . we don't talk about . . . about such things.'

'Then it's time you did. Is that why you think you will never have children?'

'Oh no.' Charlotte frowned. 'I don't think it's advisable for me to have a child after being so bad with the tuberculosis, but in any case I wouldn't want any child to inherit my mother's vindictive nature. She was so mean and spiteful. The world is a better place without such people.'

'I see,' Libby said. 'But surely . . .'

'No!' Charlotte shook her head. 'I'd never risk it. You don't know how awful my childhood was.'

'Well, even if you don't want children it doesn't stop you getting married to someone if you love him and if he loves you and understands. Does Uncle Josh know your views?'

'He knows I don't want children. He . . . he seemed to understand and agree, at least about taking risks with my health.'

'Well then . . .' Libby smiled. 'What's to stop the two of you getting married and not having children? You love Uncle Josh, don't you, Charlotte?'

'Yes, yes I do. But when people get married and love each other the children follow.'

'Not if you don't want them. Not these days.'

'I-I don't understand.' Charlotte frowned. 'It's natural.'

'I think you should tell Uncle Josh how your mother has poisoned your mind about men. Being married to the man you love is the most wonderful thing on earth, believe me, Charlotte. And there's nothing to endure. Women get as much pleasure as men. Please be honest with Uncle Josh. I'll bet he knows how to prevent you having babies after being in the RAF. Anyway, you can buy a book about it now, and you can go to the family planning clinic. I've learned a lot since I married Billy. You could call yourself Mrs Crainby and no one would know you in Glasgow.'

'Is that true?' Charlotte stared at Libby. 'Is that why you and Billy haven't had a baby?'

'It was. I didn't want a baby until I had worked for a year, but we both wanted to be married and . . .' Libby blushed. 'Well, you know . . . But we're having a baby now – at least we are in six months' time, but only Mum and Dad know just now, so please don't tell anyone, Charlotte.'

'Oh, Libby, that's wonderful news.' Charlotte hugged her.

'Mmm, we think so. Promise me you and Josh will have a talk, a proper talk, holding nothing back. Invite him to a romantic dinner for two or something. Anything so long as you get things straightened out in your own head, Charlotte.'

'I'll see,' Charlotte said, but her mind was buzzing.

The more Charlotte thought about her conversation with Libby the more her resolve hardened. As soon as she returned to Glasgow at the end of her summer holidays she made plans. Josh had already returned to work and she was due to start her new job in two days' time. She telephoned to invite him for dinner at her flat.

'If you're sure,' Josh said, surprised. He knew how diffident Charlotte was about her cooking skills. Her repertoire was limited but she had been practising and she had discovered she enjoyed creating appetizing dishes. She followed Libby's advice and concentrated on a simple meal, starting with Josh's favourite lentil soup made to his mother's recipe. She had prepared a beef casserole with plenty of vegetables, and for dessert she had made a trifle which Libby insisted was his favourite. She had also bought a bottle of wine to go with the meal. Everything was ready and the table set, including two long ivory candles in the silver candlesticks salvaged from the sale of her family's possessions.

She ran upstairs to soak in a scented bath. On the bed she had laid out the new dress that she had bought for this evening. It was a silky material in blue and white and it brought out the colour of her eyes. The fitted bodice was held in place with narrow shoe-string straps. It was cut low but it had a matching bolero which made her feel less naked. She had also bought a pair of expensive leather sandals with high heels and low fronts. They were extravagant and impractical but they showed off her legs and made her feel good.

There was an appetizing smell emanating from the kitchen when she descended the stairs in her new finery. She was tempted to take a glass of wine to settle her nerves and give her confidence until she remembered alcohol had been her mother's downfall. This evening must not be spoiled by memories of her mother. She lifted her head, her small chin set with determination. This evening was for her and Josh.

Josh and Billy had joined together to buy her one of the new record players for Christmas and she had been overwhelmed by their generosity. She loved to listen to music. She had learned to play the piano at school and it came in useful now she was teaching but she lacked the gift of a true musician. Later Josh had given her a record of light orchestral music with most of the tunes relating to the moon. She knew it was a reminder of a walk they had taken by the river when they had been enthralled by the beauty of the moonlit night. She selected the record now, intent on setting the scene for a romantic evening. She prayed Josh wouldn't think she was trying to force him into a relationship he didn't want.

Ten

Josh arrived carrying a fragrant spray of freesias. He had never given her flowers before and for a moment Charlotte wondered whether Libby had talked to him too. Her cheeks flushed at the thought but Josh greeted her with his usual quizzical smile.

'These are in honour of my first invitation to dinner and I must say it smells delicious.' Charlotte's fingers reached for the flowers but Josh lifted his free hand and imprisoned them, his eyes serious now as he studied her face. 'You always look pretty, Charlotte, but tonight . . .' His voice deepened. 'Tonight there's something more.' He searched for words and couldn't find them. Instead he leaned forward and kissed her cheek – no different to the way he had done scores of times in greeting or to say goodbye, and yet to Charlotte it seemed to have more meaning. She buried her face against the flowers.

'They're lovely, Josh. I will find a vase for them while you open the wine. At least that should be all right, but I don't know about the rest of the meal. You're used to such high standards with your mother, your sister-in-law and your niece.'

'It smells delicious. I can feel my taste buds working overtime already.' Josh grinned. 'Is that why you're nervous, Charlotte? There's no need to be, you know.'

The food was as good as it had promised and they chatted as they ate.

'We'll have our coffee in the lounge,' Charlotte said as Josh ate the last spoonful of trifle.

'Mmm, that was wonderful.' Josh stood up. 'You're an excellent cook, Charlotte. You've proved it tonight, so now you can relax.'

But she was more nervous than ever, wondering how she could talk to Josh about the things that mattered so much to both of them. Her hand trembled as she poured the coffee and Josh stood up and took it from her.

'Come and sit beside me, Charlotte, and tell me what's wrong.' Josh was always kind but he could be masterful too. She could not meet his eyes and Josh's smile faded. She felt him tense beside her. 'Have you something important to tell me?' he asked. She looked up and saw his mouth had tightened. He looked tense and wary, his blue eyes narrowed. 'Out with it, Charlotte. Have you met someone else? Is that what you're afraid to tell me? Someone nearer your own age, I suppose?'

'No! Oh no, Josh, nothing like that! I don't want anybody else, young or old. It's you I . . . trust . . .' She couldn't bring herself to say 'love'. Josh noticed but his face still showed relief.

'If you trust me, Charlotte, can't you tell me what's bothering you?'

She began to talk, stumbling over the words, hiding her face so that he wouldn't see her embarrassment. He was holding both her hands and he refused to let them go when she would have pulled away. Sometimes her words were garbled but Josh got the gist of what she was trying to say.

'You mean to tell me your mother convinced you the relationship between a husband and wife, or a man and woman who love each other, was something to be endured, at least by women? Like . . . like . . . Oh, I don't know, like some kind of suffering?' He looked at Charlotte. 'She must have loved your father once, when she first married him?'

'She never loved my father,' Charlotte declared. 'She told me so herself. I don't think my mother knew how to love anyone. Wh-what if I'm the same? How would I know unless I got married – and then it would be too late.'

'I've heard some women are frigid. Maybe that's what was wrong with your mother.' Josh frowned and his clasp tightened on her fingers. He looked her in the eye.

'Charlotte . . .' He hesitated, then hurried on. 'Are you telling me you've reached twenty-seven and you're still a virgin?' Her face flamed and she tried to pull away but he

wouldn't allow it so she looked down instead and he saw
her nod.

'You are?' he breathed. 'By all, that's wonderful! I can't
believe it.' She looked up in surprise and saw his eyes were
shining but his expression was tender.

'How can you think that's wonderful?'

'You were away at boarding school, and abroad. I assumed,
well I suppose I thought you knew all about such things. If
that's not the case then what made you decide you would
never marry?'

'How shall I know if I'm frigid and unfeeling, like my
mother? I have never had the chance to find out. Oh, Josh,
you have taught me how to trust, can't you teach me how
to love?' Josh drew in his breath, wondering if she realized
what she was asking of him. 'I don't want to be like my
mother. I don't want to be married. I couldn't bear to have
a husband who sought whatever he needed from someone
else if I'm fr-frigid.'

'Oh, Charlotte! Dearest Charlotte.' Josh pulled her into his
arms and held her against his chest. She could feel his heart
thumping against her cheek but he turned her face up to his
and his kiss was no longer that of a close friend, it was that
of a lover, searching and probing and moving down her neck
to the edge of her dress and returning to her mouth. Charlotte
found herself responding whether she willed it or not and
when Josh removed her bolero and trailed his lips over her
shoulders, nudging away the thin straps, then back to her
lips before moving down and down to the swell of her breasts,
easing her dress lower and lower, she clung even closer.

Her legs were long and tanned from the summer weather
so she had not bothered with stockings. Josh reached to her
feet and pushed off her sandals. His long fingers moved over
each toe, over the soles of her feet, then began moving up
her leg and down to her feet again. It was amazingly erotic
and Charlotte wondered how she could have so many exciting
nerves tingling in her lower limbs. He laid her back against
the cushions of her long sofa but his eyes held hers as his
hand moved over her knee and up to the silky skin of her
thigh. His breathing quickened as she parted her lips, eager
for his kiss and whatever else he offered.

'Are you sure this is what you want, Charlotte?' he asked. 'You know the first time may be a little painful?'

She didn't know. According to her mother every time was a disgusting discomfort. But she knew Josh made her feel wonderful and she wanted more.

'I trust you, Josh. I want . . . I want you.'

Josh gave a long sigh of satisfaction and eased her on to the thick woollen rug before the fire. They were the words he had longed to hear. He began to undress her, seeing her breathing quicken, feeling her response to his kisses.

Much later he carried Charlotte to the bedroom, leaving their clothes behind on the carpet. It was the first time Charlotte had ever slept beside another human being and she snuggled into him, thinking she was in heaven to be held so tenderly in Josh's strong arms. He had been right about the initial pain but Josh had made sure she shared the ecstasy which followed. Long before morning she knew beyond doubt just how wonderful it was to be loved by Josh.

'There's nothing frigid about you, my darling girl,' Josh murmured as he drifted into sleep.

In the morning he wished he didn't need to go to work. He tried not to waken Charlotte as he crept from the bed, but when he turned at the bedroom door she was watching him, a dreamy smile on her face.

'I didn't want to disturb you. How do you feel?'

'Wonderful,' she breathed and raised her arms above her head in a languorous stretch. She had no idea how inviting she looked and Josh groaned. 'I need to work today, you temptress, but I shall return tonight, shall I?'

'Oh yes, yes please, Josh.' She threw aside the bed clothes and reached for her dressing gown.

'I'll cook you some breakfast while you bathe and dress,' she offered. A little while later Josh joined her at the small kitchen table to the smell of bacon and toast.

'Tea or coffee?' Charlotte asked.

'Tea please. I could settle for this kind of service every day.' Josh grinned. He looked up at her and smiled. 'Any regrets, Charlotte?'

'None,' she answered and shook her head for good measure.

'I'm glad,' Josh said fervently. 'You were wonderful.'

'I was?' Charlotte said in surprise. 'Really, Josh?'

'You were.' He stood up and came round the table, drawing her to her feet and taking her in his arms. 'Maybe too wonderful. I . . . er . . . I know a lot of Catholics depend on the time of the monthly rhythms to prevent them having babies, but it is not always reliable,' he said, looking down into her eyes and wanting to kiss her upturned mouth. 'I think we shall have to take more precautions if you don't want babies, especially when you don't want to get married. We'll talk about it later.'

'Yes,' she nodded, savouring his kiss. Thanks to Libby she knew what to do now. She would not allow anything to stop her loving Josh now she had discovered how wonderful it could be.

It was the middle of the morning when the telephone rang. Charlotte was a little surprised to hear the voice of Morven MacRory, a young teacher who had done her probationary year at the same school as Charlotte. Morven was one of the youngest to complete all her training. She could have gone further but Charlotte suspected her decision to teach primary-school children had been influenced by her friendship with Donnie Smith. They had been students together. Donnie had been brought up in the Quarriers Homes and he had no idea who his mother had been or why he had been abandoned. He had a job as a teacher in a school on the outskirts of Glasgow.

In spite of the difference in their ages Charlotte had got on well with Morven during their probationary year but they would both be teaching at different schools in the city now and Morven wanted to meet again before the new term started. She had been brought up on one of the islands by her grandmother, following the death of her parents in a boating accident. Morven had planned to spend the summer in Glasgow to be near Donnie but her grandmother had been taken ill so she had returned to the little croft to be with the old lady. On her return to Glasgow Charlotte had found a letter waiting for her. Morven's grandmother had died peacefully three weeks after she arrived home. The neighbours had been kind and helped her clear the croft. In spite of her ability and intelligence Morven seemed naïve and innocent so Charlotte was delighted when she telephoned. She felt affectionately protective towards her, although she was far from worldly herself.

'Come for lunch,' she said. 'It will not be anything special but we can eat while we chat. I have an appointment at half past two,' she added, remembering Morven's propensity for chatter. 'Then I want to go through my work ready for the first day with my new class.'

'I've done my preparation,' Morven said. 'I'm looking forward to meeting my new children.' The amazing thing about Morven was the way she managed to hold the interest of even the most unruly children, although sometimes she didn't look or sound much older than them. Perhaps that's her secret, Charlotte thought.

Josh was astonished, and none too pleased, when he realized Charlotte had visited a family planning clinic. He had no idea how much courage it had taken for her to keep the appointment. He supposed he ought to be pleased but she had done it without any prior discussion. Was she making sure she would not be forced into marriage because of an unwanted child? He could have sworn he had dispelled her fears of married life and her mother's myths. It made him wonder whether she didn't quite trust him. He loved her and if two people loved each other, and if both were free to marry, surely it was a natural progression to get married. Josh's views had been broadened during his time in the armed services, when each day might be the last and pleasure had been seized, passions had flared and died. But his upbringing had been a traditional one and he respected Charlotte. He couldn't take her to stay at his mother's cottage and sleep with her there unless they were man and wife. In his heart he knew he would never feel fulfilled unless he and Charlotte were married. He wanted to live with her all the time, not just two or three evenings a week, but Charlotte had made her views on marriage crystal clear. She had given him no indication she had changed her views about marriage although her responses to his love-making were everything he had dreamed of.

Charlotte looked forward to Josh's visits, especially when he stayed the night. She wished he could stay every night.

He had dispelled the impressions her mother had given, impressions which could have robbed her of the joy and satisfaction of being a woman, the rapture of being united with the man she loved. She had taken Libby's advice so there would be no unplanned pregnancy to mar the spontaneity of their loving, but as time passed she had a niggling feeling there was a flaw in the bright flame of their love. She tried to banish the fear that Josh might prefer to be free to take a wife who would bear his children.

Charlotte accompanied Josh down to Darlonachie for Christmas but she was staying at Home Farm and he was staying in his mother's cottage. His silence on the drive down made Charlotte uneasy. Did he regret the time they must spend apart as much as she did, or was he growing tired of her?

They were all invited to Langmune for Christmas dinner. Libby was heavily pregnant now but it agreed with her. Her skin was clear and she seemed to bloom like a summer flower. Unlike her mother, she had no objection to going to the hospital to give birth. Doctor Ritchie's wife, June, was expecting a baby at the end of January so the two of them often went together to the clinic.

Molly was an adorable toddler and Charlotte enjoyed amusing her and singing nursery rhymes for her. She was a bright child and quick to imitate the sounds. She was affectionate too and cuddled Charlotte. Watching them together Josh thought she was born to be a mother. He wondered whether the doctors had been right to warn her about the effects of the tuberculosis, although he knew it was possible her lungs had suffered permanent damage. He shuddered. He couldn't bear the thought of losing her. Perhaps he should be happy with the part of her life she was willing to share with him.

'I don't know why I didn't see it before.' Victoria smiled, coming to sit beside him. 'Charlotte takes after her grandfather. He was a born teacher. He enjoyed imparting knowledge and he made everything interesting. He was very kind to me; he taught me such a lot. It's obvious that Charlotte loves children and she's so patient. It's hard to believe her mother was such a dreadful person.'

'Yes, I suppose so.'

'You're not your usual cheerful self this holiday, Josh. Is anything wrong?'

'What should be wrong?' Josh frowned.

'I don't know. Your work maybe? Are you still enjoying being a lecturer? Living in the city? Don't you miss the countryside?'

'Yes, I do sometimes, now you mention it,' Josh said with a note of surprise. He was tempted to tell Victoria the secret he had kept from them all, including Charlotte, but he bit back the words just in time when she came to join them.

'I was just asking Josh if he misses the country, Charlotte. He admits he does. The trouble is he wouldn't get a lecturer's job down here, I suppose.'

Charlotte looked from one to the other in dismay.

'Oh, Josh! You're n-not thinking of leaving Glasgow, are you?'

'I hadn't thought about it until Victoria asked. I suppose I could always get a job as a teacher with maths and physics . . .'

Mimi called Victoria away and Charlotte turned to him, her eyes wide and distressed.

'Oh, Josh, I don't know what I'd do if you moved away from Glasgow.'

He laughed aloud and clasped her hand where it lay on his knee. 'It was a spur of the moment answer, that's all, but to be honest I wouldn't mind going back to teaching and following the progress of the children I'd taught.'

'Oh? You've been so quiet I wondered what was wrong.'

'You're as bad as Victoria. Does that mean you'd miss me if I left Glasgow?

'You know I would.'

'Enough to come with me?' The teasing light had gone from his eyes now.

'If you asked me to,' Charlotte said, but before Josh could say any more Mimi and Lachie bounced on top of them both, wanting them to join in a game. The moment was lost.

Morven called to see Charlotte almost as soon as she returned to Glasgow after the Christmas holidays. She and Donnie had spent it together.

'I've got something to tell you,' Morven said. Her face looked young and troubled, and she was thinner.

'It sounds serious, Morven.'

'It is to me. Donnie has bought a motorbike, a big one. He's always wanted one.'

'Oh.' Charlotte felt a surge of relief. 'Is that so bad, Morven?' She had a feeling the girl was near to tears.

'It is when you've no money and we're supposed to be saving up to get married. He's used our savings as a deposit. He's paying the rest off in instalments.'

'Oh, I see.'

'My grandmother said that was the path to ruin. She said you should save up first until you had the money.'

'I suppose . . .' Charlotte chewed her lower lip. 'Your Grandmother was wise. It's what people did, but not everyone agrees. Maybe Donnie will get to see you more often if he has a motorbike?'

'That's his excuse.'

'Maybe he'll take you for rides into the country if it has a pillion?'

'It has, but I'm still mad at him,' Morven said. 'You don't disapprove of Donnie, do you, Lottie?' She sounded so young and vulnerable that Charlotte wanted to hug her.

'If you both enjoy it,' she said, 'I think it might be all right. After all, you're both young to think of marriage.'

'Yes, I know.' Morven decided not to tell Charlotte her other news. She prayed Donnie was right and she would be back to normal by the time they met again.

Eleven

On a Friday evening towards the end of February Josh drove Charlotte down to Darlonachie to see Billy and Libby's two-week-old baby son. Libby always kept a room ready for Charlotte so she knew she would be welcome.

'I'm not as good at cooking as you are,' Charlotte laughed, 'but if Billy will give it a try I'll do the cooking while I'm here to give you a rest.

'That's wonderful, Charlotte. I never expected to be so tired,' Libby said. 'It's the broken nights.'

'What are you going to call him?'

'Joseph William Crainby Lennox.' Libby grinned. 'A big mouthful for such a tot but Fraser has already named him wee Joe and his Great-Granny Pringle is delighted.'

'If it's not too cold for him I'd love to take him in his pram and walk him over to the cottage to see her and Josh,' Charlotte said. 'Then you can have a nap while we're gone.'

'That would be splendid,' Libby agreed. 'I could do with you every day. He'll be warm enough if we wrap him up. Gran has knitted him a lovely pram suit – leggings, jacket, bonnet and mitts in soft blue wool. Already he wriggles out of the mitts but if you keep the hood up and the blankets well up he'll be fine.'

'Perhaps I could phone and say I'm walking over then?'

'Of course,' Libby grinned. 'And no doubt Uncle Josh will walk to meet you.'

They met at the edge of the wee wood. Charlotte made sure the brake was on the pram as Josh took her in his arms, seizing the opportunity for a kiss and cuddle. They were unaware of Mimi and Lachie helping Peter repair a fence on the other side of the narrow strip of woodland. The trees

were bare of leaves and the twelve-year-olds had a clear view
of them and nudged Peter, stifling their giggles with an effort.

'Hush,' Peter said. 'You're not to tease. Keep it a secret.'

'Can't we even tell Fraser?' Lachie spluttered with laughter.

'Not Fraser,' Peter grinned. 'He'd be sure to tease. Anyway,
somebody might catch you at it one day.'

'They wouldn't get me being that soft,' Lachie scoffed.

Polly was delighted to see Charlotte and her first great-
grandchild.

'Take your coat off, lassie. I see you've taken to wearing
trousers like Libby, eh?'

'These are Libby's,' Charlotte smiled. 'She thought they'd
be warmer.'

'Mmm,' Josh murmured, running a hand over her rounded
hip, 'and very fetching you look in them too.'

'Well!' Polly exclaimed, her eyes almost popping out of
her head. 'You're lucky you didn't get your face slapped for
being too familiar, young Josh!'

Charlotte blushed and even Josh looked abashed. His action
had been automatic and admiring, but his mother had no
idea how intimate his relationship with Charlotte had become.

The spring term passed in a flurry of activity. Charlotte met
Morven twice at a café for a cup of coffee. Morven arrived
swathed in a voluminous winter coat which she hugged
around her as though she was cold. The second meeting was
on a fine spring afternoon just before the Easter holidays
began. Charlotte teased her about her unnecessary layers.

'I'm saving up for some new clothes,' Morven snapped,
then to Charlotte's dismay she burst into tears and dashed
out of the café. Charlotte ran after her but Morven jumped
on a bus and disappeared. Later that evening she was just
telling Josh about their meeting and Morven's strange behaviour when she telephoned to apologize.

Josh guessed the news from the one-sided conversation.

'You've to vacate your digs in three weeks? Whew! Listen,
Morven, I'm going down to Darlonachie tomorrow. As soon
as I return after Easter you must come here. We'll arrange
something, I promise.' Her expression was troubled. 'I'll telephone you as soon as I get back.'

'Trouble?' Josh said when Charlotte turned to face him.

'Yes, oh yes. Morven's in terrible trouble, Josh. I have to help her. She has no one else.' She saw him frown. She ran into his arms, throwing herself on to his knees with her arms around his neck as she rested her face against his cheek. He felt her lashes brush his skin, delicate as a butterfly wing. He realized she was struggling to blink away tears and he drew her away to look down into her face.

'Please don't be angry, Josh. I must help Morven. She has no one else to turn to.'

'What about that boyfriend of hers?'

'Donnie? I could throttle Donnie,' she said. 'He has used all their savings to pay a deposit on his motorbike and now he's struggling to make the payments. He had promised Morven he would pay back some of her money by the end of term but he can't. Her landlord asks for a term's rent in advance. She hasn't got it so she has to move out. I've told her she can come here until she can get another place to stay.' Her arms tightened, almost childlike in their urgency. 'It . . . it means we shall not be able to spend nights together here until Morven finds other digs.'

'Surely it will not be for long, sweetheart?'

'Any time is too long,' she said, then her eyes widened as though she couldn't believe she had said such a thing. Josh chuckled and held her closer. She drew a deep breath. 'There's more than just digs . . .'

'Mmm, I thought there might be from what I overheard.' Josh nodded.

'I should have talked to her, Josh. I should have given her help and advice, as Libby did for me, then she wouldn't be in such a mess. They're so young, both of them, and Donnie has no sense of responsibility. He says the baby will have to be brought up in a home, as he was.'

'My God! He can't mean that? His own child? He'll have to sell his motorbike and marry the girl. He'll have to support them.'

'That's what Morven told him but he doesn't want to think about it. She's afraid the headmistress at her school will find out too, and ask her to leave her job.'

'When is the baby due?'

'August.'

'She can't hide her condition until the end of June, can she?'

'I don't know. She's quite stocky and she's been wearing shapeless clothes for a while – probably from the minute she knew, hoping no one would notice much difference, except to think she has put on weight. Oh, Josh I don't know. I should have passed on Libby's advice and sent her to the family planning clinic.'

'Libby's advice?' Josh sat up straighter, his grip tightening. He looked into her face, his brows dark arches above his startled eyes. 'Exactly what sort of advice did young Libby give you, Charlotte?' he demanded.

'Oh . . . er . . . well it was supposed to be confidential,' Charlotte stammered in confusion, her cheeks growing hotter by the second. 'G-girl talk – you know.'

'No, I don't know.' Josh's mouth tightened. 'You tell me.'

Charlotte looked at him. He seemed tense and angry and he was waiting for an answer.

'Ages ago Libby said she was sure we were meant for each other and she wanted to know why we . . . why we didn't get married. She wasn't interfering, Josh. She wanted us to be as happy as she and Billy are. I told her about Mother saying marriage was disgusting and had to be endured, not something to enjoy. I said our friendship was very precious and I'd rather keep things as they were than risk losing you. She insisted that Mother had talked complete rubbish and if that's all that stopped me from considering marriage I should find out what was involved then make up my own mind. I w-was horrified. I thought I'd get a baby. Libby explained about caps for women and things I'd never heard about, so . . .'

'You mean Libby knows we . . . we . . . ?'

'No! Of course not, Josh. We've never mentioned things like that again. She explained how to avoid having babies. I-I thought about it a lot. I had to know if . . . if we got married whether . . . well, whether I would hate it as my mother did. In my own heart I was sure anything that brought us closer had to be good, b-but I needed to know . . .'

'I see,' Josh said.

'Oh, Josh, please don't be angry. It's the most wonderful thing that ever happened to me and I'd never have had the courage to find out without Libby's advice.'

'What do you mean "it's the most wonderful thing", Charlotte? Having sex?' Josh was tense.

'Not just sex,' Charlotte said. 'I have no fears of marriage now – at least not so long as it was with you. I don't know how it would be with other men. Perhaps my mother was right about—'

'Damn your mother, Charlotte. Are you saying you've no objections to getting married? Now you know there's nothing to "endure"? You're convinced it's all right?'

'All right?' Charlotte frowned. 'It's much more than "all right" for me. Is that all it means to you, Josh?'

'I'll tell you what it means for me, Charlotte. It means I want to marry you and make sure you're mine and that you never, ever, try finding out with any other man. You've always been so against being tied by marriage vows. I thought I'd have to settle for what we have.'

'Oh, Josh, you banished all my stupid worries the first night we spent together.'

'Let me get this straight, Charlotte. If I ask you to marry me now, tonight, would you say yes?'

'Of course I would, so long as you promise not to keep searching for a woman who would bear your children.'

'Oh my . . .' Josh shook his head in disbelief, and expelled a long sigh. 'I've known for a long time there was only one woman I want for my wife, but I thought it was an impossible dream when I discovered the real identity of a student called Lottie Laine.'

'I'm sorry about the deception.' Charlotte said, but there was a little smile curving her lips as she looked into Josh's eyes.

'Well, so long as you make sure there are no more deceptions,' Josh warned with mock severity. 'Shall we go and buy an engagement ring before we set off for Darlonachie tomorrow morning?'

'All right.' Charlotte smiled. 'If that's your wish, my lord and master.'

'It is my wish. In fact it's my command.' Josh grinned.

'We'll not tell anyone. I can't wait to see the faces of my mother, and Libby, when they first notice a ring.'

'I feel excited already,' Charlotte chuckled.

'They'll want to know about a wedding date, I suppose.'

'I suppose so, but Josh . . .' Charlotte frowned. 'I'd prefer a quiet wedding. Just your family, if you don't mind.'

'I don't care what kind of a wedding it is so long as you're my wife at the end of it. At least if we're engaged Morven and her boyfriend will realize you'll not be here much longer and they'll have to make plans.'

'She's very independent, or at least she tries to be. Her grandmother has had more influence that she realizes. She's scared of getting into debt, but Donnie has had no one to influence him. He has as good a job as Morven and I have. We manage to save a bit each month but he seems to have no self-control.' She sighed. 'I wish Morven hadn't got pregnant though. That changes everything. Donnie will have to keep them both. It will be a bad start to their life together.'

'You can't take on the troubles of the world, Charlotte,' Josh said.

'I know, but remember I've suffered the humiliation of being put out of my flat without warning. A very kind man helped me.' She smiled up at him. 'The best man in the whole world.'

Josh's arms tightened. 'When you look at me like that I'm glad you went to that clinic.' He lifted her up and carried her through to the bedroom. 'We'd better seize the opportunity while we can,' he growled softly. 'We shall be in Darlonachie tomorrow for Easter, and Morven will be here when we return. How am I to survive?'

'I'm sure you will, dearest Josh.'

'Maybe, but let's set the wedding date. How about the first week of the summer holidays, the beginning of July? I shall count the days like a child waiting for Christmas.'

'Mmm, I'm willing.' Charlotte looked up at him, her eyes already dark with desire, her lips parting to meet his own.

The following morning Josh telephoned his mother to say they would be later than expected, then he took Charlotte into the city to search for the engagement ring he wanted her to have. They chose two diamonds set in a twist of gold.

'Just like two lovers intertwined,' Josh whispered, bringing the ready blush to Charlotte's cheeks as she glanced at the sales assistant.

Much later as they approached Darlonachie, Josh reminded her of their plan to surprise his mother and Libby, the two who had been most impatient to see them married.

'I can't stop looking at it and thinking how lucky I am to have you, Josh.' Charlotte smiled. 'I'm sure they'll see me.'

When they arrived at the cottage Fraser and Peter were working in the garden and Mimi and Lachie were supposed to be helping them sow pea seeds but Lachie was more intent on chasing Mimi with a big worm.

'They sound happy anyway,' Josh chuckled as Mimi shrieked and ran towards them for protection from a grinning Lachie. Polly hurried to the door to see what all the noise was about.

'You're just in time for tea,' she greeted them. 'I was making some for Fraser and Peter. They've worked hard all afternoon but these two rascals havna earned any.'

'Oh, Gran! You promised to make us one of your buns with the chocolate icing,' Lachie said, giving her his most beguiling smile, while Mimi beamed at her.

'Oh, all right then. You'd better give Fraser and Peter a shout. I'm sure Charlotte must be ready for a cup of tea after her journey.'

'What about me?' Josh demanded, sounding like an older version of Lachie instead of a man of thirty-eight.'

Polly put her hands on her hips and regarded him. She shook her head. 'Men are always wee laddies at heart,' she told Charlotte.

Charlotte was helping her pass round the cups of tea when Polly gave an unexpected yelp of surprise and delight.

'That's a ring you're wearing, lassie! An engagement ring! Well I never.' She sat down with a thump and bounced up again, coming round the corner of the table to take Charlotte's hand and have a closer look at the two sparkling diamonds, then she hugged her warmly. 'This is the surprise I've been wanting . . .'

'It isna a surprise at all,' Lachie interrupted over a mouthful of scone. 'We knew – Mimi and Peter and me. We saw them kissing and cuddling.'

Charlotte and Josh turned to him, eyes widening with shock as their minds flicked over a dozen possible scenarios. Mimi kicked him under the table.

'You weren't supposed to tell,' she hissed.

'Well it's true.' Lachie said.

'When was this then, Lachie?' Josh asked, recovering his composure and winking at Charlotte, noting her cheeks were hot with confusion.

'We were helping Peter with the fencing on the other side of the wood and Charlotte walked over from Home Farm with wee Joe in his pram. I thought you were going to eat her,' he added.

'That's enough from you, young man, or there'll be no chocolate buns,' Polly warned but her eyes were twinkling as she looked at her youngest son. 'But I agree it's long overdue, Josh.' She was remembering the familiar way he had stroked Charlotte's hip and Josh knew what was in her mind. He grinned.

'I know. We shall not waste any time now though. Before you ask, we're having a quiet wedding at the beginning of July, but I have a few changes to make before then.'

'Aye, I suppose you will have,' Polly nodded. 'You'll be needing a proper house for one thing, and maybe a garden.'

'Something like that,' he nodded.

'He never did tell us what he was doing until he had it all worked out in his head,' she said to Charlotte and changed the subject, or so she believed. 'Mr Glenys has lost his wife. I hear he's giving up his wee farm and moving in with his sister. She lives on the other side o' Dumfries. I wonder who'll get Lintysmill, or if it will be to sell again,' she mused.

'Why are you so interested in Lintysmill, Gran?' Fraser asked, passing his cup and saucer for a refill.

'Because nobody ever heard who the Good Samaritan was who bought it and let the Glenyses stay on, for one thing, and for another the land joins Throstlebrae at the bottom. I wondered whether your father would be interested. He always says land is the best investment a man could have, in his opinion that is.'

'That's because he's a farmer.' Fraser grinned. 'He's prejudiced.'

'Aye, he was always determined to be a farmer, a bit like Peter here. Libby will be pleased you're engaged,' Polly added, turning back to Charlotte and the subject that was uppermost in her mind.

The summer term was a busy one but for Charlotte the weeks seemed to fly past. She wished she had kept the piano and a few other things from her old home as Josh had wanted her to. Instead she stayed after school to practise the songs for the end of term concert. Morven was still living in the flat with her and the girl's unhappy plight was the only thing that dimmed Charlotte's happiness. Donnie had refused to give up his motorbike. He clung to it like a small boy with a favourite teddy. Morven loved him and made the excuse that he had never owned anything of his own before, but she wished he had not chosen a motorbike, or such a powerful one. He seemed unable to make any serious plans for their future.

'Donnie is coming to get me this evening,' Morven announced wearily one Friday in mid June. 'We're going to look at a flat in the next block to where he stays. He says it's going cheap because it's in a poor state.'

'I do hope it will be suitable.'

'I doubt that, from the way he describes it,' Morven said, 'but it's the first time he's looked for a place for us.'

'We'll keep our fingers crossed. It may be better than you're expecting. Remember you can have my curtains and a few other things. Josh's mother is knitting a pram suit for the baby for the winter. Things will come all right, Morven.'

'I pray they will.' Morven was near to tears and she looked exhausted. 'I don't know what I'd have done without you, Charlotte. You're the best friend I've ever had. Here's Donnie now. I'd better go. Is Josh coming round?'

'Yes, in about half an hour.'

'We'll not be late. I hate riding pillion now that I feel so bulky.'

Charlotte listened for the usual roar as Donnie took off. It didn't come so she glanced out of the window. Morven was still standing on the pavement, Donnie was astride his motorbike and it was obvious they had quarrelled. Morven climbed on to the pillion, brushing away tears with the back of one hand and clinging to Donnie with the other. He zoomed away with more noise than usual.

Josh was pleased to have Charlotte to himself for once, although he felt sympathy and concern for Morven. She was a bright, intelligent girl and she enjoyed her work with the children. It was still light at ten o'clock in mid June so neither Charlotte nor Josh felt concerned when Morven had not returned.

'Perhaps it's a nicer flat that she expected and they're measuring up windows and things,' Charlotte suggested. At half past eleven it was quite dark and Josh was preparing to go home. They were standing together in the hallway of the flat, locked in each other's arms, when the shrill ring of the telephone startled them.

Charlotte reached out for the receiver, still within the circle of Josh's arm. He felt her tense.

'A crash? Hospital?' she repeated. 'Is she . . . Are they . . . ?' The blood had drained from her face and she was glad of the support of Josh's arm. He moved closer to listen with her.

'Ask which hospital,' he whispered. 'I'll take you. Tell them we're coming now.'

Twelve

The nurse's expression reflected Morven's grave condition.

'Miss MacRory is asking for you, Miss Crainby. Perhaps
your presence will calm her but time is precious. The doctors
are going to operate.

Charlotte stifled a gasp of dismay. Morven was barely
conscious and one eye was covered. She opened the other.

'Charlotte,' she breathed. 'Thank you . . .' Her words came
with an effort but she seemed desperate to communicate.
'My baby . . . If I die . . .'

'No, no,' Charlotte began but the nurse indicated she should
listen. 'They're going to take it away. Don't let them put it
in a home.'

'Don't distress yourself, my dear,' the nurse soothed. 'The
doctors need to operate to save your baby.'

'Not a home – not like Donnie.' Morven fixed her eyes
on Charlotte's face. 'Promise you'll . . .'

'We must ask you to leave now, Miss Crainby, Mr
Pringle. The doctors are waiting.' Morven tried to protest.
'You will see your friends in a wee while,' the nurse
soothed. She inclined her head towards Charlotte. 'There
is no time to lose. I shall come back to you in a few
minutes.'

Charlotte's eyes widened when the nurse returned accompanied by a priest.

'Morven isn't a Catholic,' she stammered.

'No, my child, but I met Donnie at the school where he
worked. He had no family, I believe. He attended services
in our church sometimes. I was here when they were
brought in.'

'I-I see,' Charlotte murmured.

'It was a nasty accident.' Josh's heart sank and he moved closer, putting a protective arm around her shoulders as the priest went on. 'His motorbike hit a telegraph pole and somer-saulted into a timber yard. I understand Donnie was killed instantly.'

'Oh no! Poor Morven.'

'I have to tell you . . .' The nurse looked at Josh, then turned to Charlotte. 'The doctors do not think your friend will live till morning. I'm so sorry. The doctors are doing all they can. It may be possible to save the baby, but it is premature and . . .' She trailed off.

'I-I see.' Charlotte's face was deathly white.

'Miss MacRory has no family?'

'No, her grandmother brought her up. She's dead.'

'She cannot realize what she is asking of you. Father Turner, may I leave you to explain?'

'What about?' Charlotte looked from the nurse to the priest.

'If Miss MacRory regains consciousness she may plead with you to care for her baby. It is difficult to refuse a request when a person is dying. As a single woman I don't think you would be permitted to adopt a child who is unrelated to you. You must not feel compelled to make promises which may distress you later.'

'Miss Crainby and I are to be married in less than a month,' Josh interrupted. 'But this has all come as a shock, Father.'

'I understand, but unless God performs a miracle, I fear there is little time to consider the implications. If you wish to avoid making promises to a dying girl I suggest you leave now.'

'I can't do that!'

'We should like some time alone, to talk,' Josh said. His arm tightened around Charlotte.

'Very well, but it is my duty to explain the commitment that would be required.'

'We work with children, Father, and we are not feckless teenagers who would take on responsibility without careful thought.'

'I see.' The priest looked at Josh with reluctant respect. 'I will ask one of the nurses to send in some tea.'

As the door closed behind him, Josh and Charlotte looked

at each other, then he enfolded her in his arms and held her close. He felt her trembling. They clung together, struggling to make sense of the night's events.

'Sometimes it difficult to believe there is a God,' Charlotte murmured. 'Where is His mercy now?'

'I know, my darling, and yet I feel there has to be.' Josh knew he would never have got through his time in the RAF had he not clung to his belief that there was a greater power than man. He cupped her face in his hands and looked into her eyes. 'Perhaps even now He is working out some purpose beyond our comprehension. Whatever you decide, Charlotte, I want you to know you have my support.'

'You mean if the baby survives? If . . . if I promise to take care of it?'

'I shall be with you every step of the way,' Josh said with quiet assurance. 'Bringing up a child affects both our lives. It must be a joint decision. I would have preferred a little time on our own together and time to consider such an important issue, but I doubt if we shall have that option.'

'Josh.' Charlotte considered her words with care. 'We have never discussed children, indeed we have just got used to the idea of getting married, but . . . but do you think you would ever have considered adopting a child?'

Josh pondered the question. 'It's not something I've thought about, but yes, I might have done. If you wanted to adopt a child I would have considered it.' He thought of his mother and knew she would be against such a proposal. 'I know how fond you are of children, Charlotte. I remember you considered teaching children who needed help.'

'Yes, ever since I was in the Swiss clinic I've thought I would like to do that.'

'Then perhaps we should consider adopting Morven's child if it becomes necessary.'

'I have the money I was saving to buy a house,' Charlotte said, considering the practical aspects, 'but I know that will not last forever. Do you think we can afford to keep a child and educate it? Would you mind the sacrifices?'

'We can afford a child,' Josh assured her. 'Money is not

an issue. In fact there are several things we need to discuss. This is neither the time nor the place, but I think we might enjoy having a small person to care for. I've seen how tenderly you look at wee Joe and at Molly.' He broke off as the nurse brought in tea. 'I'm ready for a drink. The decision will be taken out of our hands if the baby doesn't survive. We must consider that too.'

Charlotte caught her breath. She hadn't thought of that. In that moment she knew if Morven and her baby died she would feel as bereft as if it was already theirs.

They had barely time to drink their tea when one of the doctors came in.

'Miss MacRory is asking for you. She is drifting in and out of consciousness. I will take you to her now. There may not be much time . . .'

'Thank you,' Josh said. They followed the doctor.

'You may see the baby later if you wish. She has been taken to the special care unit. She is as well as can be expected in view of the trauma. The next twenty-four hours will be crucial.'

Morven had no tubes in now. She looked almost like a wax doll lying lifeless in the white bed. Charlotte moved to her side and lifted one limp hand from the coverlet. Morven opened her eye.

'Charlotte . . . you came.' Her voice was little more than a whisper. She gave a faint sweet smile, like a trusting child, Charlotte thought. She had difficulty holding back her tears. 'Baby girl,' Morven murmured, her gaze fixed on Charlotte's face. There was no doubting the unspoken question. Josh moved closer. She looked up at him in silent pleading. His eyes were filled with sadness. Morven looked little more than a child as she lay there and she seemed to be fading away before their eyes.

'We shall take care of her, Morven,' Charlotte said clearly. She felt a faint squeeze from Morven's fingers.

'Josh . . . a lovely daddy,' she whispered, her gaze moving to Josh's face and back to Charlotte's. 'Thank you.' Her eyelid closed. A few moments later she murmured, 'Lucy . . . yours now.' They were the last words Morven MacRory would utter. Father Turner stepped forward.

'We will say the Lord's Prayer together for the mother who has given her daughter into your keeping. May God grant you strength and wisdom.' They bowed their heads in prayer.

They were only allowed to look through the window at the baby. She seemed to be in some sort of glass bubble and her tiny body appeared to have tubes sprouting everywhere. Charlotte caught her breath.

A cheerful nurse came out of the unit to speak to them. 'She looks a poor wee soul just now but in a month's time she'll be just like every other baby.'

'Do you really believe that?' Charlotte asked.

'Indeed I do, m'dear. I'm not saying she doesn't need careful nursing, but we shall give her that.' She sounded so matter-of-fact that Charlotte felt hope surging through her. Josh took her arm and led her away.

'I'll stay with you tonight, Charlotte, shall I?'

'Oh, yes please, Josh. I don't think I shall sleep anyway but I don't want to be alone.'

'If I'm honest, neither do I,' Josh admitted. 'Death is such a final thing and Morven had barely begun to live her life.'

'I think Morven intended us to name the baby Lucy, don't you?' Charlotte said much later when they were curled up in bed together.

'Yes. Lucy is a nice name though. Do you mind?'

'No. I like it. Do you think we could ask the minister here to baptise her very soon?'

'I think that would be wise.'

Charlotte was glad they had settled for a quiet wedding but even that seemed to demand more time and preparation than either of them had anticipated. Mimi had agreed to be a bridesmaid so long as she could wear a long dress.

'I don't mind,' Charlotte told Mary. 'I'm wearing a ballet-length dress and I've got a frivolous little hat to match.'

'The main thing is that you're both happy, lass,' Willie said, drawing contentedly on his pipe. 'And I've never seen Josh looking so pleased.'

'Molly is going to be a flower girl,' Charlotte told them.

'It's a good job it will only be family,' Mary laughed.

'I think two-year-old Molly may take more watching than Mimi realizes.'

Charlotte was grateful when Libby and Victoria offered to deal with the arrangements to be made at Darlonachie. Everything was to take place so soon after the end of term. The school concert had to go ahead despite the grief and trauma of Morven's death. The headmistress was depending on Charlotte to accompany the children's singing but she always needed to practise her music. She was a competent pianist but she knew her limitations.

Josh and Charlotte had expected to be the only mourners at the joint funeral but there were members of staff from both schools and a number of parents were there from Morven's school. Some of them were in tears as they recounted how much their children had loved their young teacher.

During the last week of term Charlotte cleared her flat and moved her possessions in with Josh. They went regularly to see baby Lucy but for a few days they almost despaired of her survival when she developed an infection that affected her breathing. Despite the reassurance of the sister in charge, they were filled with anxiety.

'Now you go off and get married and enjoy your honeymoon,' Sister advised when Lucy began to improve again. 'The wee one will be all right with us and there's nothing you can do, even if you are here. Take my advice; you'll have plenty of work and worry when she's ready to go home with you.'

So Josh booked a honeymoon in Switzerland, knowing Charlotte wanted to pay a visit to the clinic there and also to see more of the country and the mountains. He had been quieter than usual during the last week of term and Charlotte wondered whether his mother's views on adoption were giving him cause to regret his decision. Charlotte steeled herself to ask him.

'I have no regrets. I think we shall enjoy having a child of our own. I knew my mother would not approve. She has led a sheltered life and she's a different generation. There was nearly always some relation or other to bring up an orphaned child, but that didn't always mean the child was wanted or loved. When my mother sees wee Lucy she will love her as she loves her other grandchildren, so don't you worry, sweetheart.'

'So what is bothering you then, Josh?'

He looked at her. 'Something I should have told you a long time ago,' he said. 'Several things have happened and they're forcing me to make a major decision now. I have to learn to consult you. This decision affects both of us and more than anything in the world, I want you to be happy, Charlotte.'

'I am happy, Josh. I know all about getting married, thanks to you,' she grinned, 'so I'm not nervous about it. I think Lucy will make the biggest change in our lives.'

'You're right there,' Josh agreed. 'This place is not suitable for a child for a start. Charlotte, do you remember once telling me you couldn't wait to get away from Darlonachie?'

'Yes. I thought everybody despised me because I was my mother's daughter. It hasn't been like that though. Whenever we go back people are always friendly.'

'They respect you for selling everything to pay off your mother's debts. They like you for the person you are, not for who your mother was. Just as my mother learned to love you and welcome you into her family.'

'Yes, I shall always be grateful for that. I know you couldn't have been happy if your mother had disliked me, as she did my mother.'

'It would have made things difficult,' Josh admitted, 'and I would not have asked you to make the choice I'm going to put to you now.'

'You did say you would go back to Darlonachie one day, I remember.' Charlotte smiled. 'So the answer is yes, before you even ask. If that's where you want to live, then I'll be happy to be wherever you are, dearest Josh. But what would you do about your work? I wouldn't like being left alone all week and having a weekend husband.'

'Neither would I,' Josh answered with feeling and pulled her on to his lap. It was a little while before they resumed their discussion. 'I've been offered a job as a physics teacher but I have to decide soon.'

'Wouldn't that be a step backwards?'

'Depends how you look at it. I enjoy teaching and seeing my pupils progress and helping the ones who have difficulties. I think the satisfaction will make up for a lot. Besides, there's other things I'd like to do. I miss not having a garden and I'd like Lucy to enjoy the freedom of the countryside, as we did when we were children.'

'As you and your brothers did.' Charlotte grimaced. 'You have no idea how restrained my childhood was. I wasn't a happy child, Josh.'

'I suppose not,' he said. 'You were never allowed to play or get dirty, were you?' He hugged her. 'I'll make up for that, my wee Lottie, if you'll let me, and we'll make sure Lucy has a happy childhood and we shall enjoy it with her.'

'Oh, Josh, I do love you,' Charlotte said. 'Shall we have to go house hunting when we return from our honeymoon then? I'd like to keep this flat as a base until we get Lucy out of the hospital.'

'Yes, we'll do that. Do you remember Lintysmill, the wee farm Mr Glenys rented?'

'Yes, of course I do.' Charlotte frowned.

'No one else wanted to buy it with a sitting tenant so I bought it myself. It's paid for, and now it's empty. We could sell it at a decent profit but that's not what I want to do, unless you insist. You see what I mean about the changes all coming at once? The house at Lintysmill is vacant. We need a house. We could move down there and have a large garden and an orchard. We could keep one of the fields for a pony. I'm sure Andrew would rent the extra fields from us. Even if he didn't, some of the other farmers would be glad of an extra few acres. What do you think, sweetheart?'

'I can't believe it!' Charlotte exclaimed.

'Would you move back to Darlonachie? The house needs a lot of improvements but I'm planning to change it.'

'Oh, Josh, that sounds wonderful. We could use the money I kept in the bank.'

'If we need to, but there's no harm in keeping a wee nest egg. I'm no callow youth, remember. I've worked for a number of years now and my mother brought us all up to be thrifty so I think I shall manage to make a comfortable home for the three of us. Will you mind moving back to Darlonachie, Charlotte?'

'I'd go to the end of the world, so long as we go together.' Charlotte pressed her lips to his. 'You make it all sound so wonderful. I can't believe my good fortune and it will be lovely to be near all your family. Lucy will have Molly and wee Joe for playmates.'

'And no doubt Mimi will volunteer as a nursemaid,' Josh grinned. 'I've been quite worried about telling you in case you didn't want to leave Glasgow, Charlotte.'

'Oh, Josh, I never believed I could feel so happy.'

'Mmm, there's only one thing I need now.' Josh grinned and stood up, lifting her with him. 'And that's to go to bed with my favourite girlfriend before I become an old married man.'

Although the wedding was supposed to be a quiet family affair they were both surprised by the number of people who had delivered gifts and good wishes either to Home Farm or to Polly's cottage. On the day itself Mimi was delighted when so many of the locals crowded around the wee kirk to greet them and wish them well. Charlotte felt proud of Josh. He was tall and slim and both he and Andrew had retained their thick brown hair, unlike Willie who was almost bald. Happiness leant them both a radiant glow. Everyone seemed to be enjoying the day so much that Josh had difficulty getting Charlotte away in time to get to the airport to catch their plane.

They spent a week in Switzerland but as soon as they landed back in Scotland they went to the Glasgow flat and then to the hospital. They were eager to see baby Lucy and were hoping for news that she might be allowed home soon. Neither of them could have anticipated the dark cloud that awaited them.

Josh gave a gasp of dismay as he read the letter from the Adoption Society. Charlotte moved closer to read it with him.

'But we promised Morven we would take care of her baby and give her a home,' Charlotte protested in dismay. 'They can't take Lucy away from us! What do they mean we must be approved? It . . . it was Morven's last w-wish . . .' Her voice broke and Josh knew she was near to tears. 'Oh, Josh, if they discover my mother committed suicide, or that I spent two years in a clinic with tuberculosis, they'll never approve me.' They were both tired after travelling and now it seemed their dreams of taking Lucy into their home and hearts were to be shattered.

Thirteen

B ack in Darlonachie, Peter had completed two years of practical farming at Langmune and High Bowie. He was nineteen and he felt he had reaped the benefit of his Uncle Andrew's experience and knowledge, as well as Willie's more traditional way of farming. Recently he had spent some time with Billy and Libby, listening and learning, knowing that he too must accept changes and continue learning.

'I'm not saying my way is the only way, Peter,' Uncle Andrew had told him on more than one occasion, 'but my methods work for me and for Langmune and change for the sake of change is no use.'

Cathy wrote regularly but he had heard nothing from Dinah or his stepfather during the last two years. Cathy had hoped he would attend the agricultural college at Edinburgh so that they might meet but he had not even applied there. He had received an acceptance from Ayr and from a college in Devon. He fancied seeing another part of the country and Uncle Andrew had agreed it would add to his experience. Mimi protested. She was twelve now but she and Lachie still spent their spare time following Peter and Fraser around, helping when they could.

Peter had a tender heart where Mimi was concerned; she had been like a ray of sunshine in his life from the day he arrived and she had filled the gap he had felt when parting from Cathy. When he saw her mouth tremble and the tears spring to her eyes he hugged her, lifting her off her feet as though she was no bigger than Molly.

'I shall miss you all wherever I go,' he told her, 'but I shall write and tell you about my new life and I shall look for letters from you too, giving me all the news. I'll take some photos with my new camera and send you some pictures.'

'But Devon is like going to the end of the world,' she wailed.

'Don't exaggerate, Mimi,' Mary said with unusual sharpness.

'It seems like the end of the world,' Mimi protested and her chin wobbled. Peter chewed his lip, sorry he had upset his little friend. Willie intervened.

'Come on, laddie, we'll take a walk to the top o' the hill and check yon ewe that was lame.' There was no lame ewe but both Willie and Mary knew their young daughter thought the world of Peter; they feared he had unwittingly encouraged her adoration. It was time for Mimi to grow up. Mary knew she would be hurt when she realized Peter had girlfriends who could dance and run and play hockey and tennis and badminton, not girls who walked with a limp. He had grown tall and he was a good-looking lad with his lean jaw and dark twinkling eyes. He had a fine mop of brown hair too, but it was his smile that would break a few hearts. They had heard Fraser tease him about various girls in the Young Farmers' Club, but so far none of them had been more than casual friends. Peter had been serious about his aim to save as much money as he could, and he intended to pay his own way through college, with the help of a grant towards his fees. But Mary knew he would not remain immune to the charms of the opposite sex.

The first visit Josh and Charlotte had made to the hospital had been far from satisfactory. Sister Stevens knew them by now but she was not on duty. The nurse in charge was officious and they were forced to obey her instructions to look through the window and not to go near Lucy's crib.

'Anyone would think we're criminals,' Charlotte muttered.

'Maybe she thinks we are.' Josh nodded. 'She's keeping an eye on us as though we might steel Lucy away.'

'Will Sister Stevens be on duty tomorrow?' Josh asked when she came into the corridor.

'That isn't your business,' the nurse snapped. 'The people from the Adoption Society said there was no reply on the telephone number you left and you never came in here once last week. Babies needs better attention than that.'

'But we were on our honeymoon . . .' Charlotte began.

'You're just married?' She glared at them. 'Why should you want to adopt a baby then? You'll have brats o' your own before long. They'll need to be told about that before they consider allowing you to adopt this poor bairn.'

'Did the man from the Adoption Society leave a name or a telephone number?' Josh interrupted her tirade in a cold voice.

'You'll have to wait until I've time to look for it,' she muttered.

'We shall wait all night if necessary,' he insisted but some time later he realized she had waited so long the office would be closed. 'We'll come back tomorrow to see Lucy. Maybe Sister Stevens will be back on duty then.'

Charlotte couldn't sleep that night. She tossed and turned.

'Try not to worry, sweetheart,' Josh murmured, turning to take her in his arms. 'I suppose they have to make sure we are capable of looking after Lucy. There may not be slave traders in the world anymore but there are still people who can be cruel.'

'If they deem us unsuitable,' Charlotte fretted, 'it will be my fault. I always knew what a wonderful father you would make and since we've thought of Lucy as ours I've seen how much you enjoy planning for her to come home, choosing her wee crib, the teddy bear, and buying a pram.'

'We have both enjoyed preparing,' Josh agreed. 'I'm sure they'll consider us suitable parents, especially since it was Morven's wish that we should care for Lucy.'

'I know how prejudiced and afraid some people are about tuberculosis. My mother was terrified of catching it; that's why she sent me away to Switzerland.'

'Did you hear what I said, Charlotte?' Josh interrupted. 'You go for regular check-ups, so they can't argue with the doctors over your health. They told us at the clinic that you had suffered pericardial effusion and that was the reason they were wary of recommending you should have children of your own. Mary was very ill when she was having Mimi; Willie thought he was going to lose her.' His arms tightened.

'I couldn't bear that, Charlotte. Whatever happens over Lucy, promise me you'll never take that risk, my dearest girl.'

'I promise,' Charlotte agreed, 'but it's not only my health. What if the adoption people look into those horrible stories in the newspapers about my father and Billy's mother, and then if they find out my mother was an alcoholic and sh-she c-committed suicide . . . Oh, Josh, they'll never think I'm a suitable person with my background.' She began to weep against his chest. Josh held her close and did his best to soothe her. 'Maybe your mother will be relieved if we don't get Lucy after all.'

'No she won't. She's coming round to the idea. Victoria reminded her that she and Mark had been orphans and Mark had been adopted as a baby. My mother admitted she wouldn't have missed having Victoria in our family for all the tea in China.' Charlotte knew he was doing his best to cheer her up. She could never fail to respond to his tender loving and eventually they fell asleep in each other's arms.

Neither of them had realized there would be rules and checks to be met before they had any chance of making Lucy their child. She was growing stronger by the day and would soon be ready to leave the hospital. Still nothing had been decided and Charlotte's anxiety increased. The end of the school holidays was approaching and Josh would soon be starting his new job as a maths teacher in Dumfriesshire. The tradesmen were working on the house at Lintysmill and Josh had to make frequent drives down there to consult with them. It was not an easy time for either of them but Josh was tender and kind when Charlotte burst into tears of despair or frustration and she loved him more than ever.

Sister Stevens had been off sick but when she returned she suggested they ask Father Turner to support their cause. He had been present on the night of Morven's death and he had heard her wishes.

'We haven't much time before I must move down to Dumfries to my new job. I hate the thought of leaving Charlotte alone here, and Lucy still in the hospital,' Josh fretted.

'Then ask Father Turner to accompany you when you meet the adoption people and you could suggest fostering Lucy until they reach a decision. She is almost ready to leave us and it will be better if she could start off with you. The district nurse from your own area will check up on her and give advice. As soon as they give permission you can come in every day and help with her feeds, Mrs Pringle.'

'Can I?' Charlotte's eyes shone with anticipation. 'I've met the district nurse for Darlonachie. She attended my brother's baby when he was born in February. She's very nice. I should welcome her advice.'

'Tell the folks on the panel that. Some people resent all officials, even if it is for the sake of the babies. So Lucy would have a wee cousin five months older than she is, eh? She'll want to play before you know it.'

'Oh, I do hope you're right,' Charlotte sighed.

'In wee Lucy's case I expect the adoption will follow if all goes well with fostering.'

Josh lost no time in seeking out Father Turner. He asked similar questions to the adoption people. Neither of them had been in trouble with the police, they had both worked with children and had excellent character references; Josh had an exemplary record in the RAF and yes, they could afford to keep a baby. When Father Turner asked about their respective families Charlotte confessed that her mother had committed suicide.

'I-I didn't tell the adoption people,' she admitted.

'If everything else is satisfactory they will not hold that against you, my dear child, but it's possible they sense you are holding something back. Then there is the possibility you may have children of your own and you may not love this baby as much as your own flesh and blood.'

Charlotte told him why they didn't intend to have children of their own. 'But I have had good reports from the doctors, both here in Glasgow and from Switzerland. I know how serious it would be if the tuberculosis returned, but they have discovered new medicines since I had my treatment.'

'I see.' Father Turner pondered this. Then he smiled at them. 'I will do my best. Your young friend had every faith in you. She had shared your flat, I believe?'

'Yes, for the last school term before she died.'

'I believe Sister Steven's advice to take one step at a time is sound. The reports will probably be sent to your own authority and the people down there will see for themselves how you cope with being foster parents.'

Less than a week before Josh was due to start the autumn term at his new job they heard they had been approved as foster parents for Lucy Morven MacRory.

'I must dash down to Lintysmill,' Josh said. 'The builders still have much to do and I fear you will find the house a mess, Charlotte. I must make sure the bedroom is finished, and the bathroom. We shall need a place for Lucy, but . . .'

'Dearest Josh, don't worry about the house.' Charlotte flung her arms around his neck and kissed him exuberantly. 'So long as we're together, and we have Lucy too, then I can cope with builders and a bit of upheaval. I feel so relieved, and so happy.'

Josh kissed her back and swung her up into his arms.

A while later he dropped Charlotte off at the hospital to begin feeding Lucy while he drove back to Darlonachie for a couple of days, which turned into three whole days. Charlotte wondered what could be keeping him but her heart was filled with love and tenderness each time she cradled the baby in her arms.

Charlotte sensed Josh was tense and on edge when they set out for Darlonachie on the Sunday morning with Lucy in the new carry cot on the back seat. It was almost as big as a small pram without any wheels. Josh was due to start work on Tuesday so they would just have one day to settle in. Charlotte had brought enough food to last until they could get to the grocer's in Darlonachie on Monday morning and they had an electric kettle and a tin of milk powder for Lucy. She was anxious about Lucy being too hot or too cold, too many blankets or not enough. Now they had her to themselves she realized taking care of a defenceless baby was a big responsibility. Lucy had been fed and changed before they left and she showed no signs of waking up but Charlotte still worried and peered at the tiny face.

As they drew nearer to Darlonachie she noticed the pulse throbbing in Josh's jaw and she wondered why he was so tense. Then they were drawing off the road on to the short drive up to Lintysmill. She could not stifle the gasp of dismay when she caught her first sight of the piles of bricks and sand, a cement machine, planks and rubble and various piles of rubbish.

'I'm so sorry to bring you to this mess, Charlotte,' Josh apologized. 'I underestimated the time it would take to carry out all my ideas.'

'Don't worry.' Charlotte gulped and patted his knee. 'We'll manage.'

Fourteen

It was plain that they would never get near the door but Josh drove on round to the back of the house. The track was new. Charlotte blinked. There were still bits of debris and tools lying around but there was a flagged path to the back door and a new extension.

'They must have taken off the roof! They've built up the walls . . .' She climbed out of the car and stared up at the house in amazement. 'All the windows at the back are new, Josh.'

'Some parts are finished. I hope and pray you'll think it's all right once it's completed. It seems to have taken so much longer than I expected. I wanted it to be a surprise and instead it's a muddle.' He looked like a worried small boy and Charlotte's heart swelled with tenderness. He took her in his arms and looked into her upturned face. 'I can't give you a castle, Charlotte, but I promise I shall do my best to give you a decent, comfortable home, and all my love to go with it.'

'Oh, Josh.' Her chin wobbled and her eyes filled with tears. 'I don't want a castle, even if you could give me one. All I want is you and Lucy.' They peered into the car but Lucy was still asleep.

'Come and have a quick look before she wakes and needs feeding,' Josh urged. 'The men promised to lay the carpets in the bedroom and living room. Let's see what they've done. At least I shall be here to chivvy them on now.'

'I didn't know the house very well before, except that it was a single storey and not very big.' Charlotte said, following him into what had been a small kitchen.

'I thought we'd keep this for coats and boots, and I've ordered a Bendix washing machine.' Josh looked at her

anxiously, wondering whether he had made too many decisions on his own in his efforts to give Charlotte a pleasant
surprise.

'We saw those new machines in Glasgow but the salesman
said they were automatic, all in one tub, and they're very
expensive, aren't they?'

'You deserve the best, sweetheart, and you'll have Lucy's
nappies to wash. Come and see the new kitchen. I didn't
know whether you would like a dresser so I've left that to
you.' He opened the door and watched her face. She opened
her mouth in astonishment, then took two tentative steps on
to the blue and cream Marley floor. She spun round to face
him and flung her arms around him.

'I can't believe it, Josh. It's beautiful, and it's so spacious.
It's even bigger than the kitchen at Langmune and I've always
thought how welcoming that is.'

'Yes, well, . . . it's a different shape, but the builder says
it will be easy enough to put up a partition wall if you want.'

'I love it just the way it is.' She moved towards the cooker.
'Do I smell paraffin?' she asked, running her hands over the
big silver lids that covered the hot plates. Josh moved up
behind her. 'It runs on oil. You'll never need to fill it up with
coke like Victoria and Libby do.'

'I think you're spoiling me, Josh,' Charlotte said, leaning
back against him, tilting her face up to his.

'The bits that are finished have to make up for the wilder-
ness outside and the rooms still to be done.'

'This more than makes up for it.' She twisted round to
face him, drawing his dark head down so that she could kiss
him on the mouth. It was several minutes before they drew
apart.

'We must remember Lucy is in the car.' He smiled. 'Shall
I bring her carry cot in here?'

'Not yet. Is this a brand-new refrigerator?' She opened the
door to peer inside. 'Goodness, it's all stocked up with milk
and butter, eggs and bacon. There's even a roast of meat,
and a big piece of cheese. Oh, and look, Josh. Someone has
prepared a lovely salad and a cold roast chicken.'

'All this is a surprise to me too,' Josh said. 'It must be
Libby or Victoria.'

'There's a trifle too. I'll bet that's from your mother.'

'They must have brought all this last night.'

'You have a wonderful family, Josh,' Charlotte said, her eyes wistful.

'They're your family too now, Charlotte, and Lucy's. Do you like the new unit with the stainless-steel sink? I wondered if you'd think it was a bit too modern.'

'I love it, and it will be a lot easier to clean than the wooden drainer we had in the flat.'

'I'd like to see what they've done to the sitting room and whether or not we have a bedroom to sleep in tonight,' he said anxiously. Charlotte followed him through the door into a square hall which had once been a small bedroom. It still had a bare stone floor and the green distemper was peeling off the old walls. They crossed to the opposite door and it was like entering a different house.

'That's the carpet we saw in Glasgow one Saturday.' She turned to Josh. 'You must have taken note of it. Oh, my goodness, it goes right to the walls – no wood-stained surrounds to dust or let the draughts in.'

'Someone has lit the fire in the new grate,' Josh remarked. 'It's well banked down but it will soon blaze away.' He bent to fiddle with the front.

'This is a huge room, Josh. You must have had them knock two rooms together. How lovely it is. What a beautiful view from the windows . . . Josh!'

'What's wrong?' Josh straightened up from the fire, which was flickering merrily now.

'The piano . . .' Charlotte said and crossed towards the familiar instrument. 'It is! It's the one we had in the Dower House. It's the one you thought I should keep back from the sale for myself. How . . . ? And the corner display cabinet. Oh, Josh, I always loved it. How did you manage it?'

'I left bids with the auctioneer; they have been in store until now. I knew I would give them to you as a wedding gift one day, but I always hoped it would be as my wife, and not someone else's.'

'Oh, Josh, I don't think there can be another man as kind and thoughtful as you, or as generous to me. I-I can't quite believe it.' She reached up and hugged him and he felt the flutter of her damp lashes against his cheek. If it had not been for Lucy, he thought, they would have made love there and then in front of the fire.

'I'd better bring Lucy inside in her carry cot, before we look upstairs. Then we shall hear her when she wakens. There are four bedrooms upstairs now but only one is finished. The other downstairs room was a small back bedroom. I hoped we might make it into a study where I can have peace to mark up books and such like?'

'Of course that's what we'll do,' Charlotte agreed.

'You'll have a busy time fixing curtains and cushions. We can use the chairs from the Glasgow flat until you can choose something to your liking.'

'I recognize these two small tables, Josh, and the big standard lamp. You must have taken careful note of everything I wanted to keep from the sale.'

'I knew by then you were the girl I wanted to marry,' Josh grinned, 'but I wasn't sure whether I would ever dare to ask you.'

'And I was longing for you,' Charlotte beamed. 'I'll come with you to get Lucy and carry some of her things into the kitchen. I never knew babies needed so much equipment.'

Lucy was still sleeping when Josh carried her into the warm kitchen and set the carry cot on the table.

'Come on, let's look at the bedroom before she wants a feed.'

The bedroom was furnished and someone had made up the bed and brought a fluffy sheepskin rug.

'I'll bet that was Willie and Mary.' Josh grinned. 'He cured some skins himself and I know Mimi has one in her bedroom. She says it warms her toes when she gets up in the morning.'

'I can't believe how kind everyone has been,' Charlotte said, 'and that's the bedroom carpet I admired in Glasgow too. You're so thoughtful, Josh.'

She moved to stand in front of the dormer window and gazed at the view. The corn was ready for harvesting and the fields looked like swathes of pure gold waving in the late afternoon sunshine, stretching up the side of the glen towards Langmune. Josh moved to stand beside her.

'It's so beautiful,' she said.

'What, the garden?' Josh teased, looking down on the rubble beneath their window.

'I didn't even see that.' Charlotte smiled, looking beyond it to watch the burn tumbling and burbling under the bridge at the end of their short drive. The brilliant violet blue of the wild vetch climbed up the hedgerow, while rosebay willow herb swayed in the breeze. At the edge of the cornfield poppies fluttered their crimson petals.

'I can almost smell the scent of honeysuckle from the hedge on the other side of the burn. I'm so lucky I can't quite believe it.'

'That's a relief, Charlotte. I thought you might want to turn around and go back to Glasgow when you saw the mess.'

'Is that why you were so on edge, Josh?'

'Yes. I'd hate to make you unhappy. I was a bit ambitious, but I want you to have a home you can be proud of and I wanted to give you a surprise.'

'I am happy so long as I have you beside me, Josh. You're the most wonderful thing that's ever happened in my life.'

'Wait until morning,' Josh grinned, 'when the workmen arrive.'

'Listen, I think that's Lucy stirring.' She turned into his arms and kissed him. 'That's until tonight,' she promised, her blue eyes alight with love.

Three weeks later Josh had settled down in his new job, the harvest fields had been shorn and all the stooks gathered into barns. The morning air was crisp and fresh, reminding them that summer had passed; the rowan berries shone as rosy red as the hips in the hedgerows.

At Langmune Peter was preparing himself for college and his journey to Devon. Victoria planned a family gathering for Sunday lunch to wish him well on the next stage of his journey, and to welcome baby Lucy into the Pringle family circle. Julie Dunlop was still helping at Langmune and Mimi and Lachie had promised to keep Molly amused and out of mischief while Victoria concentrated on cooking for the ever increasing number. At two years old Molly was proving to be an adventurous toddler with no sense of fear. One day Victoria had been unable to find her anywhere in the house or garden, and she was beginning to panic, fearing she had drowned in a cattle trough, or fallen down the stone steps of the hayloft. Andrew found her curled up asleep beside the collie dog in the barn.

Charlotte was nervous about taking Lucy, afraid she would not settle or that she would be sick or cry all the time.

'She'll be fine,' Josh assured her. 'There's plenty of people to keep her amused or to nurse her if she is fretful. Didn't the district nurse tell you what a fine baby she is?'

'Yes, but she is usually sleeping or on her best behaviour when Nurse Bailey calls.'

'Let's hope she can influence the adoption panel then, and get them to proceed. I don't think either of us will feel she belongs to us until we know everything is legal and we can change her name to Pringle. Did Victoria tell you that Peter is changing his name to Mark's?'

'Has he done it officially?'

'He wants to be known as Peter Mark Jacobs from now on. When he has used his new name for two years, and he has proof, he will be able to get legal documentation. I'll bet Doctor Sterling will not be very pleased when he finds out.'

'He doesn't deserve to call Peter his son the way he has treated him.'

'I agree. Victoria says he's never sent the money from Mark's insurance but Peter is determined to pay his own way through college.'

'Good for him.' Charlotte nodded. 'It shows he's got character.'

'Oh, he's got that all right, and plenty of determination. Andrew and Willie both think he'll do well whatever job he takes on. Mary says Mimi will miss him. He helps her with her maths and science. Young Lachie has no trouble with his studies. He seems to be turning into a bright student.'

'Like his Uncle Josh then,' Charlotte smiled. 'You said you always enjoyed studying.'

'Yes, I did, but in recent years I've missed not living in the country. I'm looking forward to creating a garden. I've ordered some fruit trees to plant a small orchard. We all helped my father, you know, when we were young, and I think it must be in our nature to cultivate the soil and make things grow.'

'Mmm, well it's bound to be an improvement on a builder's yard,' Charlotte teased, 'even if you do end up growing a fine crop of weeds instead of vegetables.'

'I hope I shall manage better than that!' Josh declared, then he saw the lights dancing in her eyes and seized her waist, only letting her go when one of the builders appeared at the back door requesting boiling water to make his tea.

It was a happy family gathering on that sunny September afternoon. Polly seemed as content to cuddle Lucy as she had been to nurse wee Joe and Charlotte was reassured that she was accepting the baby girl as part of her family.

'Wee Joe is growing so fast he makes my old arms ache,' she said to Libby, 'but he has a smile just like his namesake, lassie. Joe would have been proud o' the wee fellow.'

Mimi was known for her happy smile and sparkling blue eyes but today she seemed as near to being miserable as Josh had ever seen her. He sat beside her and talked in a low voice.

'Just because Peter is going away, Mimi, it doesn't mean there's no one else to help you with your homework. You know you can always come to me, don't you? If it's science or maths you need anyway; if you want help with French or German you'll need to ask Charlotte.'

'I hate science. Anyway it's not just homework, Uncle Josh,' Mimi said, turning a pair of soulful eyes upon him. 'Peter is good fun and he never makes me feel different just because I'm little for my age and have a limp, and he comes to stay with us at High Bowie and Daddy likes his company and Mum makes a fuss of him and cooks all his favourite meals. You wouldn't understand. It'll not be the same without him.'

'But he'll be back for the Christmas holidays, and all the other holidays, Mimi. They'll not be long in coming round.'

'It will seem like forever,' Mimi insisted with all the dramatic tragedy of a twelve-year-old.

'If you don't like science, what would you like to do when you leave school?' Josh asked, moving the subject away from Peter's departure.

'I want to be a farmer but Daddy says that's nonsense.'

'Well, supposing you persuade him to change his mind, you will need to study chemistry to go to college or university. There's a lot of science in agriculture, and a lot of maths too with all the calculations you'll need to do. Libby tells me you're a good wee cook. Wouldn't you like to do something like that?'

'Oh yes, I like cooking.' Mimi nodded. 'I've been first in cooking in all the exams so far.' Her wide mouth drew into a stubborn line. 'But you can't sidetrack me, Uncle Josh. I still want to be a farmer.'

'That's all right then, Mimi. I know better than to argue with a determined young woman like you.'

She began to giggle. 'Oh, Uncle Josh, you are funny.' She lowered her voice. 'And I'm ever so glad you married Auntie Charlotte and got baby Lucy. I will come to see you sometimes, and not just because I want you to help me with my homework.'

'That's a deal then. When Peter goes away you can come to tea on your way home sometimes, maybe on Fridays, eh? So long as you remember to tell your mother so she knows you'll be late home. I'll drive you up the glen to High Bowie after Lucy has had her bath.'

'I'd love that, Uncle Josh!' Mimi wound her thin arms around his neck and hugged him. He felt a pang of pity for her. She hero-worshipped Peter because he was kind to her and ignored her disabilities, but he feared she was in for some heartache in the future. It wouldn't be long before her companions at school were going to teenage dances and parties. They all seemed to be growing up faster these days. Willie joined him, packing his pipe, dragging him out of his reverie.

'I'm going outside for a smoke,' he said. 'You coming for a stroll?'

'All right, I'll come for a wee while,' Josh agreed, after glancing towards Charlotte to see whether everything was all right with her and Lucy. Willie saw him and grinned as they stepped into the yard together.

'I never thought I'd see you so smitten, young Josh.'

'What d'you mean, smitten?' Josh demanded.

'Why, with your wife, and a bairnie as weel now. You barely take your eyes off them.'

'Aye, he's got it bad,' Andrew agreed, following them outside, a wide grin on his face.

'I'm just following the example of my older brothers as usual.' Josh grinned back at them.

'Och! When did you ever follow our example?' Willie demanded.

'No getting away from it, Josh.' Andrew nodded. 'You've done it your way but you've got a fine wife in the end, even if it did take ye a long while.'

'Aye, and a fine house, tae, so Mary tells me,' Willie said. 'Ye could have knocked me down wi' a feather when I heard ye'd bought Lintysmill.'

Josh knew his elder brothers enjoyed teasing him a bit. They always had.

'Speaking of Lintysmill, I shall have about twenty acres of good land to let next spring. Are either of you interested?'

'I'm always interested in more land,' Andrew said, serious now. 'It neighbours Throstlebrae, so . . .'

'It does, and it neighbours Quarrybrae too,' Josh reminded him, hiding a smile. 'Mr Adamson called to see whether I'd thought of selling or renting a couple of fields.'

'Adamson! Did he, by Jove?' Andrew whistled. 'He doesn't miss a chance. You wouldn't favour him in front of your own brother though, would you, Josh?'

'Adamson didn't waste much time, did he?' Willie remarked. 'You'll need to watch him, Andrew. Hasn't his lassie got her eye on Fraser?'

'I don't know which way round it is,' Andrew said, frowning, 'but they seem to go around together. Well, Josh, what about it then? Do you want to sell twenty acres?'

'I don't want to sell any, but I'll rent them to you if you make me a fair offer.'

'Mmm, you're turning into a business man, little brother,' Andrew grinned. 'All right then. I'll make enquiries and see what sort of rents the farmers on the Croston Estate are paying and I'll let you know.'

'I saw you and Mimi were having quite a talk,' Willie

remarked, and Josh guessed that was the real reason Willie had wanted him outside. Andrew excused himself.

'Yes.' Josh nodded. 'I've offered to help her with her maths and science if she needs me when Peter leaves. I told her she could come to tea and see Lucy being bathed some Friday evenings. I thought it might be easier for her to ask for help if she gets into the habit of calling on us, and she does love children.'

'Aye, she does.' Willie sighed. 'She's going to miss Peter. He's a fine laddie and he has a kind heart. The trouble is she's finding they're not all like that since she moved to a bigger school. We think some of them tease her and the teachers can't keep an eye on them all the time as they did at Darlonachie.'

'There's always some who pick on their weaker brethren,' Josh nodded, 'but Mimi's such a pretty wee thing.'

'Aye, and Mary reckons that willna help her with the other girls. Looks mean a lot to females, she says. They get jealous, whereas the lads tease girls like Mimi because they're different. She's not as happy as she was and she can't keep up with Lachie either. They're in different classes now. He used to protect her a bit but they don't see each other as much as they used to. Anyway, it's not your problem, Josh, but it's not all joy having bairns, just remember that. You'd suffer for them if you could, but life isna that simple, is it?'

'No, I'm afraid it's not,' Josh said, remembering some of the bullies, and the bullied, from his RAF days. 'All we can do is help them stand on their own feet and build their confidence. Mimi has plenty of courage and determination. She may be a bit miserable sometimes but I guarantee she'll grit her teeth and learn to cope.'

'Aye, maybe you're right, Josh. You know more about bairns and their schooling than I do, and thanks for offering to help her. Neither o' us were that fond o' schooling so we canna expect Mimi to be brilliant.'

'She must be intelligent or she wouldn't have passed for the Academy,' Josh reasoned.

'I suppose so. It just seems to have been a shock to her when Lachie finds it all so easy. He hasna told Andrew and Victoria yet but he confides in Mimi. He fancies being a vet.'

'That will be a disappointment then,' Josh reflected. 'Andrew and Victoria have made a lot of sacrifices to buy Throstlebrae so Lachie and Fraser would have an equal start in farming. Still,' he shrugged, frowning, 'there's no good trying to run other people's lives. It's hard enough making the right decisions in our own.'

Fifteen

That Christmas, although Polly was making a good recovery from bronchitis it had left her very tired and weak. Peter would soon be back from college for the holidays and they were all eager to hear how he was getting on but she couldn't face a big family gathering.

The first Christmas of their married life should have been a joyous occasion for Josh and Charlotte at Lintysmill but they were still waiting for a decision on Lucy's adoption. Josh called in to see Victoria one day.

'We don't feel much like celebrating,' he confessed. 'It would break Charlotte's heart if they take Lucy away from us.'

'Oh, Josh, you don't think they would?'

'It's possible. We're only foster parents. I know they need to be careful with a young life but we don't know what they think or how they decide. They may consider me too old . . .'

'Of course it's not that, Josh. Thirty-nine isn't old to be a daddy and you're wonderful with her.'

'Mmm, well we shall see. Will you mind terribly if we don't come for Christmas dinner? If you'll not be offended we considered asking Mother to join us. It will be quiet enough at Lintysmill.'

'That's a splendid solution, Josh,' Victoria said with relief. 'I didn't like the idea of her being alone at Christmas. I've been concerned about her since this last bout of bronchitis.'

It had been Charlotte's suggestion to invite Polly but she was nervous at the prospect. 'I've never cooked a Christmas dinner,' she said.

'Mother insists on bringing one of her plum puddings.' Josh grinned. 'She had them made before she was ill. Have you seen the deep-freeze cabinet Billy has bought for Libby?'

'Yes, it's supposed to keep some foods for a year. It's unbelievable.'

'Would you like one? There's room beside the washing machine. You could put the mince pies in, and the stuffing, I think.'

'Dear Josh, you'd buy me the moon if it would help, wouldn't you?'

'You know I would, sweetheart.' Josh kissed her. 'I don't want you to be worried.'

'If we knew for certain we can adopt Lucy, I wouldn't care if the whole dinner was a disaster.'

'You needn't worry about me, lassie,' Polly assured her. 'I'd everything to learn when I married Joe.' Her blue eyes took on a faraway look. 'Not that he worried about my cooking so long as we had each other.' Josh caught Charlotte's eye and winked. 'Aye,' Polly went on with a glint in her eye, 'just like the two o' you. It was Victoria's great-grandmother who taught me to cook when I first married. She was one o' the finest cooks in the county. Victoria was brought up in the castle kitchens and she learned to cook as soon as she could hold a wooden spoon. She loves cooking. She always has, and she's taught Libby a thing or two. She's encouraging Mimi now. We all have to learn. I can see you're making each other happy and that's the most important thing to me.'

Charlotte need not have worried. The capon was cooked beautifully and the Aga cooker was wonderful for keeping all the trimmings hot. After dinner Polly fell asleep in front of the sitting-room fire and wakened just in time to hear the Queen's speech. Lucy thrived on routine and she fed and slept like an angel, then wakened for a cuddle on Polly's knee and won her grandmother's heart showing off her two tiny teeth with her baby smiles. It was a happy, peaceful day and Charlotte persuaded Polly to stay overnight rather than go home to her cold cottage in the darkness.

'That's a good idea,' Josh agreed. 'I'll take you home in the morning and help you kindle the fire and get the house warmed up. You know the cold air sets you coughing again.'

'I'm a fortunate old woman,' Polly said to them later that evening. 'I'm sorry it took me a wee while to welcome you into the family, Charlotte. You've made Josh a happy man.'

A little while later Josh and Charlotte snuggled down together in their own big bed. Through the window the stars were brilliant against the dark sky; there would be a white frost dusting every blade of grass with diamonds by morning. Safe in each other's arms they appreciated their good fortune, each knowing Lucy's adoption was the one thing they needed to complete their happiness.

The letter arrived on the last day of the school holidays. Josh's hand trembled as he opened it. Seconds later he seized Charlotte and waltzed her around the kitchen in his glee.

'She's ours! Lucy is our daughter at last. They'll never take her away now.' Minutes later Charlotte picked Lucy out of her pram and grinned at her, holding her above her head until she drooled with baby laughter, although she was oblivious to the big decision that was to seal her fate and her future.

'At last we shall get a new certificate declaring you're Lucy Morven Pringle, my precious angel,' she chuckled. Watching them, Josh felt his heart swell with joy.

In the summer of 1962 Peter finished his college diploma and passed with flying colours but to Mimi's disappointment he accepted a job on a large mixed farm in Gloucestershire.

'He'll never come back to Scotland now,' she said in despair.

'He'll come back when he's ready, lassie,' Willie assured her. 'The experience will be good for him if he wants a manager's job.'

Mimi was fourteen now and working hard at school. Josh had helped her a lot with her science and maths. He didn't just teach; he explained the reasons. So Mimi worked hard and made progress. Lachie steamed ahead, but in that year the Scottish Leaving Certificate was being replaced by a Scottish Certificate of Education, with ordinary and higher grades in all subjects. As well as his sciences, Lachie needed a good pass in a foreign language to go to Edinburgh University so he sought Charlotte's help. Andrew was beginning to realize his younger son had no inclination to be a farmer.

Wee Joe was two years old and Libby was expecting

another baby in July. Charlotte had volunteered to take care of Joe while Libby was in the maternity hospital, and Billy often brought him down so that he would be familiar with Lintysmill and Lucy.

Molly was almost four and she followed Andrew around whenever possible. She was a sturdy little girl and she seemed to have no fear. She had her own basket for collecting eggs and her own small bucket for feeding the hens and ducks; she protested if anything prevented her 'doing her work'. During the milking she sat in the cake bin and played with the lumps of cattle cake and listened to the conversation of the men as they worked, repeating their language at the most inopportune times.

One day the minister called to discuss the church fête with Victoria and he stayed for afternoon tea.

'Jem says Mr Mackie should ken it's time to milk the bloody cows and not drink tea all the bloody day,' Molly announced. She stood close beside the Reverend Mackie and looked up at him with innocent brown eyes, her head tilted sideways, waiting for his response. It came in a choking splutter as the Reverend Mackie tried to stifle his laughter. His eyes watered with the effort and Molly frowned.

'I dinna think Jem meant for ye to cry about it,' she said.

'No, I'm sure he didn't, Molly, but he is right, it is time I was going home. Do you think you will come to Sunday School when you start school next year?'

'Do you think you'll want her?' Andrew asked, doing his best to hide his own mirth.

'She's a fine, healthy wee girl,' the minister said. 'We can't blame the child for repeating what she hears. She shows great intelligence.'

'She doesn't miss anything,' Victoria sighed, wishing her cheeks didn't feel so hot.

At the end of July Libby and Billy had a daughter, Kirsty Margaret. Libby was a natural mother and she chafed at being confined in hospital for another seven days.

Polly had got over the bronchitis of the previous winter but her health was far from robust and she felt blessed to have all her family around her. Every time she went to visit Lintysmill Josh showed her his garden as he had shown her his childhood treasures. He was growing more like his father than either Andrew or Willie. He had designed a flower garden at the front of the house and a big vegetable garden to the south side. At the back of the house there was a large lawn with the washing line and Lucy's swing and the see-saw he had made for when Joe went to play. Beyond it he had planted a fruit garden and an orchard with apples, pears and plums. Charlotte shared his interest and they had bought a freezer to preserve their surplus fruit and vegetables.

'We always bottled the spare fruit,' Polly said sceptically, but she was astonished when she saw how well the vegetables had kept after four months in this amazing chest.

It seemed no time before Kirsty was celebrating her first birthday and her five-year-old Aunt Molly was starting school. It was something of a family joke that Molly was an aunt to Joe and Kirsty when she was just a child herself.

One Saturday afternoon in September Josh and Charlotte were taken aback when their district nurse called to see them, accompanied by a man and another woman. Josh and Charlotte looked at them warily and then at three-year-old Lucy who was tucking a favourite doll into her pram.

Nurse Bailey explained that they were seeking a foster home for three-year-old twin boys whose father worked on a farm on the Croston Estate. Their mother had been rushed to hospital and the couple had no close relatives. Neighbours were helping out with an older boy and girl who would be at school during the day but there was no one to look after the twins.

Josh and Charlotte looked at each other wide-eyed, remembering the apprehension and anxiety they had suffered before Lucy's adoption became official.

'Can we talk it over and let you know?' Josh asked, unwilling to let Charlotte suffer the trauma of fostering two little boys who could be whisked away at a moment's notice.

'I'm afraid there is no time,' the man said. 'You were approved as foster parents for your wee girl and you are our last hope. We do have approved families in the area but they are all full up. If you cannot take the children we must take them to the children's home.'

'Oh dear,' Charlotte said in distress. She looked at Josh.

'I wanted to teach children who needed special care. Do you think this is another way of helping children in need, Josh?'

'It's one thing to teach children and send them home at night, but it is quite another to take them into your home twenty-four hours a day,' Josh said. 'How long will the mother be in hospital?' he asked the nurse.

'We're not certain,' Nurse Bailey said. 'Three weeks in the first instance and then another two weeks to convalesce. We would be grateful. They are a decent family and they love their children. Robin and Rory are missing their mother so much.'

'Robin and Rory . . .' Charlotte said slowly. They had names; they were real people – little boys who cried for their mother, little boys with dirty faces waiting to be fed. She gulped and looked up at Josh. He smiled. He knew what she was thinking. 'The burden would be mainly yours, my dear, though I will help if you do take them in.'

'Very well,' Charlotte said. 'We'll do our best. When?'

'Today. Now, in fact,' the woman said with a sigh of relief. Her shoulders seemed to sag inside her smart jacket and Josh realized that her job was not an easy one. She had feelings too, as well as a big responsibility to the children.

Later that evening when the little boys had sobbed themselves to sleep, clinging to each other for comfort with two damp teddies squashed between them, Charlotte telephoned Victoria at Langmune. Peter was coming for ten days' holiday between the end of harvest and the potato gathering. At Langmune the harvest was not quite finished but Andrew still considered Sundays as a day of rest with only the essential work of milking and feeding to be done, so Victoria had invited the family for lunch and to see Peter again.

'I'm sorry we can't come,' Charlotte apologized and explained about Rory and Robin.

'Goodness, Charlotte, you will have your hands full, especially now Josh is back at school. I'm sure Peter will call in to see you before he goes back. If there's anything we can do to help you must tell us.'

Peter had missed Langmune and all the familiar faces. On Monday morning he volunteered to do the routine check of the cattle so that the men were free to get on with the harvest.

Andrew had bought a Land Rover to get round the more distant pastures on Throstlebrae and the two ten-acre fields at Lintysmill that he rented from Josh. Charlotte saw him driving along the track past the orchard while she was hanging the washing. She uttered a silent thank you for Josh's foresight in buying the automatic washing machine. Nurse Bailey had assured her Robin and Rory were dry at nights but both of them had wet their pyjamas and sheets. Charlotte had half expected this, knowing how upset they were.

This morning the sun was shining and they were playing in the garden but every few minutes, or so it seemed, they ran to ask when they were going home to Mummy. When Peter stopped off to say hello Charlotte invited him for coffee.

'It's such a lovely morning.' He grinned. 'Shall we have it out here?' Victoria had told him about the twins and he admired Charlotte and Josh for taking in the two troubled little boys. They approached him now, each carrying an identical toy tractor. Lucy followed with her doll.

'I'll bring it on a tray then, and some juice and biscuits,' Charlotte said, glad to have a brief respite from the pleas of the sad wee brothers. Robin and Rory seemed to take to Peter and they didn't want him to leave.

'I think they would enjoy having a sand pit,' Peter said. 'My boss has four children and the younger three play all kinds of games in their sand pit. The two girls make pies for tea and the boy makes silage pits which he rolls with his tractor.'

'That's a good idea,' Charlotte said. 'I'll suggest it to Josh. We shall have the boys for five weeks so it will be worth it. It must be dreadful for their father. The foster people advised him not to visit in case he unsettled them.'

'I could make them a sand pit,' Peter offered, 'if you're sure Josh will not mind.'

'Josh will be as grateful for your help as I am.' Charlotte smiled. 'I'll phone and tell Victoria you'll have lunch with us, shall I?'

'That's fine.' Peter smiled at her. 'You know, I feel more part of the Pringle family than I ever did in my stepfather's house, even before Mother died. And after . . .' He frowned, remembering. 'Afterwards I felt like a cuckoo in the nest.

I can't tell you how wonderful it is to come home to Langmune, and to be made so welcome here and at High Bowie and at Home Farm. It's as though I've known all of you all my life.'

'I do understand,' Charlotte said. 'I feel the same, Peter. There's a warmth and generosity in Victoria. Libby has it too. It seems to extend to all those around them. Marrying Josh and being part of his family is the most wonderful thing that's ever happened to me.'

'Yes.' Peter looked at her. 'Yes, I think I can believe that.' He stood up and looked down at the three expectant faces. 'Will you promise to be good until I come back with some wood and the sand?' They all nodded, trailing after him as far as the gate, then running back to play again.

'You'll pass the road end into Croston Estate and the cottages, Peter. By the time you return it will be almost lunchtime so you might catch Mr Dunnett. I'm sure he would be relieved to hear his boys are settling down.'

'All right, I'll tell him,' Peter agreed.

Charlotte watched the Land Rover drive away. *What a fine young man Peter has turned out to be*, she thought, *and what a tangle of relationships we have between us all*. His grandfather would have been the nephew of Sir William Crainby, Billy's and her grandfather.

Each morning of his holiday Peter called in at Lintysmill after he had counted and checked the cattle for Andrew. He enjoyed his morning coffee and he always entertained the children for an hour or more. They looked forward to him coming. On Saturday he brought Mimi too. She was fond of children and the pair of them amused the three youngsters most of the day, giving Charlotte a welcome break.

'We shall all miss you when you return to work on Monday, Peter,' Charlotte said over lunch.

'I've enjoyed seeing everyone.' Peter smiled. 'And to be honest I'm sorry I work so far away but I've plenty to keep me busy. Some of the men refuse to work at weekends but I don't mind. Mr Draper has a small flock of pedigree Suffolk sheep so he'll be pleased to see me back. He has given me two of his pedigree ewe lambs instead of cash for working weekends. He lets me run them with his flock, and this autumn they will go with his ram. He paid four thousand pounds for him last year. He's a fine specimen. If I get a couple of lambs by him I shall count myself lucky.'

'Dad is pleased about your sheep.' Mimi grinned. 'He thinks he's responsible for awakening your interest.'

'I have a lot to thank him for.' Peter nodded. 'He taught me all the basics, even if the Suffolks are a different breed.'

'What will you do if you want to move on?' Josh asked. 'Not many bosses would allow you to keep your own sheep.'

'I'd have to sell them, I suppose,' Peter said. 'But I'll cross that bridge when I come to it. Mr Draper knows he can trust me to look after his sheep if I have some of my own. He goes to the NFU meetings in London. He's some sort of official.'

'You do seem happy there,' Josh remarked.

'I am, but there's no future if I stay; Mr Draper has a son to follow him. He'll not need a manager.'

'Well, make sure you come back to Scotland when you do move,' Mimi said. Josh and Charlotte smiled at her youthful command.

None of them could have foreseen the changes another year would bring, or the effects they would have on Mimi's young life. Although she would always walk with a limp, Doctor Ritchie still regarded her as his special protégée and he had made sure she had the best treatment. She still saw the physiotherapists and she had always been conscientious about the exercises. At fifteen she showed promise of developing into a pretty young woman with her fair curly hair, sparkling blue eyes and ready smile.

Sixteen

Peter always glanced over the situations vacant in the farming press but the following May there was one in the *Farmers' Weekly* that grabbed his full attention. It was for a working farm manager at Croston Estate, to be responsible for the day-to-day organization of its three farms and to liaise with the factor.

'I saw it,' Mr Draper said, greeting him with a wry smile as soon as he saw him crossing the yard. 'I've just been saying to Mrs D, "If Peter sees this we shall be losing him, like as not." She has always said you'd head back to Scotland one day.'

'I don't think I've enough experience for such a job yet,' Peter said. 'But it's so close to where I belong that I must have a go. You do understand, Mr Draper?'

'I do, lad. We don't want to lose you but you can't keep a good man down. You've worked hard while you've been with us and you're reliable and honest. I shall miss you, but you deserve a good reference so you can count on me for that.'

Peter was pleased to be offered an interview. His two Suffolk ewes had produced three ewe lambs and a ram lamb between them. He would have to sell them all if he did get the job at Croston and that would be a blow. He decided to let fate decide.

'It will likely be young Mr Gerald and the factor who will interview you,' Andrew told him. 'Lord Croston has handed the estate over to his son, but he still lives up at the Manor himself. His son must be about forty, I think, but he's not married. He spends a lot of his time abroad, or so I hear. You can borrow the car to go for the interview.' So far Peter had resisted buying a car of his own. He never lost sight of his dream to rent a small farm so he saved his money.

* * *

On the day of his interview, Peter arrived in good time and parked beside two more cars a short distance from the farm office. He wondered if the cars belonged to other applicants. The farm steading appeared to stretch out behind the office. He was early so he strolled to the side of a track, which seemed to lead to the fields. He hoped he would get a look round the estate even if they didn't offer him the job. It looked tidy and well maintained as far as he could see. He was deep in thought so he didn't pay much attention when he heard a tractor chugging down the track towards the steading. It was almost abreast of him when he looked up and saw the tractor and trailer slowing, ready to turn towards the farm buildings. Everything seemed to happen in a split second. In the instant he recognized John Dunnett as the driver, a small figure hurled itself from the tractor, shrieking his name. Peter dived forward instinctively. His fingers clawed at the child's jacket, not a hair's breadth away from the massive rear wheel. He hauled him into the air. They fell backwards together, Peter still clutching the boy.

'My God, Rory Robin, don't ever, ever do that again!' he gasped. 'You could have been killed.'

'You still call me Rory Robin,' the boy chortled, heedless of his brush with death. 'I'm Roryeee.'

Peter scrambled to his feet and saw the white face of John Dunnett above him, half out of the tractor, clutching the other twin by the back of his jacket. Apparently he had been about to follow. He closed his eyes again, trying to shut out the picture that flashed through his mind. He was mortified when his stomach lurched and he knew he was going to be sick. He released his grip on Rory and jerked aside. When he regained control he found John Dunnett had climbed down from the tractor and was holding the boys firmly by their collars. His face was chalky white and he looked apprehensive. The door of the farm office had opened and two men were standing there. The older of the two looked furious.

'Dunnett!' he bellowed. 'I've told you before you're not to have those brats of yours with you on the tractor. It's far too dangerous.'

'I-I'm sorry, Mr S-Stacey,' John Dunnett mumbled. 'Rory recognized Peter. Before I realized h-he . . .' He couldn't go on. Like Peter, he was visualizing what had almost happened. Peter was surprised the twins still remembered him. He knew they had had two more long periods with Charlotte while their mother was in hospital but it must be eight or nine months since he had last seen them.

'Is your wife in hospital again, John?' the other man asked.

'No, Mr Gerald, sir. B-but she's not well. I-I brought the boys out with me because Doctor Ritchie is coming in to see her.'

'I see. And how do the twins know –' he looked at Peter – 'Mr Jacobs, is it? You are here for an interview?'

'That's right.' Peter nodded, still shaken, and embarrassed by his reaction. There was no chance they would be offering the job of manager to a man who reacted like a girl. John Dunnett was explaining how the twins knew him.

'I'm surprised they remembered me,' he mumbled.

'I take them to visit Mr and Mrs Pringle and wee Lucy,' John Dunnett said. 'They always hope ye'll be there. Bairns don't forget folks who are kind to them. My two have had a rough passage since my wife took ill.' He looked towards Mr Stacey and there was faint reproach in his glance. Gerald Croston saw it but he knew his factor deserved his support.

'We sympathize with your family troubles, John, but we can't allow you to have the boys with you on the tractors,' he said.

'I understand, sir, but I think my wife will be going back into hospital today. We're hoping Mrs Pringle will foster them again. They'll be starting school in the autumn.'

'I see. Well do your best to keep them out of danger.'

'Aye, Mr Gerald, thank you.' He turned to Peter. 'I dinna ken how to thank ye. You saved my laddie's life,' he said.

'Yes, he did. I expect a cup of hot coffee would be welcome, Mr Jacobs?' Gerald Croston suggested.

'I'll not waste your time, thank you, sir,' Peter said.

'But you are here for an interview?' Croston asked in surprise.

'Would you still consider me after such a display?'

'That was quick thinking and courage, man.'

Peter looked at him. He had acted on instinct. Now his

suit was a dusty mess and he felt as though he'd been turned inside-out.

'I suggest we all go up to the house for a drink of coffee. After that we shall take you for a drive round the three farms, Peter Jacobs. Our questions can wait. You may have a few of your own to ask.'

'Thank you,' Peter said, dusting down his one decent suit.

It was a long morning of exploring and questions and at the end of it Peter felt drained and the beginnings of a headache throbbed in his temple. It was two o' clock by the time he returned to Langmune but Victoria had saved his dinner. He felt better when he had eaten. He began to tell her about the disastrous start to his day, and his subsequent interview.

'They said they would let all the applicants know by the end of May. Whoever is successful would need to start at the beginning of August.'

'Oh, that's splendid,' Victoria said. 'You would be able to give Mr Draper two months' notice and I know you didn't want to leave him in the lurch.'

Peter laughed at her enthusiasm. 'They haven't offered me the job and I don't think they will. They said they would prefer someone older and married. There's a house available. I told them I live in a cottage on my own in Gloucestershire but they didn't seem impressed. The manager has to live on the estate.'

'Well that would be all right, except for your sheep, of course,' Victoria said. 'You could continue renting out Ivy Cottage while you live rent free in a tied cottage. Alma is so settled in Darlonachie I think she hopes you will sell her the cottage one day.'

'Mmm, we'll have to wait and see. The housekeeper remembered me from that time I found Lord Croston injured in the woods. Do you remember? Mr Stacey made some joke about me making a habit of rescuing people. I think he was being sarcastic.'

'He has a good reputation as a factor, I think,' Victoria said. 'Andrew will know. He's eager to hear about the estate.'

'They said it was in my favour to have Andrew Pringle for my uncle and to have had my pre-college experience at Langmune,' Peter told her.

'Did they?' Victoria beamed with pride.

'They were not happy about me having sheep of my own though. Mr Draper had mentioned them in his reference. Mr Stacey made it clear I wouldn't be permitted to keep them on the Estate if I did get the job. I've been lucky with the Drapers.'

'So you'll not feel all is lost if you don't get the job, Peter?'

'We-ell . . . it would have been good to be back near everybody and the pay would be half as much again, but there would be so much more responsibility.'

Later that evening Charlotte telephoned to say Mrs Dunnett had been taken into hospital again and she had the twins staying.

'Mr Dunnett told me about Peter saving Rory's life,' she told Victoria. 'He's tremendously grateful. He asked if I would tell Peter again.'

'Mmm,' Victoria murmured. 'I think Peter played that bit down. He was more concerned with being sick in front of them all and showing himself up.'

'From the way I heard it they all thought it was his prompt action that saved Rory from being crushed under the tractor wheel. It would be wonderful if he gets the job and moves back up here.'

Mimi prayed that Peter would move back to Darlonachie but she was busy studying for her Scottish Certificate of Education. Lachie had had excellent passes at ordinary level last year and he was studying hard for his higher grades this year.

Victoria's first thought was that there had been an accident when Peter telephoned long distance in the middle of the morning towards the end of May.'

'There's nothing wrong!' Peter laughed aloud. 'I just had to tell somebody. I've been offered the job at Croston Estate.'

'Peter! Oh, how wonderful!' Victoria almost wept at the news. 'We'll phone you tonight so that Andrew can congratulate you too.'

'All right. I shall be coming back up to Scotland when I finish working for Mr Draper at the end of July.'

Later that evening, after he had finished congratulating

him, Andrew announced, 'I have another bit of news for you, Peter. I've been down to see Josh since we heard your news. He's willing to rent his fields to you if you want to keep your sheep. He says the rent will be the same as I pay now.'

'B-but won't you mind giving up the twenty acres, Uncle Andrew?' Peter asked in astonishment.

'Not now. Lachie has made up his mind to be a vet and I have plenty with Langmune and Throstlebrae. If it hadn't been Josh who was renting out the two fields at Lintysmill I wouldn't have bothered anyway.'

'I can't believe it!' Peter said. 'I long to keep my sheep and Lintysmill fields would be ideal. They're not far from where I shall be living at Croston.'

'There's no shelter for the ewes for lambing,' Andrew reminded him, 'and I imagine your pedigree Suffolks are a lot softer than Willie's Blackface ewes.'

'We-ell, Mr Draper pampers them a bit because they are quite valuable.'

'Josh says he'll help you erect a shelter in the field near his orchard if you like. It would have to be at weekends though and he doesn't want to encourage you to neglect your work as manager.'

'Oh no, that would never do. I must look after my bread and butter job first. Don't worry, Uncle Andrew, much as I enjoy having my few sheep I hope I shall never neglect my work.'

Peter returned to Darlonachie in the summer of 1964. As soon as he crossed the Solway Firth and saw the four tall towers of Scotland's first atomic energy plant a few miles from Annan he knew he was almost home. Home, yes Darlonachie was his home now.

Mimi was delighted when she knew she had passed all her ordinary level exams with excellent grades. Lachie had done exceptionally well in his higher grades too. The results were good enough to gain an acceptance at university but he was still only seventeen. His teachers advised him to spend another year at school but Lachie had other ideas. He decided he would work for a year at Langmune if his father would pay him a wage. He would go to Edinburgh University to study veterinary science when he was eighteen.

Fraser thought they should have a celebration of all the good news, but it was Peter who suggested Mimi should accompany them to the Saturday night dance. Willie was dismayed.

'Mimi willna be able to dance. They'll make a fool of her, and then she'll be left sitting at the side. I can't . . .'

'Hush, Willie, don't say that,' Mary urged. 'The boys wouldn't offer to take her with them if they were going to abandon her. Anyway, I don't think the dancing is the same as it was when we used to go, and not all the boys are experts like you and George were. Mimi's got to grow up . . .'

'She's still a bairn.'

'Oh, Willie!' Mary sighed with unusual exasperation. 'She's sixteen. She's not your wee girl any longer. Haven't you noticed she's a pretty young woman, even if I do say it about my own daughter.'

'I don't care. She's not going to the dancing,' Willie declared and stomped out of the house. He and Mary seldom disagreed and when they did it was never more than a mild difference of opinion. Her heart ached for Mimi. She knew how much she wanted to dress up and go to dances like other girls. Unknown to either of them Mimi had heard their quarrel and she stole out of the house to hide her tears.

She knew it was Peter's idea to take her to the dance and she longed to go with him, but deep down she knew her father was right. Who would want to dance with a girl who limped all the time? Before she knew it she had walked further than she realized and she found herself near to Home Farm. Libby had always comforted her when she was little and Mimi sought her now. When she heard what had happened Libby was as annoyed with her beloved Uncle Willie as Mary had been.

'Most of the dancing these days is doing your own thing. The girls don't wait for a partner to ask them either. Anyway, Peter would never take you and then leave you alone. Shall I talk to Uncle Willie?'

'N-no.' Mimi shook her head and the tears swamped her blue eyes again. 'H-he's right. I'll never be able to dance like everyone else. I'd better be going home now.'

'Stay for tea,' Libby urged. 'I'll phone and tell them you're here. You can help me bathe Joe and Kirsty and I'll run you home later.'

'All right.' Mimi brightened a little; she loved helping with the children. A while later Libby left Mimi having fun with her two boisterous offspring while she telephoned her mother.

'The trouble is, Willie will not accept that his wee girl is growing up,' Victoria said. 'Maybe he's right about her not being able to dance as well as other girls but I'm sure she would manage and she has to find out for herself. Mimi's never lacked courage.'

'How can we persuade him to let her go then, Mum?'

'I doubt if anyone can make Willie change his mind when he gets an idea in his head – except, perhaps . . .'

'Perhaps what?' Libby prompted.

'Peter might be able to persuade him. He could take our car and tell Willie he will bring Mimi home if she isn't enjoying it. Fraser has his own wee car now.'

'Will you be seeing Peter?'

'Of course. He's coming up tomorrow for his lunch. There's plenty of time before Saturday.'

Peter was dismayed to hear Mimi had been upset. He went over to High Bowie as soon as lunch was over. He had to get Willie on his own. It would never do if Mimi heard them discussing her again.

He and Willie walked to the very top of High Bowie hill and still Peter hadn't managed to broach the subject that was uppermost in his mind.

'Come on, laddie, get it off your chest, whatever it is that's bothering you. You have a frown like my old granny. Is there something the matter with your sheep?'

'No, no, they're fine. Mr Draper arranged the transport and they travelled without any bother. They had a compartment of the lorry to themselves. You'll have to come and inspect them soon and give me your opinion.'

'Opinion!' Willie echoed with a bitter laugh. 'Nobody wants my opinion on anything else it seems. Not even Mary.'

'Oh? Have you had a disagreement?' Peter pretended ignorance.

'We had a wee difference of opinion over Mimi.'

'Speaking of Mimi . . .' Peter seized his chance. 'We're

hoping she'll agree to come to the dance with us to celebrate her success in her exams. Aunt Victoria says I can borrow their car so I can bring her home when she's had enough, or if she doesn't enjoy dancing.' He hurried on, allowing Willie no chance to argue or interrupt. 'She told me a while ago she's never been at a proper dance so we thought it was a good chance to take her when we're all going to be there to look after her.'

'Och, I dinna think it's a good idea.' Willie scowled. 'I told Mary that. She's only sixteen. Anyway I ken what young fellows are like. You'll forget you've taken her and leave her sitting on her own at the side of the dance floor. I've seen many a miserable lassie—'

'You must have a very poor opinion of me.' Peter pretended to be hurt and angry. In truth he was disappointed that Willie didn't trust him to take care of Mimi. 'Can you believe I'd take Mimi then forget about her? When I first came to Darlonachie Mimi was like a ray of sunshine in my life. I was so bloody miserable and she cheered me up every time I saw her smile. I owe her for that.'

Willie looked at him sideways. He knew Peter never used even mild swear words as a rule. He frowned. 'Er . . . We-ell, laddie, it's not that I don't trust you, but I know what young fellows are like when you get together . . .'

'You're forgetting I've been away for most of the last four years. I shall be like a stranger. Mimi and I will be good for each other. We'll stick together. Tell her I'll pick her up about eight o' clock. I don't know whether Lachie is coming with me or if he's going with Fraser. Oh, and tell Mimi it's an ordinary dance so most of the girls will be wearing trousers and a fancy top.' Willie opened his mouth to protest but no words came and Peter hurried on to another topic. 'I'd like you to come and see my ram lamb. I'd like to have kept him since he's so well bred, but he's too closely related to my three ewe lambs.'

Willie knew he was being deliberately side-tracked but he liked Peter. If anyone could be trusted with Mimi it was him. He sighed. He loved her so much but he couldn't visualize her ever enjoying life like other young women and having boyfriends.

*　　*　　*

'Don't worry if you can't dance all of the time,' Mary said to her daughter when it was agreed she could go to the dance. 'We often sat out, but it is a good place to meet other young people and to chat. Your father and Uncle George were mad about the dancing when they were young so your father thinks that's the way it is for everybody, but they're not all like that. Would you like to go into Dumfries on Saturday morning and buy some new trousers and a pretty blouse?'

'Oh, Mum, could we?' Mimi's eyes shone with excitement. 'Will Dad mind?'

'Of course not. You deserve some new clothes when you've done so well in your exams. I'll tell you what, I'll leave the dinner ready for your father and we'll have ours in Binns. It will be a treat for me too.'

Mimi knew she would always remember that day. It was so rare for the two of them to go shopping together, or for her mother to enjoy herself away from High Bowie. It was a happy day. She persuaded her mother to buy herself a new skirt and she helped to choose it. Her mother seemed to want her opinion and she treated her as a companion. She began to feel she had left her childhood behind at last.

'It seems strange to see girls dressing up in trousers for a dance, but I'm glad you didn't choose one of those miniskirts that are in fashion these days, Mimi,' Mary remarked, her eye fixed on a tall girl with the shortest of skirts.

On the night of the dance, Peter arrived in Andrew's Volvo to collect Mimi, who was ready and waiting.

'How will you get back to Croston when you return Uncle Andrew's car?' Mimi asked.

'Don't worry about that.' Peter patted her knee. 'I cycled up to Langmune but Uncle Andrew suggests I take the car home tonight and come for Sunday lunch. I'll cycle home in daylight tomorrow. I'm thinking of buying myself a second-hand car if I get a good price for my ram lamb. I've got my eye on a Morris Minor.' As they drew nearer the dance hall Peter sensed Mimi's nervousness.

'You're looking lovely tonight, Mimi,' he said. 'Your blouse is the same deep blue as your eyes. I can see I shall have to fight off half the fellows there.'

'Oh, Peter, you know very well no one else will want to dance with me so don't pretend,' Mimi said. 'And don't think I expect you to be my nursemaid all evening. I know you haven't had many evenings to yourself.'

'Listen to me, Mimi, you pay too much attention to your father's opinion on dancing. It's different now. Even if we do get an odd slow waltz or a Scottish dance or two you'll manage fine, but everybody does their own thing for the dances these days. You must have seen them on the tele-vision, dancing to the Beatles. You can do what suits you, so don't worry. Quite often the girls dance with each other if the lads are slow to join in. Some of the lads get very ener-getic, of course, swinging their partners over their shoulder. Just promise me you'll tell me when you've had enough, or if you're tired. Promise?'

'All right, I promise, but I don't want to ruin your evening.'

'The only way you'll do that is if you desert me for a young handsome fellow.'

'You do talk rubbish.'

Mimi laughed but when she looked at him he seemed serious. She was surprised and warmed when he met her glance and nodded. 'I mean it, Mimi. I wouldn't have asked you to come if I hadn't wanted you for my partner.' Peter had said the words intending to reassure her but he realized they were true. He was looking forward to taking Mimi to her first dance. He loved to see her smile and the way her eyes lit up when she was happy. It always made his spirits rise.

Fraser, Lachie and his friend Tom Adamson were already there. Close behind them was Tom's older sister, Jade Adamson. Mimi's heart sank. Jade had been a prefect at the Academy when Mimi first started there. She was bossy and spiteful, quite unlike her younger sister, Iona, who was the same age as Mimi, although she was in a lower year. Jade Adamson was tall and sophisticated, dressed in a bright red miniskirt and a low-cut black top that clung to her slender curves. She was wearing a lot of make-up round her eyes and Mimi felt young and gauche in comparison. She wanted to turn round and go home. Peter sensed her uneasiness though he had no idea of the cause.

'Don't be nervous, Mimi,' he said in a low voice, bending close to her ear so that she felt his breath caressing her cheek. 'Come on.' He drew her on to the floor and moments later Jade Adamson was forgotten as she became absorbed in the rhythm, the beat, the noise, following Peter's manoeuvres and improvising her own. He grinned down at her, tugged at her hand and drew her around him with a twirl. Mimi grinned back. She was beginning to discover a whole new world. Sometimes Lachie drew her on to the floor, sometimes Fraser, but she knew Peter was never far away.

'Come on, you must join in this one, Mimi,' he chuckled. 'It's just a bit of fun.' He clasped her round the waist and she saw him looking around the dance floor. He caught Fraser's eye and jerked his head. They exchanged a grin and Fraser beckoned Lachie. They both came to join in, with Fraser on her other side. She was imprisoned by two strong arms at her back. Other lines were forming across the hall now. A young man came up to Fraser, hoping to join their line.

'So you've shaken Jade off at last, have you, Frase? Who's the new chick?' His eyes were on Mimi and she blushed. 'She's a real looker. Haven't seen her before . . .' Fraser glanced at Mimi, his eyes filled with laughter. He was just about to introduce her, but the light died from his face as Jade Adamson pushed herself into the line between him and Lachie. The other fellow raised his eyebrows. 'What's her name?' he yelled over the increasing volume of the music.

'She's his cousin. She's a cripple, that's why you haven't seen her around,' Jade Adamson said dismissively and shrugged. Mimi heard the words and felt Fraser tense. He scowled.

Peter had heard too, and now he met Fraser's angry glare. 'We'll show the lot of 'em,' he said.

'Aye, we will that.' Fraser nodded, his jaw clenched, then he relaxed and grinned. 'Just follow our steps, Mimi.' He nodded to Peter and they lifted their arms. She was a foot above the floor. 'You're light as a feather.' He ignored Jade and her expression grew sullen. The lines of dancers began. Step to the right, step to the left, so many steps forward half as many back. She recognized the old nursery rhyme 'Horsey, Horsey' as one of the tunes. Mimi was lost in no time and

Fraser and Peter delighted in swinging her off her feet. When the dance finished Fraser moved away, determined to lose Jade, but Peter retained his hold around Mimi's waist. She fitted so snugly beneath his arm; her head just reached his shoulder.

'We'll have one more dance and then we'll leave, shall we?' he said above the noise. She nodded, trying to glance at her watch. 'It'll be ending soon and there's always a rabble to get out. I don't want anybody to bump Uncle Andrew's car,' Peter explained.

She nodded. 'I can't believe the time has flown so fast.'

Outside the air was crisp and cool after the heat of the dance hall, and it was quiet and peaceful with just the two of them. Peter settled her into the car but he didn't drive away. He turned towards her.

'How did you enjoy your first dance, Mimi?' He wondered if the Adamson girl's remark had spoiled her evening, but he need not have worried.

'I loved it!' she said, smiling, her eyes shining. 'Thank you for taking me, Peter.'

'It was my pleasure. Maybe we'll be able to do it again. I know your father thinks you're a bit young yet so he'll not want you to go too often, and you'll be busy studying for your higher grades this year and I shall have to earn my salary as a manager, but maybe we could go to the Christmas dances, if you'd like that?'

'I'd love it,' Mimi said, her young heart soaring. Little did she realize the changes that could turn a life upside down in a few short weeks.

Seventeen

Time passed quickly, and soon Mimi was working hard towards her higher grade exams. She often went down to Lintysmill to practise her French conversation with Charlotte on Sunday afternoons. She enjoyed amusing Lucy and the other foster children Charlotte often seemed to have around. Rory and Robin considered it their second home.

'What do you want to do when you've got your Higher Grades?' Josh asked one Sunday over tea. 'You're very patient with the children, Mimi. Would you like to be a teacher?'

'I don't know. I don't want to go away to training college.' She caught Peter's eyes and he smiled at her across the table.

'Two years soon passes if it's what you want to do.'

Most Sundays Peter spent time tending his sheep in the Lintysmill fields and Josh often went with him. He had bought a second-hand maroon Morris Minor although he had not sold his prized ram lamb. Instead he had followed Willie's advice and bought some more pedigree Suffolk ewes to run with the well-bred ram and he had accepted Mr Stacey's offer to run the three related ewes with the Croston flock. They were commercial ewes but the Suffolk rams were pedigree and it was the best arrangement Peter could afford.

The days were short and dark as November drew to a close and Uncle Josh often strapped Mimi's cycle to the back of his car and ran her home to High Bowie. On this particular Sunday, however, Peter offered to take her home instead.

'You haven't forgotten you promised to come to the Christmas dances with me, have you, Mimi?' he asked when they were almost back at High Bowie. Mimi had dreamed of little else since he first mentioned the dances but she smiled and said of course she remembered.

'There's one on Christmas Eve and another on Boxing Day, but I'll be seeing you before then to make proper arrangements. Do you like my little car? There'll be no problem about collecting you and seeing you home.'

December came round and countdown to Christmas began. When Mimi mentioned the dances Willie was filled with doubts again. This time his objection was that she was too young to be gallivanting. Mary just smiled and winked at Mimi. Her look said 'leave him to me'.

'It's only a fortnight to Christmas. I think I'll drive to Dumfries on Monday and do some Christmas shopping,' she said. Later she asked Mimi if she would like a new dress to wear for the Christmas dance.

'You think Dad will let me go?' Mimi asked.

'He will when I've talked to him. I know you'll be safe with Peter. I suppose Fraser and Lachie will be there too?' Mimi nodded and hugged her mother.

Mary drove to Dumfries on Monday morning and spent a happy few hours browsing around the shops. She saw a dainty hexagonal watch on a gold bracelet in the window of one of the jewellers. She had promised to buy Mimi a gold watch for her eighteenth birthday, which was more than a year away, but she stared at the watch for a long time. It would look so good on Mimi's slim wrist. It was more expensive than she had intended to pay but she might never see anything as lovely when she wanted it. Mimi deserved a few pretty things to give her confidence. Mary would have done anything she could to compensate for the blow life had dealt her beloved child.

She hurried back to the car. She had been longer than she intended. It would be almost dark by the time she got home. She could feel a headache coming on. She ought to have stopped for something to eat, or at least a cup of tea, but she hated going into restaurants alone. She would have a drink at home before she tended the hens, she decided. She heaved a sigh of relief as she drove through Darlonachie and up the track, past Home Farm and on to High Bowie. She had no recollection of driving out of the town, but she was almost home. It was going to be a cold night. She blinked, trying hard to clear her vision. The car swerved violently as it caught the edge of the track; she managed to get it under control but the shock made her shiver. If the car had rolled over the edge . . . 'Don't think about what might have happened,' she muttered to herself. It was a relief when she drove into the familiar yard. She gathered her packages and carried them inside, dumping some on the table while she poked up the fire with her free hand. She shoved the kettle on for tea. She was clutching the long narrow package from the jeweller's as she climbed the stairs.

Mary had no recollection of leaving the car slewed across the yard, or of climbing the stairs to her room and removing her hat. The house was in darkness when Mimi arrived home from school. If Mary had been thinking clearly she would have waited in Darlonachie to give her a lift. Instead she had passed though the village only minutes before the school bus arrived. Mimi found the kettle steaming away on the side of the fire but there was no sign of her mother and no answer when she called. She went outside to look for her. Some hens were still scratching outside their huts, waiting for their afternoon feed although dusk was falling.

Willie was collecting the buckets to feed the pigs.

'Where's Mum? Have you seen her, Dad?'

'Not since she went to Dumfries about mid-morning, love.' He walked beside her towards the house. He frowned and paused beside the car. 'She must have been in a hurry to get indoors. She never leaves the car like that.' Mary was neat and tidy in everything she did. Willie felt his heart beats quicken. Some sixth sense warned him there was more than an abandoned car to worry about. He set down the buckets and hurried into the house, switching on the lights as he went.

Mary was still wearing her winter coat, sprawled half across the bed where she had collapsed in the cold darkness of the December afternoon. As soon as he saw her, Willie knew she had had a stroke.

'Telephone the doctor, Mimi, get an ambulance . . . Hurry, lassie!' Gently he lifted Mary's arm and then her leg on to the bed and opened the buttons of her coat.

'B-but, Daddy . . .' Mimi felt young and helpless.

'Hurry, lassie,' Willie urged brusquely. 'I think your mother has had a stroke.'

Mimi rushed down the stairs to the telephone.

Mary opened her eyes but there was no recognition in them. She tried to speak but all she could utter were unintelligible noises. Willie stroked her brow gently and murmured soothing noises but his heart was heavy. He had known a stroke to ruin the life of the strongest man. Mimi was only forty-seven. *Please God don't let it be serious*, he prayed silently, but in his heart he knew it was. Her mouth was pulled to one side and she couldn't move her left side. She was clutching a slim package in her other hand. She seemed agitated but no words would come.

'Doctor Ritchie is visiting at one of the cottages at Home Farm. They're sending him straight up,' Mimi said breathlessly as she ran into the bedroom. She threw herself to her knees beside the bed, holding her mother's lifeless hand.

It did not take Steve Ritchie long to get up to High Bowie. He had seen all sorts of illnesses but he felt his heart contract with pity when he looked down at Mary, and at Mimi kneeling beside her, holding her hand. He could see by her clothes that she had been away from the farm. He asked Willie a few short questions as he bent over his wife.

'She seems agitated.' He frowned. 'What's this?' He touched the slim package clutched in Mary's other hand. Her brain was incapable of making her fingers release it but she turned her head in the direction of Mimi's voice. 'I think she wants you to have this, Mimi. Listen, that's the ambulance. Bring them up, Willie.' Mary seemed more agitated now. Doctor Ritchie prised her fingers from the package and handed it to Mimi. 'It looks like jewellery – a gift, perhaps. Put it away in your room, Mimi.' Mary seemed to grow calmer as he gave Mimi the package, but Doctor Ritchie had seen more than Mimi and he ushered her out of the bedroom. 'Make way for the stretcher, Mimi. I'll go in the ambulance with your mother. Be brave now. Follow in the car with your father.' Mimi hurried to her room and tucked the package beneath her handkerchief case where it lay forgotten. She wanted to speak to her mother, to kiss her cheek before they carried her to the ambulance, but Doctor Ritchie stood between them. His eyes met Willie's. 'I'll see you at the hospital,' he said.

Later they were told that Mary had died in the ambulance on the way to the hospital. There was nothing anyone could have done. All the way there Willie had been shaking like an aspen leaf. Mimi knew there was no way he could drive them home. She felt cold and remote. A nurse told her where to find the public telephone but she had no change. She dialled Langmune and reversed the charges. After the initial shock Victoria said, 'Wait at the hospital, Mimi. We're coming. Fraser can look after Molly. Andrew will drive your car back.'

Mimi put the receiver back in place, then she began to tremble. She was vaguely aware of a nurse talking to them, bringing a cup of tea, asking her father questions, but everything else was a blur.

Eighteen

Christmas came and went unnoticed at High Bowie. It didn't occur to Mimi to return to school. Her father needed her. In the beginning friends and neighbours called to offer their sympathy. Peter came several times but it was plain to all of them that Willie preferred to grieve alone.

'I hate to think of you alone up here, Mimi,' Peter said, 'but I feel your father considers me a nuisance just now, although we have always got on so well.'

'No, I'm sure that's not true,' Mimi said. 'He's the same with everybody, even me. He blames himself. It-it's as though he lives in a different world.'

'It will pass,' Peter comforted. 'But I will stay away for a while and give him time and space. Lift the telephone and I shall come if you need me.'

'Thank you, Peter. You're a good friend,' Mimi said in a low voice. She did need him, but she understood how unwelcome he must feel.

'My first ewe lambed on New Year's Day,' he said, 'and the rest are due anytime so I expect they'll keep me busy.'

'I understand, Peter,' Mimi said, and she did. He drew her into his arms and held her close. Then he kissed her tenderly before he left. It was a precious memory that brought comfort when her thoughts were dark with despair in the months that followed.

Victoria, Libby and Charlotte took turns at inviting them for Sunday lunch but Willie always made an excuse and Mimi couldn't leave him on his own. She doubted whether he would eat at all if she didn't put food under his nose.

Peter wrote to her and she treasured his letters, telling her about his work, or what was happening at Lintysmill.

Sometimes he telephoned but if her father answered he was polite but distant and he never called Mimi to the phone.

In March Mimi had her seventeenth birthday but she had already left her girlhood behind in the three months since her mother's death. She watched over her father even more carefully than Mary had done. She heard him tossing and turning in the room next to hers. He seemed to have withdrawn into a world apart. He cared for his animals, he worked, he ate, and he slept when exhaustion claimed him. He welcomed the bitter winds of March, and the longer, lighter days, and the constant care needed by lambing ewes.

Mimi was growing concerned about the growing pile of letters. Her father had always paid the bills himself but now he set them aside unopened. In desperation she telephoned Langmune and asked Aunt Victoria for advice.

'Pile all the letters into a carrier and come over here as soon as you've finished the essential jobs, lassie.' Victoria's tone was brisk. There was no arguing. 'Leave your father a snack and you can have your dinner with us, then we'll sort things together. And bring the cheque book. Willie can't opt out of his responsibilities for ever.'

Mimi felt a surge of relief now that she had confided some of her worries. She had begun to wonder if her father wanted to shut her out of his life along with the rest of the world. She kept remembering a conversation she had overheard at her mother's funeral. The two women were strangers to her but she had overheard the younger one remark, 'He thought the world o' his wife. Remember how ill she was when she was expecting the bairn. I remember him telling old Doctor Grantly he must save his wife's life and sacrifice the babe if it came to a choice between the two o' them.'

'Yes, I remember,' the older woman sighed. 'But Willie Pringle will be thankful he has a daughter now, poor man.'

'Aye, maybe, but I wish my man thought as much o' me as he did o' his wife.' The women had moved away then. Mimi sometimes wondered if her father still wished she had been the one to die, if only he could have her mother back.

Victoria helped her sort the letters into piles. Some were just duplicates and reminders of neglected bills and she threw them in the fire.

'See, there's not so many now,' she said, 'but here's one from the Academy, asking why you have not been attending school. Have you any regrets about giving up your education, Mimi?'

'Not when Dad needs me, though he is so silent and withdrawn, I'm not sure he knows I'm there half the time.'

'I'll answer that letter then and explain what has happened. If you write out the cheques and address an envelope for each one all your father needs to do is sign the cheques ready for you to post. You must make sure he does it. You must insist. I know your mother never nagged but sometimes you have to be firm.'

'I'll try.' Mimi nodded, but without conviction. 'I'll have to be getting back home now but I do appreciate your help.'

'Wait for a scone and a cup of tea. Here's Uncle Andrew and Lachie and Fraser coming in for theirs before the milking.'

'Mimi, I wonder if you could cope with Lachie if I send him over to High Bowie to get some experience in lambing ewes?' Andrew asked. Mimi wondered if he was serious. She frowned.

'I can feed Lachie, if he can put up with my cooking,' she said, 'but are you sure he wants to come? Dad is so uncommunicative. I don't know whether he would explain about things.'

'If Lachie is going to be a vet he'll need to learn and I can't think of a better man to teach him than your father.'

'Peter said your father taught him all he knows about sheep,' Lachie said. He grinned at her. 'You're not such a bad cook are you, Mimi?'

'I think you'll survive.' She smiled back at him. 'But I do have a terrible job getting the oven hot enough sometimes.' She frowned. 'I thought I might ask Granny Pringle if she understands about the flues.'

'You need to rake them right out,' Victoria said, 'every morning if you have time, before you do your black leading. It can still be a problem when the wind is in the wrong direction. I remember the struggles we used to have with the old range at the castle.'

'But that's a ruin now,' Fraser said. 'Even Granny P has

a modern range.' Andrew and Victoria exchanged glances. It was too bad of Willie to expect Mimi to do everything Mary had done. She never saw her friends since she stopped attending school. A few days later Victoria mentioned this to Polly over a cup of tea.

'I feel so sorry for Mimi,' she said, 'but Willie does need her. He seems to be so depressed. She says he looks the same on the outside but he's like a snail that's gone away and left its shell behind.'

'Is that what the bairn said?' Polly asked with concern. 'That's just how Joe's father was when his wife died. The doctor said it was the shock of losing her; he got very low in spirits. It's not good for Mimi being up there on her own if Willie is like that.'

'Andrew is sending Lachie to stay for the lambing; we think some young company will be good for Mimi. They've always got on well. Willie didn't sound too enthusiastic though when Andrew phoned to suggest it.'

Polly was at Langmune when Lachie arrived home for his Sunday dinner, bringing his dirty washing with him.

'Mimi would be offended if she knew I'd brought my washing home,' he said, 'but you've no idea how hard she has to work. She still lights a fire for the boiler on a Monday and she has to turn a handle over the wash tub. She doesn't even have an electric ringer. She turns it by hand.'

'Mmm, that's the way we used to wash.' Victoria nodded. 'I'm glad I've got an electric washing machine with this dirty wee rascal though.' She seated Molly in a seat beside her grandmother but the little girl just gave her impish grin.

'It's not only the washing. Mimi has an electric kettle and that's about all. Do you think Uncle Willie can't afford anything more modern to make her life easier? After all, she's given up school to look after him. She milks the two cows morning and night and she feeds the hens and cleans and packs the eggs.' Lachie had always felt deep affection for his cousin and he was angry and indignant now.

'Why didn't you ask him whether he can afford more modern equipment for Mimi?' Andrew asked. 'He can't be that poor. He has no labour to pay and he gets subsidies for his sheep.'

'I wouldn't dare ask him.' Lachie frowned. 'Uncle Willie
has changed. There's no fun in him now. He used to tease and
tell jokes and interesting things about his dogs and the countryside. Now he only speaks if he has to. It must be miserable
for Mimi. I don't know how she sticks it.'

'Maybe she'll not stick it if Willie doesn't snap out of his
despair,' Andrew said, anxious for both his brother and his
niece. He couldn't imagine his own life without Victoria.
She and Mary had been the same age. He shuddered and
pushed the thought away.

Polly listened and made a silent resolve. She was Willie's
mother. She could give him a piece of her mind and risk
offending him, or even hurting him, but she couldn't stand
by and let Mimi suffer. In a few weeks she would be seventy-
six. There was no time to waste.

Mimi couldn't believe it when she saw her grandmother plod-
ding up the track with her stick in one hand and a basket in
the other. It was a fine April morning and Polly had wakened
early. She had baked some fresh scones and packed them in
a basket for Mimi. This was her excuse for calling, if she
needed one. Along the hedgerows the primroses were blooming
in profusion, lifting their lovely faces to the sunshine and her
spirits lifted too.

'Granny! How did you get here? You didn't come across
the burn?'

'Aye, I did. It's a beautiful morning and I baked a fresh
scone for ye, lassie.' She handed Mimi the basket. 'I nearly
missed the last stone, but here I am.' Polly didn't add that
she'd had to sit on a log until her heart stopped thumping after
she had nearly fallen in. She would not attempt that again.

'It's lovely to see you,' Mimi said with real pleasure, 'and
I'll take you home in the car. I haven't passed my test yet
but we shall not go on the road. Aunt Victoria persuaded me
to get my provisional licence and I've got the L plates.'

'That'll suit me fine, bairn, but I'd like a chat with your
father before I leave. D'you think you could leave us alone
after he's had his dinner?'

'Of course, but he normally eats up and goes back to work
before we're even finished.'

'I shall detain him today if you and Lachie make your-selves scarce.'

'All right. You sound as though you mean business, Granny.'

'Aye, I do. He's moped long enough, and I shall tell him so.' She looked at Mimi's anxious young face. 'Don't fret, lassie.' She patted her granddaughter's arm. 'Remember he was once my bairn and sat upon my knee. I don't mean to hurt him, but neither can he go on the way he is, shutting out the world and everybody in it. I shall remind him he hasna been to see his old mother for more than three months for a start.'

At dinner time it was just as Mimi had said. Willie cleared his plate and pushed back his chair to go out as soon as he'd finished. Mimi had already whispered instructions to Lachie and they rose too.

'It's a long while since I've seen ye, Willie,' Polly said. 'Have ye no' a minute for your old mother?' Willie turned to look back at her in genuine surprise. She nodded at him. 'Sit ye down again until I drink my tea. I'd like a chat with ye.'

Willie frowned but he did as she asked, barely aware that Lachie and Mimi had left the kitchen and closed the door behind them. He sat in silence, staring into space. Polly's heart sank. There seemed to be no soul in a man who stared so vacantly. But she'd made the effort to get here. She was not going to hold back now.

'When will you stop being so selfish, Willie?'

'What?' He stared at her, startled and indignant, but it was a reaction at least.

'You heard what I said. Moping about, never speaking, refusing invitations, feeling sorry for yourself, I suppose. You're not the first man or woman to lose the one you love. You'll not be the last either.'

'I ken that.' He rose from his chair, intending to leave.

'Mimi's lost her mother. Why are you treating her so cruelly?' Polly demanded.

He turned back and stared at her. 'Cruel? Cruel to Mimi? I'd never hurt a hair o' her head.'

'It's not her hair I'm talking about,' Polly snapped. 'It's her poor work-worn hands and the way she's a slave to ye,

Willie Pringle. She's just had her seventeenth birthday and here she is struggling to do a woman's work. Still lighting up the copper to boil clothes, and a wash tub little better than the posher and peggy tub I used years ago when I was first married. Libby and Victoria and Charlotte all have electric washing machines – aye, and they don't have a range to black-lead and flues to clean before they can cook a Sunday roast, or coals to carry and cows to milk, not to mention looking after the poultry and packing the eggs for the egg man.'

'Has Mimi been complaining?' Willie asked. It had crossed his mind that he should give up High Bowie and move to the town and let Mimi finish her education, but he had drifted on, not knowing what else he would do with the rest of his life.

'Mimi never complains. You should know that. She's like her mother. Mary never complained either and the lassie is trying to carry on where Mary left off, but Mary was your wife. You made each other happy and it was the life you both wanted. What is Mimi getting out of this life? You don't even make an effort to take her out for Sunday dinner when the family asks you.'

'Mimi could go without me . . .'

'Ye ken she wouldna leave ye on your own without a Sunday dinner!' Polly scoffed. 'Now listen to me, laddie, this is 1965 we're living in. I get an old-age pension now and it's going up from three pound seven and six a week to four pounds. I can manage fine on that with the help I get with milk and bacon frae Langmune and a bit of lamb now and then frae you. If ye're that short o' money I'll draw out the bit I've got put by in the bank. You can have it to buy an electric washer for Mimi, or a cooker like Charlotte has. It never—'

'God damn it, Mother! I don't want your money!'

Polly kept her head lowered and pressed her lips together. She thought that might sting his pride. There was silence. Polly raised her head a little to peep at him. She was dismayed and filled with remorse. Willie was holding his head in his hands; she wondered if he was weeping. She got to her feet and moved round the table to his side. Tentatively she stroked the thin strands of his hair.

'I'm sorry, laddie. Maybe I shouldn't have been so . . . so blunt wi' ye. I ken ye're grieving for Mary still.' Willie sniffed hard and gulped over the lump in his throat, but it was almost his undoing when his mother pulled his head against her bosom and patted his back as she used to do when he was a young lad.

'You're right,' he said at last, struggling for control. 'I've been blind, aye, and thoughtless, where Mimi's concerned. I should give up the farm, move into the village—'

'Oh no, Willie! High Bowie is your life. You've worked so hard for it. No . . .'

'It's not the same without Mary. And you're right about Mimi. This is no life for a lassie, being a drudge on a place like this, away frae her friends and young company.'

Polly chewed her lip. Had she gone too far? Said too much? 'Mimi wouldn't want to leave ye wherever ye live, Willie. I'm sure she'll be happy enough staying here if you could see your way to making her life a bit easier – aye, and maybe accepting some o' the invitations. They'll stop asking if ye never accept.'

Willie was silent for a while, thinking, and then he lifted his head and straightened in his chair. He turned to look his mother in the eye. 'Did you walk over here especially to get me back on the road?' There was a light in his eye – not the old twinkle, not yet, nor quite his old smile either, but a relaxing of his mouth. He shook his head several times. 'I can't believe how blind I've been.'

'Can ye afford to make things a bit easier for the lassie?' Polly asked.

'Aye, I can afford it. We've always put a bit by for a rainy day, ever since the first year when we couldn't find the rent.' He shuddered at the memory.

'That was when Mary was so ill though, before Mimi was born.'

'Aye,' he nodded. 'But I wouldn't touch that. We always said it would go to Mimi if we didn't need it.'

'I reckon Mimi would appreciate things to make her life easier now, more than the money in forty years' time,' Polly said.

'Aye, but what I mean is, I don't need to touch our wee

nest egg yet. We both had a life insurance to draw out when we were sixty five, for our old age, or to pay off the farm if anything happened to us. The land is ours now and neither o' us thought of anything like this happening. The insurance company paid out Mary's money a few weeks ago. It's in the bank. I couldn't see what good money is when Mary isna here to benefit from it.'

'I think Mary would be pleased to know Mimi was getting the benefit if it makes her life easier, don't you, Willie?'

'Aye, I suppose you're right,' he sighed. Then he looked up at her with a wry grimace. 'Mothers are supposed to be right, or so you used to tell us.'

Polly hoped and prayed she had been right over this. For a few minutes there she had wondered if she had driven Willie right over the edge. She gave his shoulder another pat and went back to her chair.

'Mimi tells me she's got a provisional licence to learn to drive the car. She said she would take me home after tea. We'll not be on the main road. I'd like to see more of her when she's time to come for a wee visit. After all, I shall be seventy-six soon.'

'I'll look into things,' Willie promised, 'and I'll make sure she has time to visit ye, Mother, but we're getting into the lambing. That always makes us too busy to do much visiting.'

'Aye, but the lambing will pass, and then you must make time, Willie. I didn't want to go on living without your father, but here I am – and I'm glad to be here now.'

Later that evening Josh telephoned High Bowie.

'Have you been speaking to Mother?' Willie demanded immediately.

'Not for a couple of days. Is something wrong?' Josh asked. 'Is she ill?'

'No.' Willie took a deep breath, knowing he shouldn't jump to conclusions. 'She's fine,' he said.

'There's a couple of things I wanted to ask you, Willie. Charlotte has the Dunnett twins this weekend. Mimi is a grand help at bath time, and we wondered if you would both come to lunch on Sunday, before you get too busy with the lambing. I expect Lachie can cope for an hour or two just now?'

'Uhm . . . er . . . ah . . . Yes, I suppose we could come,' Willie said without enthusiasm, but mindful of his promise. 'What else did you want?'

Willie was abrupt, Josh thought, but at least he'd agreed to visit. 'The other thing concerns Peter. I think he would welcome a bit of advice but he seems afraid of bothering you and I'm no use to him when it comes to farming. Besides, you'll know better than anyone, being a sheep man.'

'I'd say Peter knows just about as much about sheep as I do myself now,' Willie said. 'He's doing well with his few Suffolks anyway.'

'He's keeping last season's ewe lambs for breeding so his numbers are increasing. He said something about the fields getting a build up of disease. Is that right?'

'Aye, the lambs thrive better on clean pasture,' Willie agreed.

'I often go round the sheep with him at weekends and I try to keep an eye on them during the week. He has a good job at Croston but he would still like to rent a farm of his own, even though it would mean more risk and less money. He's a hard worker.'

'Aye, I ken that. So what's the problem?' Willie's tone was brusque.

'He's been offered forty acres of land to rent but the man is already a tenant on the Croston Estate. He'd be subletting. Peter thinks there might be a conflict of interests, him being farm manager and answerable to Mr Stacey. He's considering grass lets as an alternative but I don't know about seasonal grazings and growing hay. We'll see you Sunday then? You'll talk it over with him?'

'Fair enough,' Willie said. 'Oh, and thank Charlotte for her invitation.'

Nineteen

Mimi was delighted when her father agreed to visit Uncle Josh. Lachie said he would cook his own lunch; it would be good practise for when he became a student.

She hoped Peter might be there too. She knew from his letters that he went to Lintysmill most days and that he worked with his Suffolks at weekends if they needed dosing, foot trimming or shearing. Between his own small flock and his work he seemed to have no more free time than she did herself but her heart soared when she saw him standing by the garden fence chatting to Uncle Josh. Behind them, Lucy and the twins, Rory and Robin, were romping on the grass.

Charlotte had cooked a delicious dinner with a creamy leek soup, followed by roast beef and Yorkshire pudding with several vegetables, making a colourful pattern on the children's plates and a game to see who could eat the carrot petals first, and then the cabbage grass. The pudding was a raspberry sponge with custard. Mimi enjoyed it as much as the children.

'You're a grand cook, Charlotte,' Willie remarked. 'These raspberries taste like fresh ones, but I suppose you bottled them in the summer?'

'No, they're from the deep freeze,' Charlotte told him. 'That's a lot easier than bottling. In fact Josh grows so much in the garden that we're going to buy a bigger freezer.'

'You are? I'll buy yours for Mimi, if you're selling it then.' They all looked at him in astonishment. High Bowie didn't even have a fridge yet. Willie grimaced, well aware of their reaction. 'I . . . er . . . I'm thinking we need to modernize a bit, and Mary . . .' His voice roughened with emotion, just mentioning her name. 'She was insured. The money has come through. It's time Mimi had things a bit more modern.'

He looked across at Mimi's surprised expression. 'Your Granny Pringle gave me a long lecture, lassie.' He gave a glimmer of his old wry smile. 'Your Uncle Josh is supposed to be the brainbox in the family. We'll get his ideas and we'll do it right.' Mimi couldn't believe her ears. She caught Peter's eye. He winked and grinned at her.

Charlotte declined Mimi's offer to help wash up.

'You get plenty of that every day. If you take the children into the garden I'll soon clear away the dishes.'

'I'll help Charlotte with the washing up,' Josh said. 'I believe Peter wants to pick your brains, Willie.' He grinned at his older brother, determined to get him involved. 'And I expect you would like to see how his lambs are coming along?'

'Aye, I would that. They were born early – January some of them?'

'Well, the pedigree Suffolks need to be well grown before the sales,' Peter said. 'Josh helped me erect a prefabricated shed. They run in and out and I've fed them in there all winter. I'm looking forward to the grass though.' He grimaced. 'The feed has cost quite a lot over the last three months. I shall need to sell some at a good price if I'm to break even with them, but I have two good ram lambs, or at least I think they're good. I'd like your opinion, Uncle Willie.'

Willie looked into Peter's earnest face. 'I reckon you'll be as expert at judging a Suffolk ram as I am by now, laddie – maybe better in fact. And there's no need for the "Uncle" any more. Willie will do.'

Peter realized he was being accepted as man-to-man and he was pleased.

Charlotte and Josh had finished washing up ages ago and were settled before the fire with their feet up, the Sunday paper divided between them, enjoying a rare bit of peace and quiet. Mimi loved amusing the children and they enjoyed having her sole attention. Rory and Robin Dunnett were as familiar with Lintysmill now as they were with their own home. Although they didn't realize it, their mother had a serious blood disorder and frequent visits to hospital were a necessity to prolong her life. She and her husband, John, were eternally grateful to the Pringles for their help with the boisterous twins.

Eventually Josh and Willie came back from their inspection of the sheep. Mimi had seen them standing still, deep in discussion, then strolling on again round the field, gesticulating with their hands now and then. Charlotte set out scones and gingerbread for tea but the moment he had finished, Willie said he must be getting home. Mimi's heart sank.

'Can Mimi stay to help me bathe the children?' Charlotte asked. 'Josh will run her home afterwards.'

'Please, stay!'

'Please stay with us, Mimi!' echoed the childish chorus.

'All right.' Willie nodded but Mimi was torn between her father and her longing to stay. 'You'll be back before bedtime, lassie. I'd rather not leave Lachie to do everything at High Bowie. I'll see you later,' Willie said. He had heard Mimi's laughter when he and Peter were in the field, and he realized it was a long time since she had had reason to laugh. He turned to Josh. 'Maybe you'll come up next weekend and give us your ideas on the house?' He looked around the kitchen. 'You've made a good job of your own. I heard you'd drawn some plans for a couple in the village. Lachie says they're pleased with your ideas.'

'I'll come next Saturday afternoon then,' Josh agreed. 'It's better in daylight.'

Mimi loved helping to bathe the children. All three went into the bath together amidst much splashing and giggling. Then they were all wrapped in fluffy warm towels and carried downstairs to be dried in front of the sitting-room fire. Peter had stayed too and he and Josh dried the wriggling boys while Mimi dealt with Lucy. Charlotte made supper for them all.

Afterwards, as Mimi had hoped, it was Peter who drove her home.

'It seems ages since I saw you, Mimi, or had a proper chat.' He smiled at her. She responded shyly. Peter was very much a man now, and an attractive one at that. At twenty-four he was seven years older than her and she wondered whether he still thought of her as a child. When he smiled like that the stirrings in her stomach and the beating of her heart bore no relation to the trusting friendship she had felt for Peter as a child.

'It seems a lifetime since the dance,' she sighed.

'It was fun, wasn't it? But there'll be other chances,' Peter said. 'Josh says it's a big step forward persuading your father to leave High Bowie today.'

'I think that's Granny's influence,' Mimi admitted. 'But I'm so glad he listened, both for his sake and mine. I can't believe he's going to buy Charlotte's freezer, or that he's asked Uncle Josh for ideas about our kitchen.'

'He has helped me decide what I ought to do with my sheep,' Peter said. 'I'm glad he came. I'm not going to rent the forty acres from the Croston tenant now. I was uneasy about that anyway.'

'Does that mean you'll need to sell this year's lambs then, Peter?'

'Only the ram lambs, I think. Your father knows the owner of Darlonside, the farm that lies between Home Farm and the place where he used to work. It's a Mr McNay. He's going to let most of his land for seasonal grazing in the spring. He has two sons and neither of them wants to farm.'

'It's an unfair world, isn't it?' Mimi said. 'With you desperate to farm, while they and Lachie throw away the opportunity.'

'There are compensations though.' Peter grinned and patted her knee, bringing the colour to Mimi's cheeks. 'If I get some seasonal grazing, as your father suggests, I would have the use of the land from March to November and I wouldn't need to worry about fencing or buying fertilizer and a tractor as I would if I rented the forty acres all year round. I could still rest the fields at Lintysmill to keep one fresh for flushing the ewes before putting them with the ram. The other would be clean for the young lambs. I'll buy hay as I need it. If I made my own I'd need all the machinery for handling it, then I'd have to cart it in myself. I can't afford to neglect my job as manager. Mr Stacey is very understanding and so is Sir Gerald when he's at home, but I don't want to take advantage.'

'I'm sure you'd never do that,' Mimi said.

'No?' He gave her a teasing smile. 'Maybe not over my work.' He drew the car to a halt at the side of the track leading up to High Bowie and turned to look at her. 'I've missed you, Mimi. We're such good company together. You're so easy to talk to and you never pour scorn on my hopes and dreams.' He lifted one of her hands in both of his. 'I hear you're learning to drive?'

'Yes. I've got a provisional licence, anyway. I don't know when I shall get any practice. I've been up and down the track with Libby twice and once with Lachie, but I've never been on the road.'

'I'm sure you'd manage this little car of mine. D'you think your father would let me take you driving?'

'I'd be scared of damaging your car, Peter.' Mimi looked at him wide-eyed, but she couldn't hide her excitement. He grinned at her.

'It could be fun, don't you think? It would have to be at weekends though, or in the evenings when the days get longer.'

'I wouldn't like us to quarrel if I did something stupid,' Mimi said.

'I can't imagine quarrelling with you, Mimi. We've always been friends, ever since I first arrived at Langmune.' He lifted a hand to her cheek and stroked it. 'You were always so happy and smiling. I long to make you smile again. Would you come to the pictures with me sometimes? That is if your father agrees?'

'I-I don't know. I know he likes you a lot, Peter, but I hate to leave him alone. Sometimes he looks so . . . so forlorn and bereft. It frightens me when he stares into space and doesn't speak; when he's like that he doesn't even hear when I speak to him. Maybe we should wait a wee while and see how he is.'

'All right; you're very loyal to him, Mimi, and I admire loyalty.' This was true, but supposing Mimi was making an excuse not to go with him? 'I had a visit from my sister Cathy last week.'

'Oh, Peter, that's wonderful! It's ages since you've seen any of them.'

'I never hear anything from Dinah or my stepfather. Cathy enjoyed looking round the estate and seeing what I do for work, and going round my sheep. She loved the lambs and Charlotte invited us both for tea. She couldn't believe how friendly everybody is.'

'I'm so glad,' Mimi said.

'I think she'll come again when she gets some holidays. She's training to be a nurse so I expect that pleases her father, although she says he only has eyes and ears for Dinah because she's chosen to be a doctor.'

'If ever I have children I hope I shall not favour one more than the others,' Mimi said vehemently.

'Others, eh?' Peter's dark brows arched and he smiled. 'How many are you going to have, Mimi? Have you chosen the lucky man who will be their father?'

'O-oh, you know what I mean, Peter,' Mimi said, blushing.

Peter trailed his fingers down her cheek and bent his head. His mouth sought hers and she did not draw away.

'I hope I understand you, Mimi.' He sighed. 'It's hard to remember you're only seventeen. We'd better get you home or your father will wonder where you are.'

Willie was half asleep in front of the kitchen fire and Lachie had gone across to Langmune to take his washing and collect his clean clothes. He was eager to tell his parents that Uncle Willie had gone to Lintysmill for his Sunday dinner. He had been more cheerful when he returned and he had showed him how to lamb a ewe when two lambs were entangled and coming together. Lachie admired his skill and his patience. He was beginning to realize there was more to being a vet than passing exams at university. He would need a lot of practical experience if he was to be a good vet.

The following Saturday, Willie was irritated to find Josh had not arrived when he came in for his afternoon tea.

'He said he wanted to see things in daylight,' he grumbled, 'so what's he playing at? It's three o'clock already and I've a lot of things to do before dark. The ewes are lambing faster now. Josh should know we don't keep hill sheep inside at lambing time. They take a lot of getting round, and Lachie's away at the football match this afternoon.'

'Maybe Uncle Josh has forgotten he promised to come,' Mimi said. But before Willie had buttered his scone there was the sound of a car. Mimi's heartbeat quickened as she looked out of the kitchen window. It was Peter's car and Uncle Josh was sitting beside him. She hoped her father would not be too grumpy and short-tempered with them. She met them at the door and Josh raised his brows in silent query but he understood when Mimi chewed on her lower lip. He hurried into the kitchen.

'Sorry we're a bit late, Willie, but I know you've a lot to do so I've brought Peter with me to hold the measuring tape while we make a note of sizes. We'll not hold you back. Once I've got everything measured up it will give me time to see what can be fitted in and then we can decide what you want.'

'I told you, I'm doing this for Mimi,' Willie said. 'You should know what's needed to make things right for her. I want her to have things as modern as Charlotte and Victoria and Libby. And if you've any other ideas while you're here you can tell me.'

Mimi drew in her breath and frowned. 'I thought we were only having a new cooker and electric washing machine.' She tried to banish her unwanted thoughts but a shadow clouded her blue eyes. Her father would be hurt and Uncle Josh would consider her ungrateful if they knew what was on her mind. Josh smiled at her.

'We'll discuss it,' he said. 'I thought Peter might take Mimi for a driving lesson after supper while you and I talk over my suggestions, Willie? I've brought some catalogues from Dumfries to show you.'

'Sit down first and have a cup of tea,' Mimi urged. 'I've just brewed it for Dad.'

'Thanks, Mimi. That's just what I need,' Uncle Josh smiled at her and gave her a wink. 'Charlotte has taken my car into Dumfries to get Lucy some new shoes. It's not often she has Lucy on her own these days so it's a good chance for her to do some shopping.'

'I'll leave you to it then,' Willie said, pushing his chair back. 'I like to have a last look round the hill while it's still light.'

Josh and Peter praised Mimi's scones and gingerbread and helped her clear the table.

'I've the hens and things to tend,' she said, 'so I'll leave you now.'

'Hey, Mimi, before you go.' Peter put a hand on her arm. 'How would you like to drive into Dumfries and go to the cinema? If we went to the first house we wouldn't be late back. That would be all right, wouldn't it, Josh?'

'It's all right for me.' Josh nodded. 'I'd like a good talk with your father, Mimi. I'm wondering if he knows what he's letting himself in for, with the upheaval and the expense.'

'Please don't let him spend more than he can afford, Uncle Josh. It would be lovely to have a cooker like yours and an electric washing machine but I don't need anything else.'

'All right,' Josh promised. 'Don't look so anxious, Mimi. I'm sure Willie will never get into debt over house improvements, though I know he wants the best for you.' He grinned. 'And who can blame him, eh, Peter?'

'Who indeed?' Peter smiled at her. 'We'll need to eat early if we're going out . . .'

'That's all right. I'll go and see to my hens and collect the eggs. I've boiled a piece of ham for supper and there's lots of chutney in the pantry.' Her face clouded, thinking of her mother bottling the summer fruits and making the chutney and jam. She would have to deal with all those things this year. Peter saw her pensive face.

'We don't have to go to the cinema if you don't want to . . .'

'Oh, I do! I-I was just thinking about . . . about Mother making the chutney.' Her voice shook.

'Well, Charlotte has already ordered a bigger freezer so I'll be bringing you ours soon. You'll find that a lot easier,' Josh said. 'It's hard to believe you've just left school the way you cope, lassie.'

By the time Mimi returned with her baskets of eggs Josh and Peter had measured the scullery and kitchen, the pantry and the wash house and there were sheets of paper and sketches littering the table.

'Goodness, you seem to need a lot of measurements!' she exclaimed.

'I want to do it right while I'm at it,' Josh said.

'Oh, Uncle Josh, I don't think we ought to make many alterations.'

'Don't worry, Mimi! You'll be proud of your house by the time I'm finished.'

Mimi looked at him. She would never be able to share the thoughts that were in her mind.

'I'll go and milk the two cows and then we'll have supper if you clear the table.'

'You still milk the cows? Couldn't Fraser bring you a can of milk from Langmune every couple of days? It would save a lot of time, Mimi.'

'I don't mind,' she said.

'Do you use the downstairs bedroom?' Josh asked, his thoughts reverting to his plans. He had discovered he enjoyed this sort of project since he and Charlotte had almost rebuilt Lintysmill. He studied the planning regulations and he was getting well known with the local planning department. They knew he didn't take shortcuts.

'The bedroom?' Mimi frowned. 'No, of course we don't. We haven't used the dining room or the sitting room either since . . . since . . .'

Josh nodded, understanding. 'It'll not always be like this, Mimi,' he said gently, and she wanted to cry. 'Someday you'll want to entertain your own friends, or have the family for a special dinner. Then you'll be pleased if you have a nice house.' Mimi chewed her lower lip and didn't answer. She was struggling to hold back her tears so she made her escape to the two cows in the little byre with the familiar smell of sweet hay and animals. One of the cats had kittens in a spare stall and they were adorable, two fluffy black ones with white bibs and paws, almost like twins, and the other was a tabby like a miniature tiger. She loved all the animals and she loved her home and her way of life, but did she want to stay at High Bowie forever and become an eccentric spinster? She felt restless in a way she had never experienced before. She had enjoyed each day and each season and she had never looked to the future or yearned for anything different.

'Something's troubling Mimi,' Josh said, frowning. 'I thought she would be delighted that Willie is planning to improve the house and make things easier for her. She must know he'd never do anything he couldn't afford. It will be cheaper in the long run if he does all the alterations at the same time, if he can afford it. I'm going to ask him whether he's considered putting in central heating. It's quite a decent house. It will never be anything like Home Farm and

Langmune, of course, but it's a damned sight better than Lintysmill was before we added an upstairs.'

Peter nodded. His thoughts were on Mimi, wondering what was on her mind. Was he going too fast, pushing her to go out with him? Would she tell him outright if she didn't want to go to the pictures? The last time he mentioned taking her she had said she didn't want to leave her father alone, but tonight she didn't have that excuse when Josh was here; he had seized the opportunity to have her to himself.

Twenty

Driving demanded all of Mimi's concentration and she was slower than an experienced driver would have been but Peter was patient. When Mimi parked the car between two others in the town she expelled a huge sigh of relief. Her eyes were shining as she turned towards him.

'Did I do all right, Peter?' she asked. 'I'm so relieved I didn't scratch your car or anything.'

'You did well,' Peter said, feeling his spirits rise again as he looked at Mimi's animated face and sparkling eyes. Whatever had been troubling her earlier, it couldn't have been the prospect of coming out with him. She gave him the keys but he kept hold of her hand as he locked the car and they hurried into the cinema together. The short film was in black and white and it had already begun but the usherette showed them to a couple of seats near the back. Mimi had only been to the cinema two or three times before and she gave the screen all her attention and was soon absorbed in the story, but when the heroine seemed likely to be killed she grabbed Peter's arm with both of hers and turned her face into his shoulder.

'Tell me when it's safe to look,' she whispered. Peter decided it was a good enough excuse to put his arm around her and hold her close for the rest of the film. Mimi seemed content to stay that way even when the main film came on in all its glorious Technicolor. It was a love story but there were some sad moments before a happy conclusion and Peter sensed Mimi was trying hard to prevent a few tears running down her cheeks. He wanted to gather her in his arms and kiss away her tears but he contented himself with holding her closer.

It was dark when they came out so Peter drove home, much to Mimi's relief.

'Thank you for taking me out tonight, Peter,' she said as they left the town behind and the headlights carved a path of light. 'I hope you weren't too ashamed of me for being scared. I mean, I know it's stupid and I know it's a story but it seemed so real.'

Peter gave his warm deep laugh and glanced at her. 'I can't imagine ever being ashamed of you, Mimi.'

'Can't you?' Mimi's tone was bleak. Her thoughts returned to High Bowie and all the money her father was going to spend on the house to make her life easier. She shuddered as her earlier misgivings returned. Peter would be ashamed of her if he knew how selfish and ungrateful she felt. Peter sensed her change of mood like a heavy curtain coming down. They drove on in silence until they turned on to the track leading up to High Bowie. He drew the car to a halt in the shelter of some trees.

'Did you want to come out with me tonight, Mimi?' he asked, turning towards her, his voice low and intense. He had to know, even if he didn't like her answer.

'You know I did!' Mimi turned to him in surprise.

'Would you tell me if you didn't? I mean, tell me straight, no using your father as an excuse.'

'Of course I would, Peter. But you know I don't like leaving my father alone too often. He's better since Granny talked to him but he still has awful dark times when his eyes go blank and I know he's thinking of Mother.'

'Then what is it that's troubling you? I do understand you must miss your mother too, but it's not just that, is it? You've been so brave about everything.' In the dim light of the dashboard and the sliver of silver moon Peter saw Mimi's small face twist in a spasm of pain, but then she set her firm little jaw and turned towards him.

'There's nothing troubling me, Peter. You're imagining things.'

'Is there someone else you'd rather go out with, Mimi?'

'Oh no! Of course not!' She had always loved Peter, but the way she felt now was different to the adoring ten-year-old she

had been. He would think she was crazy if she told him
though. He'd always treated her as his young friend, almost
as an adopted cousin. She chewed her lower lip.

'Then can't you tell me what's bothering you?'

'I told you there's n-nothing . . .'

'And I know you too well to believe that, Mimi. I
thought we were friends, and good friends confide in each
other.'

'We . . . we are friends.' In the dim light he saw her mouth
tremble and two tears squeezed beneath her thick lashes. He
couldn't bear to see her hurting and not know why. He pulled
her into his arms and with the pad of his thumb he wiped
away each tear in turn.

'Do you want to come out with me again, Mimi – for a
drive or to the pictures or a dance?'

'You know I'd love to, b-but I can only come when it's
c-convenient.'

'Your father, you mean?'

'Yes. Oh, Peter, I'm not a reliable companion for you. I
can't leave my father when he needs me. He loves me so
much – too much perhaps,' she added in a low voice, but he
heard.

'Nobody can ever be loved too much, Mimi. So long as
I know you want my company we'll arrange something to
suit both of us.'

'Shouldn't you be taking your girlfriends out instead of
wasting your time with me?' It hurt Mimi to say the words
and she knew her voice sounded high and brittle.

'I'll tell you when there's a girl I want to take out, Mimi
Pringle,' Peter said. 'Right now all I want is to see you happy
again.'

'I'm not a little girl anymore, Peter, skipping through days
of endless sunshine and smiling all the time.' Her tone was
as cool as his.

'I know damn well you're not a little girl!' he growled
and clasped her chin, lifting her face to his. His mouth was
hard and his kiss none too gentle but she didn't draw away.
Instead she lifted her arms and clasped them around his neck.
In the confines of the car she was pressed against his chest
and he felt her firm young breasts against him. His loins

clenched and his kiss deepened. Just as suddenly he drew away and Mimi felt as though a chill wind had swept through the car.

'I'm sorry, Mimi, I shouldn't have done that,' he said. He started up the car. They drove up the rest of the track in silence but Peter knew he couldn't leave her like that. He laid a hand on her arm as she was about to get out.

'If Josh is coming to see your father about the alterations to the house, will you come out with me again, Mimi?' She hesitated for a split second and Peter rushed on. 'I'm sorry about tonight. I promise I shall not treat you so—'

'I'd like to go out with you again, so long as Uncle Josh is here,' Mimi said. How could Peter be so blind? She longed to be with him. He had awakened some primeval desire in her and she wanted more.

When Josh and Peter had gone Willie showed Mimi a rough sketch of the changes Josh had suggested. She was dismayed.

'He's measured everything up, lassie. He thinks you would be happier if the washing machine and the deep freeze are in the scullery. He suggests we should build up the outside door and make the pantry into a downstairs cloakroom with a toilet and washbasin. The plumbing and drains are convenient for that and we could make a door into the hall. It would be right next to the downstairs bedroom.' Willie sounded enthusiastic but Mimi was silent. 'There's room for a refrigerator in here and we can still keep the big kitchen table if we put cupboards round about as Josh suggests. What d'you think, lassie?'

Mimi knew her father was expecting her to be pleased and excited. 'Won't it cost an awful lot? We don't need so many changes . . .'

'Don't you worry your head about the money, Mimi. Josh is getting estimates. The insurance money will pay for most of it. You're all I have and this will all be yours one day so I want to do things right. By the way, did you know Libby's friend, Alma, is going out with Jim MacLean, the plumber?'

'I heard a rumour,' Mimi said, but without much interest.

'Maybe Peter will need to look for a new tenant soon.'

'Mmm, maybe. I think I'll go up to bed now. Goodnight, Dad.'

''Night, lassie. Sleep well,' Willie said, his eyes returning to the plans Josh had left. He thought Mimi seemed dejected rather than enthusiastic, but maybe she was tired.

Lying in bed, alone in the darkness, Mimi's thoughts went round and round. She felt trapped, as though her life was already mapped out for her. She loved her father and he loved her, but he had always regarded her as a fragile child, ever since the polio. He was convinced she would never live a normal life as other women did, just because she was small and had a limp and a weakened hand. She had coped with most things at school, including some cruel taunts when she couldn't run as fast or jump as high as the rest of the class, but she had gritted her teeth and survived. Now she was doing most of the work her mother had done. But it was true she had never climbed to the top of the hill or gone herding the sheep with her father as she had longed to do.

Her thoughts returned to Peter. Did he realize she was no longer the little girl who had welcomed him so eagerly? Did he know about the feelings he aroused whenever he touched her, let alone kissed her? Even if he did know, and even if by some miracle he could feel the same, there was nothing to be done about it. She couldn't desert her father. She was all he had; he needed her but his life centred on High Bowie and he would never want to leave it. He was planning to modernize the house, spending a small fortune on it, and all to keep her here and happy, but she was beginning to feel as though it was a prison closing in on her. She knew she should be grateful, and she was, but the ties that bound her to High Bowie were growing too strong to be broken. She would never be able to leave. As the thoughts went round in her head she felt mean and wretched.

She thought of Peter's house, which she had been in twice. It was intended for a married man with a family and it was roomy with a small walled garden. Peter had furnished one bedroom and the kitchen and even they contained the minimum a single man required. She longed to make it into a cheerful, happy home for him but he had made it clear he had no intention of staying there as a manager for ever. His ambition was to rent a farm of his own where he could breed his sheep, graze his own land and harvest his own crops. He was prepared for a struggle and sacrifices so long as he achieved his dream. Where would he go? Would he return to Gloucestershire? It was unlikely he would ever ask her to go with him, but even if he did . . . Mimi stifled a sob and punched her pillow with a small clenched fist. Her thoughts had come full circle: even if Peter asked her to go with him she could never leave her father alone at High Bowie.

'Oh, Mother, why did you have to leave us?' she wept. In the four months since her mother's death she had managed to suppress her own sorrow and sense of loss. She had sensed that her father was struggling with his own black devils and he needed her. Now he seemed to be climbing out of the trough of despondency but Mimi felt she was slipping into it. Her mother had done her best to make sure she lived her life like every other girl her age. As a little girl she had made her persevere with the exercises which Doctor Ritchie had promised would help overcome some of the effects of the polio, and as she grew she had been diligent about buying her special shoes to help her walk straight. When her father had thought she should be wearing pretty dresses her mother had understood her desire to wear trousers to disguise the fact she had one leg thinner and less shapely than the other. She had bought her the smartest trousers she could find and several pretty tops and she had persuaded her father to let her go to the dance with Peter. Without her mother there was no one to make her father see she was growing into a woman with a woman's feelings and desires. The polio had done nothing to lessen the thrill she felt at Peter's kisses. She longed for more, even if she longed in vain.

As soon as the lambing was finished Lachie returned to Langmune and Mimi missed his company more than she had expected. They had always been good friends and shared the same sense of humour. Lachie could often make her laugh with no more than a twitch of his dark eyebrows, and he had never treated her differently from the rest of his friends.

Sometimes Aunt Victoria had remonstrated with him and told him to be more considerate but he only grinned and went on as before, and she had been more than happy to tag along. Even then she had hated to be different.

Over the weeks, a steady stream of tradesmen began to appear at High Bowie. The house seemed to be in constant upheaval but Mimi was surprised to find her father enjoyed their chats when he came in for meals. They were all local to the area and they had worked on Josh's house. Jim MacLean, the plumber, was a pleasant man and he was considerate too. Mimi mentioned this to Libby one afternoon when she called to collect a blouse that Libby had been altering for her. Mimi admitted she was not very handy with a needle, except for sewing on buttons and doing rough repairs.

'I suppose Uncle Willie welcomes their company,' Libby sighed. 'It stops him thinking so much and missing Aunt Mary. What about you, Mimi? I've never seen the watch your mother gave you.'

'No, I know. It's beautiful but I've only worn it twice. It reminded me of Mum so much I want to cry and I know she intended me to be happy. It cost ever such a lot. I know that because it was in the cheque book and we couldn't help but see it when Aunt Victoria helped me get Dad's bills up to date when he was so depressed. If I pass my driving test I thought I might enrol for evening classes in accounts at the technical college. I'd like to learn to type as well.'

'I think that's a splendid idea,' Libby said. 'In fact if there's a suitable class for me on the same night we might go together. I fancy learning to make sugar flowers or cake decorating. Mum says it's just practice but those things come naturally to her.'

'I'd like it if we could go together.' Mimi grinned. She felt the gap in their ages seemed to have lessened since her mother died. She was no longer the little schoolgirl cousin seeking help with homework.

'Speaking of driving lessons, I hear Peter has been teaching you, Mimi. If you see him, will you tell him my friend Alma is going to marry Jim MacLean and they'd like to buy the cottage? It has a big garden and Jim thinks they could extend it if it was theirs. I think it was love at first sight,' she chuckled.

'I'll tell Peter.' Mimi nodded. 'It wasn't like that for you and Billy, was it? You had always known each other, like I've known Peter for ages.' Mimi's cheeks grew pink when Libby gave her a startled glance.

'Oh, Mimi, you don't think you're in love with Peter?' she said with consternation.

'I do love him,' Mimi said with conviction.

'But, Mimi, you're only seventeen . . .' She broke off. She had not been any older than Mimi when Billy kissed her for the first time and awakened her feelings for him. She wanted to ask Mimi if Peter had kissed her but she couldn't.

'I expect you think the same as Dad, that no man will ever marry me with my lame leg and gammy hand,' Mimi said.

'No! I never thought anything like that, Mimi.' Libby got up and hugged her. 'You're so pretty; lots of boys would love to take you out. But you've never been anywhere to meet them yet. It's time Fraser and Lachie started taking you with them to some of the Young Farmers' meetings. I'll have a word with them.'

'No, Libby, please don't do that,' Mimi said. 'I can't leave Dad on his own too often in the winter so one night at the evening classes will be enough.'

'Does he watch the television?'

'He and Mum used to watch the quizzes sometimes. He doesn't have much interest in anything except the farm now. That's why the company of the tradesmen is good for him, I think. But to me, the more they do, the more it feels like a trap, binding me to High Bowie forever and ever.'

'A trap? Whatever do you mean, Mimi?'

'Granny Pringle only meant Dad to buy an electric washing machine and a cooker like Charlotte's. That would have been plenty, but he's making great alterations and spending a lot of money.'

'I know. Uncle Josh was a bit surprised at how much he wanted to do to make a nice home for you. He says it will be lovely when it's finished. You'll be real posh.' She laughed lightly but Mimi didn't. Her chin wobbled.

'I'm not bothered about being posh, and I know it sounds ungrateful and selfish, but Dad has always believed I'd never get married like other girls do. He's spending all this money so that I shall be happy to stay with him at High Bowie forever.'

'I see . . .' Libby said, chewing her lower lip. She knew Uncle Willie had convinced himself years ago that Mimi would never have a husband and children. Her mother had often argued with him about his protective attitude, and she knew Aunt Mary had been determined to give Mimi every opportunity to go out and meet people and enjoy herself like other teenagers, but Aunt Mary was no longer there to fight for Mimi. 'I think the company of the young farmers would be good for you,' she said with an air of determination. 'In fact I'll ask Mum if she'll have my two rascals to stay overnight with Molly and we'll all go to the next big dance. That will be the Harvest Home Dance. I expect Peter will be there too.'

'Dad doesn't think I'm able to dance. I'm not very good at it either, but Peter is so patient.'

'Yes, I can imagine he would be.' Libby nodded.

Now that the seed had been sown, all sorts of things fell into place. She wondered if Josh had already guessed how Mimi felt about Peter. He didn't miss much and he had rather encouraged Peter to go to High Bowie and to take Mimi for driving lessons. Her heart ached for her cousin. She wondered whether Peter had any idea how she felt. She couldn't bear to see Mimi hurt.

Libby realized she could understand why Mimi might regard the improvements to High Bowie as a trap. Uncle Willie would never mean to be selfish but it wouldn't occur to him that Mimi might want to leave High Bowie to marry. He wouldn't intend to hurt her, or deprive her of a husband; it simply wouldn't enter his head. But he would not live forever either, and what would Mimi do then? Billy had told her how lonely his mother had been when he was a small boy and she lived at High Bowie.

Libby's resolve hardened. Between them they must make sure Mimi got out more and met other people. She vowed to talk to her mother about Uncle Willie's protective attitude. Her young cousin might have one leg and one hand weaker than the other but she could do most things and she was intelligent too. She had a slender figure, which most women would envy, as well as a lovely face and pretty blonde curls. Mimi had always had a happy, unselfish nature. Libby could imagine her being very happily married if she met the right man, but he would have to be a very special person to win Uncle Willie's approval.

Twenty-One

Mimi passed her driving test and by the beginning of September the improvements at High Bowie were almost complete, even down to hiring a painter and decorator for some of the rooms, something Willie would never have contemplated if Josh had not persuaded him. Mimi had to admit everything was a vast improvement and so much easier to look after. Her father had even sold the two cows; they bought milk from Langmune now instead.

Peter sold six pedigree ram lambs at the Kelso sales and achieved one of the best averages. He was becoming known as a breeder of good Suffolk stock. Willie had accompanied him to the sale and enjoyed the experience. The Croston Estate lambs had also done well and earned Peter high praise from Mr Stacey, the factor. He was always careful not to neglect his work as manager in favour of his own small flock and the factor appreciated his reliability, even while he accepted Peter's ambition to move on to a farm of his own.

Libby and Mimi started attending evening classes at the end of September and Mimi was surprised when her father said he would drop her off at Home Farm and collect her there on his way home.

'He didn't say where he was going,' she said to Libby. 'He doesn't often go out in the evening.'

'Maybe he met some of the farmers at the market,' Billy suggested. 'He enjoys selling his lambs, doesn't he?'

Peter was surprised when he answered a knock at his door to find Willie Pringle on the step. He ushered him inside, apologizing for the sparse comfort. 'Would you like to have a look around the farms before it gets dark?'

'Aye, I'd like that, laddie. We can talk as we go. I knew

all the farms on Darlonachie Estate, but I've never been round the Croston Estate before. I don't want to be too late though. Mimi has started her evening classes and I said I would pick her up at Home Farm on my way back. I don't want Libby dropping her off and finding nobody at home.'

'The nights are drawing in now. It will be dark by the time the classes finish,' Peter agreed.

'Aye.' Willie climbed up into the Croston Land Rover that Peter used for work. 'I can't say that I'm looking forward to the winter nights,' he admitted, 'especially when Mimi's out.' He shuddered. 'I was never known for my imagination when I had to write stories at school, but my God I think I have too much now. When the house is dark and silent up at High Bowie and I'm there on my own . . .' He shook his head, frowning. He didn't go on but Peter had always been sensitive to other people's feelings.

'I know how you feel,' he said. 'After Mother died it was easy to imagine she was still there, leaning against the door of my bedroom the way she used to do, or I would hear the stairs creak and think she had called goodnight.'

'That's it exactly!' Willie said. 'It's a damned silly notion for a man of my age,' he muttered, 'but when it's dark you hear the old house creak, or maybe there's mice in the walls . . . I don't know, but more than once when I've been half asleep I've thought it was Mary, and then I've come to my senses. Anyway, I didn't come here to talk nonsense,' he said, sitting up straighter in his seat. 'You've a fine place here, laddie, and there's a lot to manage.'

'We have good men – well most of them – and the dairy has just been modernized this summer. I picked Uncle Andrew's brains, and Billy's, then Mr Stacey picked mine, but in the end we've settled for a milking parlour instead of a new byre. I think it is the way things will go now more of the milk is being collected by tanker direct from farm bulk tanks.'

'I was never much interested in dairying myself,' Willie admitted, 'but I like to see a tidy place and good stock. Andrew always wanted to breed dairy cows; he didn't seem to mind milking twice a day, seven days a week. Victoria helped him from the beginning. They've been a great partnership. Even when he was young he knew he wanted to marry her . . . Ah, here's the sheep. Have we time for a walk through them before it gets too dark?'

Peter drew the Land Rover into the field gateway while they strolled around the flock.

'There's one with a bad foot.' Peter frowned. 'I'll need to get the shepherd and take a look at her tomorrow.'

'There's not many days when you don't find one with something wrong, even in the best tended flocks,' Willie agreed. 'Much as I like my sheep I often think if you look at one the wrong way it'll cock up its feet and die, just to spite ye.' They both chuckled, knowing how true it was.

'Before I forget, Peter, Jim MacLean was back up at High Bowie this week to replace a washbasin. He asked if I'd have a word with you to see whether you've decided about selling your cottage. He says they don't need to buy until the spring but he'd like to get plans made. They're getting married in March.'

'Mmm, Mimi told me they're keen to buy.'

'Mimi? Has he been getting at her too? He did say he'd offer a good price.'

'He didn't talk to Mimi. It was Alma who mentioned it to Libby and she asked Mimi to mention it to me. To tell you the truth, I don't know what to do, Willie.' He fell silent, frowning. The light was fading now.

'There's nothing worrying you, is there, laddie?' Willie asked.

'We-ell.' Peter hesitated. 'It's a long story . . .'

'Maybe we should go back to the house now then. I've enjoyed looking around. Maybe you'll show me the rest if I come down next week while Mimi's at her class?'

'Yes, I'll do that,' Peter agreed.

Once back in the house Peter was conscious of the lack of comfort as he settled Willie in the only armchair, an old one from Aunt Victoria. He settled himself at the table, undecided whether Willie would want to listen to his problems when he had plenty of his own, but Willie sensed his uncertainty.

'Are ye having trouble with your work then, laddie?'

'Oh no, it's nothing like that,' Peter assured him. 'I suppose you haven't seen Mr McNay recently?'

'No. I used to see him when I was selling lambs but he has none to sell now his farm is all in seasonal grass lets.'

'He's not very happy with some of the seasonal tenants,' Peter said. 'He's considering letting the whole farm in March with a five-year lease. He asked if I would be interested.'

'That's just what you want, isn't it, Peter? What's the problem?'

'He hasn't quite made up his mind,' Peter warned, 'so I'd rather you didn't say anything yet. The trouble is he wants to keep twenty-five acres and the new stables that he built, and the house and garden.'

'Ah, of course, his wife is a pony woman. I remember now. She came from the city – Birmingham I think. Her father was a lawyer but she did well with the horse jumping. That's how Tom McNay met her. He thought she would enjoy being a farmer's wife but she never had much interest except in her ponies. I think their two sons must be the same.'

'Yes, they are, but Mr McNay is still hoping his youngest son might change his mind and decide to come home. If I took on the tenancy I'd have almost all the land and buildings, but no house. That's why I can't decide what to do about Ivy Cottage.'

'It would be too far away to be any good, wouldn't it?' Willie said. 'McNay's place is the other side of Home Farm. The two places neighbour along most of the southern boundary.'

'I know.' Peter frowned. 'That's the problem. It would be a good chance to rent the land and if I sold the cottage I could afford to buy some of McNay's machinery. I have enough capital to buy some commercial breeding sheep and a few beef cows, but I'd have no place to live. Or I could keep the cottage and sell my pedigree Suffolks to raise the capital to set up in farming.'

'Och, you would never do that, would you, Peter? You're just beginning to make a name for yourself.'

'I would sell them if it meant getting a tenancy of a farm like Darlonside.' He sighed. 'I never expected getting into farming would be all roses so I'm prepared to make some sacrifices and I know the Suffolks would bring in a fair bit of capital now I've more of them. If I don't take on the tenancy I shall be dependent on getting seasonal grass somewhere else in order to keep the number I have now.'

'Mmm, I see it's not an easy decision.' Willie frowned.

'Well, now you see why I can't make up my mind about Ivy Cottage. I've told Mr McNay I would need to know what his son intends to do by the end of January at the latest so I can give Mr Stacey decent notice if I'm leaving, but I've already mentioned what's on the cards. He says he appreciates my dilemma and my honesty.'

'Aye, I'm sure he will. Goodness me, is that the time? I'd better be off. Come up and talk things over whenever you feel like it, Peter. You know I'm no gossip. But I'd like to come down next week and see around the rest of the Croston Estate while you're here and I have the chance.' He grinned at Peter and the years seemed to fall away from his lean face.

Mimi and Libby enjoyed their weekly drive into town and the couple of hours at their respective evening classes. Willie went twice more to Peter's for a tour of the Croston Estate, but as the nights drew in Peter fell into the habit of going up to High Bowie instead.

'You have a fine comfortable house now,' he said. 'You'll not find much comfort in mine but I didn't see the point in wasting money when I knew it wouldn't be permanent.' Sometimes they had a game of chess or drafts but more often than not they discussed the state of farming, and sheep in particular. Although he went to High Bowie to see Mimi, Peter found it easy to talk to Willie about his own affairs but he was no nearer reaching a decision. Tom McNay didn't want to make any changes until he had talked to his son during the Christmas holidays.

'I doubt he's hoping in vain,' Willie said. 'The lad would know by now if he wanted to farm. Their mother insisted on sending them both away to boarding school when they should have been helping their father around the farm and learning all the time.'

Even in winter Willie was an early riser so he was ready

for bed by the time Mimi returned from her classes and made them all a drink of cocoa. Mimi looked forward to these quiet interludes with Peter in front of the fire, but he was finding it more and more difficult to curb his desire when Willie left them alone together. He longed to discover whether Mimi might learn to love him as he loved her, but he had to keep reminding himself that she was still only seventeen. After an evening spent with Willie, in his home, his conscience wouldn't allow him to betray her father's trust, but each week he looked forward to his evening up at High Bowie.

When they went to a dance or the pictures he felt more relaxed but he was finding it difficult to control the passion that writhed inside him when Mimi's soft mouth yielded willingly to his, and her body moulded against him in the most satisfying way, but he knew she was as innocent as dew on the daisy. He hoped and prayed she would never go out with any other man who might take advantage of her youthful innocence.

Two days before Christmas Tom McNay rode his stallion down to Croston to see Peter.

'That lad o' mine doesn't want anything to do with the farm,' he announced. 'If I'd any sense I'd sell up, but my family have been tenants at Darlonside for four generations. I bought it as a sitting tenant when Darlonachie Estate was sold. My wife had the stables built to suit her so she doesn't want to move away. Anyway, Peter, if you want to rent a farm without a house I'll have my solicitor draw up a tenancy agreement and a lease. There is one cottage but Hughie MacNaught has worked for me all his life and he'll be staying on to help with the stables. I can't turn him out. Do you understand, laddie?'

'Yes, I see how you're placed.' Peter nodded, chewing his lip. 'I have a cottage in the village but it's too far away when there's stock to look after, especially in the winter and during lambing and calving.'

'Aye, I understand. If you do decide to take it the rent will take account of there being no house available.'

'Thanks, Mr McNay. I'll think it over and I'll let you know by the seventh of January.'

Although the family gathered at Langmune for Christmas it was a quiet affair, bearing in mind it was just a year since Mary's death. Willie's spirits were low and Mimi's heart ached. She was wearing her pretty gold watch but every time she looked at it she was reminded of her mother. Peter had to return to Croston early. He had agreed to do the milking to allow the herdsman to have a day off with his family. Andrew and Fraser also had their cows to attend to and Lachie, home from university, went with Billy to have a look around outside.

'Perhaps we can make Hogmanay a livelier affair this year,' Libby said to her mother when the menfolk had gone to work and Mimi and Willie had returned to High Bowie. Josh and Charlotte were sitting side by side in front of the fire, watching seven-year-old Molly entertaining Lucy, Kirsty and Joe with a new game that Joe had been given for Christmas.

'I'd like to be at home at New Year,' Charlotte said. 'We're often asked to take in a child for temporary fostering at this time of year. Some of the parents seem to overindulge and there's always the odd one who turns violent and mistreats their children. We wouldn't mind keeping these wee ones overnight on Hogmanay though, would we, Josh?'

'Whatever you say, sweetheart,' Josh replied, squeezing her hand where it lay between them.

'That would be super,' Libby said. 'Fraser and Lachie and the rest of the younger ones could come to us at Home Farm. I could make a buffet supper about nine o'clock and then we could all see the New Year in. Peter will be off for New Year so he could stay overnight. I know he's careful about not drinking too much if he has to drive back.' She frowned. 'But I doubt if Mimi will come and leave Uncle Willie alone.'

'How about you and Andrew coming down to us, Victoria?' Charlotte asked. 'If you bring Willie he wouldn't be on his own and we'll see the New Year in together.'

'That's a splendid idea.'

'You could bring Libby's children and Molly with you. They can all go to bed together when they're tired.'

'All right, we'll do that.' Victoria nodded, then chuckled.

'I hope you know what you're taking on with our wee madam though, Charlotte.'

'I heard that, Mummy!' Molly said in the nearest her child's voice could manage to a growl. 'I am not a madam, I'm a girl.'

'So you are, poppet, but you knew who I meant, didn't you?' Victoria laughed.

'She doesn't miss much,' Josh agreed, watching his youngest niece with amusement. 'I think she might turn out to be the brightest of them all yet.'

'She's the most determined of my four,' Victoria said.

'Molly's always well behaved when she comes to us, and she's a great wee helper with the younger ones,' Charlotte said. 'In fact she's far more reliable and sensible than you'd expect for a seven-year-old.'

'Mmm, strange that. She tells us she's going to be a farmer like her daddy. She tells her teacher that too, at least once a week from what I can gather.'

'No harm in dreaming at that age,' Josh said.

Mimi was looking forward to Hogmanay and the party with Libby and Billy at Home Farm.

'You'll be there, Peter, won't you? Will you see her home?' Willie asked. 'I expect it will be into the early hours so you may as well stay here for what remains o' the night. You did say you wouldn't be working at Croston . . .'

'No, I'm not. Half of us worked at Christmas and the rest of the staff will be working over New Year. I'll bring my car then but if it's dry we'll leave it here, at High Bowie, and walk to Home Farm and home again afterwards. What do you think, Mimi?'

She nodded. 'I'll get my winter boots out and carry my shoes.'

'Aye, it's safer not to be driving, even on the track, if you've had a bit to drink,' Willie agreed. 'And that's what Hogmanay is all about for you young folk.'

'Oo-oh,' Mimi said, 'it's not just the young folk who like a drink at Hogmanay, Dad. I heard Aunt Victoria saying she would drive you and Uncle Andrew back from Lintysmill because neither of you would be fit to get behind the wheel.'

Willie and Peter were sitting at the kitchen table when Mimi came downstairs dressed for Libby's party. Her eyes held faint anxiety as she met Peter's and she was relieved to see admiration flare in his dark gaze. He gave her the quizzical smile and lift of the eyebrows that always made her heart beat faster, but it was her father who commented.

'Haven't you a dress to wear when it's a party, lassie?'

'I don't want to wear a dress, Dad. Miniskirts are all the fashion and I hate wearing short skirts. It's bad enough having curly hair when everyone else has short straight bobs – at least they do in all the glossy magazines.

'Oh, Mimi, your hair is lovely,' Peter said involuntarily. 'Why should it matter what's in fashion?' He turned to Willie. 'Trousers will be warmer for walking home.'

'Aye, I suppose you're right.' Willie nodded and sighed. 'The girls all wore pretty dresses, even to go to the pictures, when I was a young man. These days I don't know which is which when I'm in the town.' Mimi and Peter exchanged wry smiles.

'I'll just get my coat and gloves,' Mimi said. 'Listen! That will be Uncle Andrew's car to collect you, Dad.'

'All right, love, I'm ready. Enjoy the party and leave some lights on in the house for when we come back.'

Peter stood up as soon as Willie closed the door behind him.

'I think you look lovely, Mimi,' he said, his eyes running over the new skinny-rib sweater that clung to her slender figure like a second skin, emphasizing her firm young breasts and narrow waist. He slid his hands down her arms and clasped her fingers, holding her arms wide while his eyes travelled down to her toes. 'Are they new trousers? I should think they're wide enough to get two legs in each hole.' His dark eyes danced.

'Bell bottoms are all the fashion!'

'Don't be indignant, Mimi. If you were wearing sackcloth I'd still be pleased you're coming with me,' he whispered and drew her closer. She looked up then and the expression in his eyes made her heart race. He lowered his head and kissed her, parting her lips as his arms tightened, holding her close against the length of his lean, hard body.

'Promise me that's just for starters,' he said. 'Everybody kisses everybody at Hogmanay, so I'm booking my quota.' He reached for her winter coat and held it while she slid in her arms then he enfolded her from behind in another embrace before he turned her around to button it up, tilting her chin and stealing a quick kiss when he reached the top button. 'Wear your furry hat, Mimi; it will be cold walking home.'

She pulled it on and made a face at him. 'You're as bad as Dad.'

'It's because we lo— We care about you.'

The house at Home Farm was well lit up and they could hear a Dusty Springfield song playing in the background. Fraser and Lachie were already there with Tom Adamson, but Mimi was relieved to see Jade was not with them.

'I'm glad to see your smiling face, Mimi. At least you haven't changed while I've been away.' Tom chuckled as he hugged her exuberantly, lifting her off her feet, oblivious to Peter's raised eyebrows.

'You've only been away a term, Tom.' She laughed back at him and returned his hug. He had spent so much time at Langmune when she and Lachie were younger that he was almost like an extension to the family. She couldn't have guessed what a struggle he'd had to escape without Jade tagging along, or that Mimi's laughter was the perfect anti- dote to his sister's sullen scowl.

'Go on through to the sitting room,' Libby called. 'Steve Ritchie and June are in there and so are Jim MacLean and Alma. I've threatened to put them out if they mention selling Ivy Cottage to you tonight, Peter.' She noticed how he kept a protective arm at Mimi's back as Billy handed them a drink and led them across the hall.

'There'll be some people you know and some you don't,' Billy said cheerfully. 'Young farmers from our day, younger ones you and Fraser know. And there's an old friend of mine from Yorkshire, Mick Butler. He would like to meet you, Peter. He's interested in your Suffolk sheep and he'd enjoy a look around the Croston Estate if you can find time during the holiday.'

'Hey, no talking shop tonight,' Libby warned. 'Mimi, you

put a stop to it if they begin.' Billy grinned and ushered them over to where his friend was chatting to Fraser and one of his friends.

'Mimi?' Mick Butler said, surprised, jumping to his feet and grasping her hand in both of his before bending his tall bulk to kiss her cheek. 'My goodness, you were just a young lass the last time I saw you and now you're the prettiest young woman I've seen in a long time.' He beamed down at her. 'Don't you remember me from Libby's wedding?'

'Yes, I do remember.' Mimi smiled up at him, overwhelmed by his extravagant compliments.

'Just you watch him, Mimi,' Billy warned. 'He gobbles up pretty girls like you for tea.'

'Eh,' Mick protested. 'Anybody would think I was a wolf, and I thought you were my friend.' He was still hanging on to Mimi's hand and Peter frowned.

'You are a wolf, at least where pretty women are concerned.' Billy grinned. 'That's why you've never settled down with one.'

'I've been waiting for Mimi to grow up.' He winked at her. She laughed but she drew her hand from his firm clasp, reassured to feel Peter close behind her.

'Whew!' she breathed as she turned to him.

'Larger than life, isn't he?' Peter smiled. 'Come and talk to the bunch over there. You will know most of them, I think.' He bent closer and whispered in her ear. 'But he's right, Mimi, you are the prettiest girl here tonight. I'm glad it was me your father trusted to see you home.'

Mimi blushed. 'Peter, you're as extravagant with compliments as he is and this is your first drink.'

Libby had made a delicious buffet and Mimi was pleased to assist her with helping everyone to food and drink. Afterwards someone helped Billy wind up the long dining table and move it to one end, setting the chairs around the walls to clear the floor for those who felt like dancing. There was no doubt the house lent itself to partying better than most. It seemed no time at all before glasses were being charged to drink a toast to the New Year on the stroke of midnight, and then everyone was singing 'Auld Lang Syne' and hugging and kissing everyone else.

Fraser, Lachie and Tom were going to first-foot Granny Pringle and then down into Darlonachie village to meet more of their friends. It would be morning before they were home. Mimi was surprised to receive so many offers to see her home but she was glad Peter was with her. She was not used to alcohol and although she had not drunk a lot compared to some of the other women she felt a little light-headed as she kissed Libby goodnight and thanked her for a lovely party.

Outside it was freezing after the warmth of the house and she was glad when Peter reached out his arm and pulled her close as soon as they were clear of the lights streaming from the windows of the house. The frosty grass crunched beneath their feet and sparkled like jewels in the beam of the torchlight. Mimi felt snug and safe, tucked against Peter's broad shoulder with his arm around her waist. There was no need for conversation; they enjoyed the silence and the freshness of the night air and the closeness of each other's bodies.

They had reached the outer wall of High Bowie farmyard before Mimi said, 'It was a lovely party. I never thought I could feel so happy without Mother. Do you think she would have minded me feeling like this, Peter? And your mother, would she have been happy for you to be with us at the start of another year?'

'Dearest Mimi, I'm sure both our mothers would rejoice for us. The world would be a very sad place if we had to go on grieving for the rest of our lives.' He held open the gate for her. On the outer edge of the farm yard there was a row of stone cart sheds, built with their back to the prevailing wind and rain. Before the war they had been used to store the wooden carts and the few farm implements, but now they were used as shelters for bales of hay and straw. Peter drew her into the nearest of these and encircled her in his arms.

'All night everyone seems to have been kissing you except me,' he laughed. 'Can I take my turn please, my sweet Mimi, before we go inside? I expect your father will be home by now.'

Mimi was always honest and without pretence, and tonight

the alcohol had relaxed her inhibitions. She spoke from her heart. 'You know I would rather have your kisses than anyone else's, Peter.'

'I didn't know, Mimi, but I hoped. You were so popular I was jealous.'

'You couldn't possibly feel jealous, Peter. No one else would be as kind and patient with me as you are.' She reached up and clasped her arms around his neck.

'You don't realize how lovely you are, Mimi.' He kissed her parted lips, but tonight one kiss was not enough. He reproached himself for feeling jealous but he couldn't deny the pang of dismay he felt at the prospect of losing Mimi to other, younger fellows. Apart from her lovely face and blonde curls, her ready smile and warm sincerity would make it easy for any man to forget whatever physical disability she might have. His arms tightened. 'I don't know if I have enough patience, Mimi. I keep reminding myself you're only seventeen.'

'I shall soon be eighteen, and I don't see what age has to do with anything anyway.'

'Your father wouldn't agree,' Peter said, but he unbuttoned his coat and drew her into it, holding her close. He glanced towards the lighted windows on the far side of the farmyard, aware that Willie trusted him implicitly. Mimi slipped her arms inside his jacket and held him tightly. Then she drew back and pulled off first one glove and then the other with her small even teeth, stuffing the gloves in Peter's pocket. 'Now I can feel your ribs,' she chuckled, running her finger-tips up and down the thin material of his shirt. The effect of the wine blew away her usual shyness but she was unaware of the sensations she was arousing in Peter.

'I think two can play at that game,' he whispered against her ear. He began to open the buttons of her coat. Mimi didn't resist, nor did she object when Peter's fingers imitated her own. His arms were warm and strong and as he held her his lips moved over her soft skin, nibbling her ear lobe and nuzzling the soft hollow at her throat. He drew back a little but it was impossible to see Mimi's expression in the darkness of the shed. She snuggled closer, returning his kisses as he eased her jumper from the waistband of her slacks so

that his fingers could explore her silky skin. Mimi drew in
her breath as his fingers reached the thin material of her bra.
Peter's desire mounted like molten fire in his groin.

'You're so beautiful, Mimi,' he murmured hoarsely against
her neck. The pads of his thumbs moved over her breasts,
feeling her nipples harden in response, but still there was
that flimsy barrier and he reached around and undid the two
small hooks that held it in place. Mimi gasped against his
neck as the material was released. He hesitated then but her
arms tightened and she gave a small whimper, willing him
to go on. Everything about Mimi was so neat and perfectly
proportioned. He lowered his head and nuzzled the silky soft
skin until his mouth found the hardened nipples. He could
feel Mimi's fingers in his hair and her response was no longer
that of a girl. She was a woman, and everything he could
desire.

'Dear God, Mimi, have you any idea what you do to me?'
he groaned as he lifted his head and found her mouth again.

'I-I think so,' she whispered, and her hand moved to the
hardness he couldn't disguise. He held her closer, his hands
cupping her neat little buttocks, pressing her to him. Mimi
moved her hand between them, fumbling at his buttons.

'No, Mimi, no,' he gasped.

'N-no?' she whispered uncertainly.

'I love you, Mimi. I think I've always loved you, but this
. . . this is . . . Do you know what you're doing to me?

'I want to make you feel as . . . as wonderful as you
make me . . .'

'You are. You're driving me wild with desire for more,
and more. I want all of you, Mimi.' He buried his head against
her breast. 'I love you and if I let you have your way I
couldn't be responsible for the consequences.'

'But it is what you want, Peter?' Mimi asked. He heard
her uncertainty.

'It's what I want more than anything in the world, Mimi,
but not like this, my love. I'd never forgive myself if I took
advantage of you now, tonight, when we've both drunk
enough to drown discretion. When I take you, Mimi, I want
it to be as my wife. I don't want you to regret anything we
do.' He was speaking urgently now. 'God knows I'm tempted,

sorely tempted, to make you mine. But I can't betray your
trust, sweet Mimi, or the trust your father has in me. My
aunt and uncle have made me welcome as part of their family;
I can't let them down. Please Mimi, don't tempt me further,
for I can't guarantee I can resist.' He took her hand and held
it against him. 'Do you understand the way you make me
feel, Mimi, my darling?'

'Yes,' she whispered and her lips tickled his ear.

'We'd better go in or your father will be coming to search
for us.' They fastened each other's buttons, stopping several
times to exchange a lingering kiss. Peter hoped he had dusted
the wisps of hay from her coat.

'You must be sure to check before you wear it again,' he
warned as they made their way hand in hand towards the house.
'You can't tell folks you feed the hens in your best winter coat.'

Mimi was surprised but relieved to find her father was not
home yet. She felt everyone must know she had been kissed
and loved. She didn't feel in the least bit sleepy as she set
a pan of milk on the cooker to make cocoa. Half an hour
later as they sipped their drink at the kitchen table they heard
singing in the yard.

'I belong tae . . . Glasgae! Dear auld Glasgae toon . . .'

The back door crashed open and shut again. There was a
loud hiccup.

'There's something the maeter wi' Glasgae . . .'

Mimi's eyes met Peter's as she clasped a hand over her
mouth to stifle her laughter.

'Dad's drunk! I've never seen him drunk before.'

'He's happy tonight,' Peter chuckled. 'I don't know what
he'll be like in the morning though.'

'Whatever is he doing?' Mimi wondered and went through
to the back porch to see her father struggling to remove his
wellingtons. 'Where did you get those, Dad? You went in
your shoes . . .'

'Andrew's,' he muttered. 'We's cam 'cross th'burn. Carried
ma shoon tae kep 'em dry.' He held up one shining leather
shoe but there was no sign of its mate. Mimi guessed he had
dropped it on the way and hoped it was not in the burn. She
helped him into the kitchen. Peter stood up, keeping his face
straight with an effort.

'Happy New Year, Willie!' He held out a hand. Willie took it in both of his, blinking as he sought to focus on Peter's face.

'Th-thappy New Yer, tae 'oo tae.'

'Do you want a mug of cocoa, Dad?'

'Cocoa,' Willie echoed with a frown, as though he had never heard the word before. He blinked. 'It's ma bedtime, is't? Th-think I'll tak a g-g-glass-ss thwater.'

'You'd better drink it before you go up then,' Mimi said, hiding her smiles as she filled him a glass of cold water. He wobbled precariously, clung to the table with one hand and drank the glass dry with the other.

'Shall I help you upstairs, Willie?' Peter offered. Willie leered at him with his head on one side and began to grin. Peter guided him to the stairs and they stumbled up it awkwardly. When Peter returned to the kitchen he was grinning.

'He's sleeping in his suit. I reckon you'll need to press his trousers before he can wear them again. We're not quite as bad as that, are we, Mimi?'

'No,' she giggled. 'They must have had a good night, Uncle Andrew and Uncle Josh and Dad together.'

'Probably reliving their youth, but at least they've helped your father get through into another year, though I'll bet he has a sore head in the morning.'

'It is morning,' Mimi reminded him, 'and we're supposed to eat one of Aunt Victoria's dinners later on. You know you're sleeping in the downstairs bedroom, Peter?'

'Yes. But I'd love to tuck you up in your bed like your father used to,' he teased. He drew her into his arms and felt her tremble. His kiss was gentle. 'One day,' he said, 'we shall go to bed together with a wedding ring on your finger and your father's blessing – at least I hope so . . .'

When the euphoria of the New Year celebrations had passed and life had returned to normal Mimi realized she had allowed herself impossible dreams. She couldn't abandon her father to live in isolation at High Bowie. She could never leave him. How could he spend the day out on the hill tending his sheep, and come home hungry and weary to an empty house?

He didn't know the first thing about cooking, or washing or cleaning, and who would look after the poultry and collect the eggs and clean and pack them every day? She shivered. Her conscience wouldn't allow her to do it.

She and Libby resumed their evening classes. Libby sensed her younger cousin's dejection but she made no comment. Mimi had enough problems to sort out without her prying.

Peter couldn't believe how undecided he felt over McNay's offer of the tenancy of Darlonside land. Now that he knew Mimi returned his feelings he longed to be married to her, but even when she had her eighteenth birthday, would it be fair to tie her down to married life so soon, even if her father would agree? He had seen Mimi twice since Hogmanay and she had been subdued. Worse, she seemed to avoid being alone with him. She had denied him any opportunity to steal a kiss. He had an uneasy feeling that she was already regretting her eager responses at Hogmanay, and yet she had seemed so sure, so sincere, even allowing for the effects of the wine. He yearned for her more than ever now. He had a good job that he enjoyed; it was well paid and secure, with a substantial house which only needed a woman's touch and a little money and effort to make it into a comfortable home. He could picture living there with Mimi, just the two of them.

Until now his sole ambition had been to farm on his own, but a rented farm carried no guarantees of security or a regular income. There would only be him to do the work and no paid holidays or free weekends. He would be responsible, but that is what he had believed he wanted more than anything else in life. All his capital, and more besides, would be needed to buy stock and machinery, seeds and fertilizers, and he wouldn't even have a house if he sold Ivy Cottage to finance his venture. Who could tell what the future held? If there had been a house included with the tenancy at least he would have had some hope of offering Mimi a home by next year . . . He groaned. How could he wait a year when he loved Mimi so much?

He chewed hard on his lower lip. He had been fortunate to be welcomed by his Aunt Victoria, and he had been accepted as part of the wider Pringle family from the beginning. It was wonderful to belong and the last thing he wanted was to betray their trust by taking advantage of Mimi.

When he went to see Willie on the first night Mimi returned to evening classes he still hadn't made up his mind what to do. Willie was sympathetic.

'It's a big step to take, laddie, but if it's what you want you should seize the opportunity and don't let anything stand in your way.'

'Not even a wife?'

'A wife?' Willie's eyes widened and he stroked his chin. 'You're thinking of taking a wife are you, Peter? You've met the right girl?'

'I know who I want to marry,' Peter said, 'but I know I must wait a year.'

'It takes a lot longer than that to make your mark in farming, laddie.' Willie thought back to the time he had gone to Maggie Lennox and begged for more time to find the rent. He shuddered. 'I reckon if the lassie is the right kind o' wife she'll work beside ye and help ye, as my Mary did. There's no joy for a man living on his own on a place like this. I could never have made a go of High Bowie without Mary.'

Later, when Willie had gone to bed and he and Mimi were sitting sipping their cocoa, he sensed she was uneasy and he wondered if she was afraid he would want to love her as he had out in the cart shed on Hogmanay. He sought to re-assure her.

'Don't look so anxious, Mimi. I shall never do anything you don't want me to do. I shall not be coming up here for the next few weeks anyway. My own ewes will be lambing and I must keep as close an eye on them as I can. I love you, and I want you for my wife, but I know I must wait until you're older and I promise you can trust me until then.'

'Oh, Peter, it's not that. I do trust you. B-but you're wasting your time with me . . .' Her mouth trembled and he realized she was near to tears.

'What is it then? Are you regretting what happened between us? We did nothing so bad, you know?'

Mimi shook her head and her voice trembled. 'I can never marry you, or anyone else, Peter. I can't leave my father here at High Bowie all alone.'

Willie's words echoed in Peter's brain: 'No joy living on your own on a place like this.' He remembered Billy saying something similar about his mother too. He liked and respected Willie Pringle, but surely it wasn't right that Mimi should sacrifice her own life in order to look after her father. Or was he just being as selfish as his stepfather had always accused him of being? All he knew was that Mimi was the girl he loved and he longed to make her his wife.

Twenty-Two

Peter sighed as he considered Mr Stacey's question regarding his decision.

'Well, Peter, you know both Mr Gerald and I would like to keep you here as manager. You're doing a good job and you're not afraid to lend a hand. The men like that in a boss. But when a man has made up his mind that he wants another challenge, sooner or later he's going to move on. I have a proposition to make.'

'Oh? What sort of proposition?'

'Well, I can understand that if you sell your own cottage it would release extra capital and get you off to a good start at Darlonside. You will have to move out of your house here if you give up your job as manager. We shall need it for whoever takes your place.'

'Oh, I understand that,' Peter assured him.

'Of course you do, but Mr Gerald is willing to rent you the wee cottage down Fellow's Lane. It isn't very handy for Darlonside either but it's only half a mile further for you to travel than your own cottage would be. To be honest we both think Mr McNay should have sold the lot and bought himself and his lady a bit of land and built new stables, but . . .' He shrugged. 'That's not our business. Fellow's Cottage will be a few shillings a week for rent, or you can do a relief milking weekend once a month instead; it's very small, just a butt and ben with the addition of a small kitchen and a water closet. Anyway, you can think about it but let us know soon if you're thinking of leaving at the end of March.'

Peter did think about it. Nothing was ideal, neither a farm without a house nor a cottage more than two miles from his stock, but he only had himself to consider. It seemed he had no prospects of taking a wife. Billy had told him the land on Darlonside was every bit as good as Home Farm, according to the late Sir William Crainby. Everybody had to start somewhere. He made up his mind to see Mr McNay that evening, five days later than he had promised.

McNay seemed relieved he was taking on the tenancy. He was ready to retire and would have moved away except for his wife's insistence on keeping the stables and twenty-five acres. He had found the seasonal grazing tenants a headache and more trouble than he wanted. Peter wondered whether he was in good health. He seemed to have little interest in anything and he had lost weight.

'What would happen to my lease, Mr McNay, if you decided to move and sell the farm?'

'The farm goes to those lads of mine when I'm done with it, even though they've done nothing to deserve it,' he added. 'If it would ease your mind, lad, I'll extend the lease to seven years and have it written in that it can't be broken. If the farm was to sell in that time it would have to be with you as a sitting tenant until your lease expired.'

'I'd be happier with that guarantee,' Peter said.

'I realize things are not ideal for you as they are and you're giving up a good job to have a go at farming on your own, but I've talked it over a dozen times and my wife insists we stay in the house and keep her stables.' He gave a wry smile. 'And I have to live with her. The rest o' the buildings are not up to much. They were neglected when the farm belonged to the Darlonachie Estate. Since I bought it most of my money has gone on the stables and horses.' He sounded weary.

'You'll put it all in writing, and it'll be signed by both of us?'

'Aye, that's fair enough.' McNay nodded. 'I'll get the lease drawn up without delay and you can get your lawyer to check it before we sign, but I'm a man of my word and if I'm any judge of a man's character I reckon you're the same, from what I saw of you last summer. Willie Pringle has a good word o' you as well.'

On his way back from McNay's Peter saw Jim MacLean's van outside Ivy Cottage so he called in to tell Alma he was prepared to sell the cottage if their offer of two thousand five hundred pounds still stood. He knew that was five hundred pounds more than a similar cottage had made a few months ago, but Ivy Cottage had a much bigger garden and it would allow them to extend the house and build a shed at the back for Jim's plumbing business. Besides, he needed all the capital he could get if he wanted to keep his pedigree Suffolks. Alma and Jim were delighted he had reached a decision in their favour. Peter envied them being all set to enjoy a happy married life but he sent up a silent prayer to his unknown benefactor and to Aunt Victoria for passing on the cottage to him. His ambition was not for himself but for Mimi. He longed to be able to make her his wife.

At the end of March he received an invitation to Jim and Alma's wedding. It was a happy affair, with all the Pringle family invited.

'I'm like you, Peter,' Alma laughed. 'I'm happy to adopt them as my family. Josh is already drawing up plans for us to extend the cottage, you know.'

As they were leaving for their honeymoon, Alma tossed her bouquet over her head, in the general direction of Mimi. Molly jumped high in the air and caught it amid a great deal of laughter.

'That means you're going to be the next bride, little sister,' Libby teased.

'I'm never going to get married!' Molly declared. 'I'm going to be a farmer like Daddy.'

'That bairn o' yours has some firm ideas in her pretty head already, Andrew,' Willie chuckled.

Andrew laughed. 'I hope you appreciate how lucky you've been to have such a good-natured lassie as Mimi for your daughter. She'll make some lucky man a fine wife.'

The smile died from Willie's weathered face and his eyes were filled with sadness. 'I doubt if she'll be that fortunate,' he said. 'Unless it's somebody with his eye on her inheritance.'

'Och, Willie, don't say that. Mimi's a lovely lassie, and she's too discerning to be taken in by a scoundrel who only wants her for her money. It would be impossible for her to manage High Bowie on her own but it would make three times what you paid for it, especially now you've modernized the house. It's been a good investment whatever happens.' They went on talking but Peter moved out of ear shot and set off home.

He settled into the tiny Fellow's Cottage at the end of March and took over the tenancy of Darlonside on the first of April. He and Mr McNay had each had a valuation of the machinery, the sheep and the remaining stock of hay and straw and they reached an amicable arrangement. Peter would take over everything and dispose of anything he didn't want to keep. This saved Mr McNay the bother of arranging a farm sale. Peter was convinced the man was either ill or suffering from depression. He seemed to have no inclination to tackle anything that required effort or organization. Neither of his sons came near the farm. His wife was old enough to be Peter's mother but she was a smart woman and didn't look her age. She also fancied herself as attractive to all the opposite sex, whatever their age. Peter began to feel uncomfortable whenever she was around and he tried to avoid going near the dilapidated buildings if he knew she was in the vicinity of the stables.

Mimi finished her course in book-keeping and passed the exam. The lecturer announced that he had been asked to recommend someone for a part-time job doing the books for a small building firm. The business was growing and the young builder needed help to send out estimates, bills and keep a check on materials. Some of the other students were married women preparing to return to work, and they wanted more than two half days. Mimi considered and decided it might be interesting to have an outside interest and earn a little money as well. She approached the lecturer.

'I thought you would be going on with further studies, Wilhelmina,' the lecturer said in surprise. 'Either the next stage with evening classes or full-time accountancy. You are by far the brightest student in this group.'

'Oh no, I don't intend going any further. I wanted to learn the basics so that I can help my father with his accounts, but two half days in a different business might be interesting.'

'I'll give you the name and address of the builder then. He is a hard worker and his business seems to be doing well so you will have to be careful he doesn't give you too much to do for the time he is allowing.'

Mimi was surprised and delighted to get a job at her first attempt. It was a scruffy little office in half of a Portakabin in a corner of the builder's yard in a village near Annan. When she told her father, he was flabbergasted.

'You have plenty of work here, lassie. Do you need more money for yourself? I could make you an allowance . . .'

'No, no, Dad, it's not that. I thought it would be good for me to be a bit independent and it will be interesting to meet other people. The work should be quite easy, I think.'

Willie's car was getting old and he had been considering changing it for a Land Rover but now that Mimi would need a vehicle he thought he might need to settle for another car. He mentioned this to Josh as they relaxed after their Sunday dinner.

'Peter is buying a Land Rover so that he can pull a small sheep trailer and move his Suffolks between Darlonside and here at lambing time. Why don't you ask him how much he wants for his wee Morris? It would be just the thing for Mimi.'

'Aye, so it would,' Willie agreed, 'and I'd like a Land Rover myself. I'll see what Peter says when he comes back in from seeing his sheep. I think Mimi must have gone with him,' he added.

Josh eyed him speculatively and shook his head at the blindness of his brother. 'Mimi is with Peter. They get on well together.'

'Aye, he's always been a pleasant laddie,' Willie agreed. 'I can't understand that father of his never getting in touch with him. He never did give him the money he was due from that insurance.'

'He seems to be managing well enough without help from anybody,' Josh reflected. 'If anything he might have too much independence. He's very proud. He'll make a good husband and father one day. Don't you agree, Willie?'

'I suppose he might, if he ever gets time to look for a wife. We haven't seen so much of him since he took over the tenancy. I expect he's too busy working, but I miss his company.'

'Yes, I expect Mimi misses him too. It must be quiet for a young girl up at High Bowie.'

'I expect that's why she's taken on this job for the builder,' Willie said. 'I hope she doesn't do too much. He's a nephew of Mr Blake, who used to be manager at Home Farm in Sir William's time. His name is Ian Blake. He seems quite easy about the time Mimi starts and finishes so long as she gets the work done.'

'Is he married?' Josh asked.

'No, he lives with his mother and a younger sister. Mimi says he's the same age as Peter so he has plenty of time yet.'

'Mmm, I don't know about that. These days they don't wait as long as we did, and I don't blame them. What would you do, Willie, if he wanted to marry Mimi and take her to live in Annan, or wherever he has his business?'

'Marry Mimi?' Willie stared at him askance. Josh was not serious but he wanted to make Willie wake up and realize that Mimi was an attractive young woman as well as being capable and intelligent. She would be an asset to a businessman. Willie scowled and stared into the fire. 'Och, you're talking rubbish, man!' he growled.

Josh suppressed a smile but sometimes he wanted to shake his elder brother and tell him to open his eyes. He had sown a seed, however, and he hoped he had said enough to make Willie take notice where Mimi was concerned.

Peter sold all of his Suffolk rams at the autumn sales and he had an excellent trade. He was jubilant. He went up to High Bowie to discuss the sales with Willie since he shared his interest in sheep.

'I'm real pleased for ye, laddie, but you deserve to do well; you've worked hard since you got Darlonside.'

'I nearly sold off all my Suffolks, thinking I'd never have time to give them enough attention, and I thought I needed the capital. I'm glad I kept my ewes and sold the cottage instead.'

'What are you going to do with the money?' Willie asked.

'I'd have liked to build a decent shed.' Peter frowned. 'But when the farm is rented I don't think it would be wise. I'm certain Mr McNay is not in good health. I'd never get proper compensation for any improvements if the farm was to sell. And I wouldn't like Mrs McNay for a landlord either. I can't stand the woman.' He shuddered, remembering his last encounter with her.

Her name had come up during a conversation with Libby and Billy and he had mentioned his dislike of his landlord's wife; he was surprised at the knowing look Billy gave him. Later, when they were alone, he grinned and remarked, 'So McNay's wife made a pass at you, did she, Peter?'

'How d'you know that?' Peter asked. 'I never . . .'

'You didn't have to. I've met her and I soon got the message.'

'Mmm, well it's getting harder to avoid her. She always seems to know when I shall be around the farm buildings. Yesterday morning she appeared in the barn in her skin-tight jodhpurs. You wouldn't think she was the mother of two grown-up sons to look at her, would you?'

'No, she keeps herself in shape,' Billy agreed, 'but she has a fair conceit if she thinks fellows our age would be interested in her.'

'Well she does. She had her shirt open to her waist band and she wasn't wearing anything underneath it. She must have known I was in the barn because she came straight towards me and held her arms out wide. Of course that left nothing to the imagination. I backed away but she just came closer. She gave that flirty laugh and then she said, "Don't be shy, Peter. I would enjoy teaching a boy like you a thing or two." I didn't know where to look or what to say. I just muttered something about having a girlfriend of my own and darted past her and out of the farm yard. I tell you, Billy, I'm not looking forward to our next encounter.'

'No-o, I suppose it is a bit awkward. You weren't tempted at all then? I mean, a woman scorned and all that . . . You don't want her as an enemy in the circumstances.'

'I don't want her at all, enemy or otherwise! I just wish she would keep out of my way.'

'Maybe you should take Mimi with you to Darlonside sometimes. She's young and pretty. It might convince Mrs McNay you're not interested in a woman old enough to be your mother.'

'That's not a bad idea,' Peter agreed.

It was a cold Saturday afternoon towards the end of October when Peter drove Mimi over to Darlonside. He had taken her because he longed for her company, rather than for the

benefit of Mrs McNay. Indeed when they arrived he was
taken aback to find Mrs McNay in the barn with one of her
horses, holding him by a rein while he ate his fill from one
of Peter's bales of hay.

'Hello, Peter,' she purred in the throaty voice she seemed
to assume at will. 'I guessed you would be coming back to
feed your precious sheep this afternoon. Nero was a little
peckish but I knew you wouldn't mind if he had a teeny bit
of your hay while we waited for you. It's such a cold wind
out there . . .' She broke off as Mimi came into the barn,
cradling one of the cats she had stopped to stroke. 'Who are
you?' Mrs McNay demanded, the throaty voice discarded
for a haughty tone. Peter turned to smile a welcome at Mimi
as he reached out to draw her to his side, his dark eyes warm
with love and pride.

'This is Wilhelmina Pringle from High Bowie. Mimi, meet
Mrs McNay, the wife of my landlord. She is stealing some
of my hay for her horse, even though we filled the spare
stable for her use.' He turned to face the older woman and
his tone was cold. 'Your husband said it was as much as you
would need for the winter. He bought it from me so that
there would be no need for you to steal.'

'Oh, for goodness' sake, the way you say that anyone
would think I was committing a crime.'

'You are. My hay crop is precious and if we get a bad
winter it will all be needed. So you stick to your supply and
I'll stick to mine.' Mimi sensed the chilly atmosphere between
Peter and the woman but she knew how hard Peter had worked
to get his hay in. Uncle Andrew and Billy had each sent a
man to help him after they had finished their own but he
had insisted on paying for the labour. When it was baled and
carted inside they had all come to High Bowie to help her
father with his. She walked over to the big horse.

'You're a handsome fellow, aren't you?' she said, patting
his glossy neck. He snorted and Mimi laughed her warm low
chuckle. 'And hello to you too.'

Mrs McNay stared at her happy young face and flawless
pink and white complexion. She was lovely even without a
trace of make-up, and her blue eyes sparkled with pleasure
as she looked at the horse. Brenda McNay felt sickened by

her youthful innocence and beauty. She gathered the reins, vaulted on to the horse's back and galloped him out of the barn so fast that Mimi had to jump back to avoid being trampled underfoot.

Peter grabbed hold of her, pulling her against him, making sure she didn't fall. He gathered her into his arms and kissed her. Mimi liked the strength of his arms about her. She knew he had been as startled as she was by Mrs McNay's sudden departure.

'She's a selfish bitch,' Peter muttered. 'Thank goodness Mr McNay is nothing like her.'

They had arranged to go to the cinema but by the time Peter had finished attending to his animals a thick damp fog was beginning to envelop everything, making it difficult to see more than a few yards.

'It's not a nice night for driving far,' Peter said with an anxious frown as they made their way to his Land Rover.

'I'd be quite happy to stay home and watch the television if you would like to stay for supper. Dad has a filthy cold so I expect he'll go to bed early.'

'I'm sorry your father is ill, but there's nothing I'd like better than staying in with you, Mimi.' Peter grinned at her. 'All week I've looked forward to us having a wee bit of time together.'

Mimi smiled in the darkness. Her fear was that Peter might get tired of waiting for her. She didn't think she could bear it if he went off with someone else, even though she had told him he shouldn't wait for her.

They were both surprised to find Willie huddled over the sitting-room fire before his day's work was finished. He was shivering and he said he felt cold but his weathered cheeks showed twin patches of burning colour and his brow felt hot and clammy when Mimi rested her hand on his forehead.

'I think it's more than just a cold, Dad,' she said with real concern.

'Aye, I reckon I'll feed the pigs and bullocks, then I'll have a hot toddy and go to bed, if you'll see to the rest, lassie?'

'I'll feed the pigs and attend to the bullocks, Willie,' Peter intervened. 'I don't think you should go out again on a night like this. Tell me what they need.'

'Thank you, laddie,' Willie accepted wearily. 'I can't remember feeling so groggy before. A good night's sleep will help put me right. If the fog doesna lift you should stay the night. It's not much further to travel to Darlonside from here in the morning.'

'Thanks, I might just do that and I'll feed your livestock before I leave.'

'Don't you want to wait for supper, Dad?' Mimi asked.

'No, I'm not hungry, but maybe you'd make me a drink of hot milk and brandy, please, lassie?'

Later Mimi and Peter sat side by side in front of the sitting-room fire, glad to be in from the raw October night. They ate generous helpings of the fish pie Mimi had left cooking in the oven, followed by steamed syrup sponge and custard, a favourite of Peter's. As he spooned up the last mouthful he sighed with satisfaction.

'If only we could sit side by side like this every night at the end of the working day.' He set aside their empty trays and drew Mimi into his arms, looking forward to spending the evening together in comfort. He was grateful for Willie's invitation and relieved he wouldn't need to drive home to a cheerless house on such a foggy night.

Later, lying in bed, knowing Peter was sleeping downstairs, Mimi ached with longing. Peter had aroused her desire, taking her to impossible heights, only to draw back before either of them could reach the fulfilment of belonging. She understood why he always felt guilty when he came near to betraying her father's trust in him, especially here, under his roof, but he had also told her about his parents, how his mother had pleaded with his father to make love to her before he went to war and he had been the result.

'Somehow we must find a way to belong to each other as man and wife. First I need to establish myself as a farmer and prove that I can keep a wife. Maybe if I can do that your father will help us find a solution.'

Mimi had had to be content with this but when she was alone her heart sank and she couldn't visualize any solution that wouldn't make her feel torn between the two people she loved most in the world.

Willie's feverish cold took its toll and it was almost a

week before he felt well enough to attempt the steep walk,
even halfway to the top of the High Bowie land. Peter had
attended to everything on the Sunday morning but Uncle
Andrew had despatched Fraser to herd the sheep each day
after that, knowing Peter had his own work to do.

'Herding sheep up there is harder work than I realized,
Uncle Willie,' Fraser declared after the third day he had been
on the hill.

'Aye, this is the first time I've been unable to do it myself.'
Willie nodded. 'It's made me realize I'm not as young and
fit as I used to be. Did you notice whether they've started
planting trees over the top to the north of us, Fraser?'

'Is that what they're going to do?' Fraser asked, startled.
'I saw all the lines of ridges. It looks as though they've
ploughed deep furrows or something.'

'They're going to plant all the land further up.' Willie
nodded. 'They must be making a start.' He sighed. 'They
wanted to buy High Bowie peak as well but it's a fair area
of land to lose so I turned them down. Now I'm wondering
whether I should sell it while I have the chance. They wouldn't
come offering again once they move on. They want large
areas all together. Makes sense for the planting and for felling
the timber.'

'I didn't know they were doing any planting around here,'
Fraser admitted in surprise. 'Does Dad know?'

'No, I didn't even consider it at the time. Now I'm not so
sure. Maybe you'll tell your father I'd like to talk it over. If
I lost the hill acres it would mean going in for a smaller
flock of sheep and a different breed.'

'How would you feel about that?'

'I suppose we should all be prepared to change. I've had
time to consider these past few days. Mimi could never
manage to herd the hill and it wouldn't pay to employ a
shepherd.'

'No-o, I suppose not. I hadn't thought of that. Dad will
enjoy a talk with you. He might even decide to sell our top
field along with yours. It's pretty steep and it borders yours
and he knows I'm more interested in cereals than sheep.'

It was almost inevitable that Mimi would suffer from the
same feverish infection as her father and it kept her from

going to work at the builder's yard the following week. When she returned she was dismayed to find a pile of bills and invoices waiting for her attention. She hated getting behind or in a muddle. She decided to take sandwiches and continue working into the afternoon to catch up.

'I do appreciate you doing this for us, Mimi,' Ian Blake said, popping his head round the door of the small space he euphemistically called an office. He smiled at her. 'Keep a note of your extra time. I'm off to look at a job as a subcontractor for two new houses. I shall not be back until about six o'clock.'

'That's fine.' Mimi nodded and returned his smile. 'I'll stay until four o'clock, then I've jobs to do at home. There's plenty to keep me going here.'

She worked hard all day and felt a glow of satisfaction as she closed the last of her ledgers. The November day had never been light and now darkness was creeping in fast. As she bent to slip the ledger into its proper place she heard the door opening. 'I wasn't expecting to see you back so early, Ian,' she called without looking up. There was no reply and she glanced over her shoulder as she stood up and reached for her jacket from the back of her chair. Dick Pearson, the plasterer, stood with his arms folded, his back against the closed door, almost as though he was standing guard to keep her prisoner. Mimi felt a quiver of uneasiness. She didn't like the young plasterer, although Ian had told her he was excellent at his job and very skilled. He always made her feel uncomfortable. It was the way his eyes followed her if ever she had to cross the yard when he was loading his materials into his van. He had a fair complexion, with short red hair and green eyes. He could have been quite attractive but Mimi didn't like his receding chin and thin, rather cruel mouth.

'Is there anything I can get you?' she asked as she slid her arm into the sleeve of her jacket.

'You'll not need that on!' He grabbed hold of her and swung her round to slam her hard against the door. She gave a yelp of pain. The door was old, salvaged from some derelict building. It had an old-fashioned latch with the sharp end pointing to the inside. It pierced Mimi's shoulder. Pearson was oblivious to her pain. He was pressing her back against the door with the length of his body. She thought she was going to faint as the metal sank deeper into her flesh, even through her shirt.

'The latch,' she gasped. He didn't seem to hear but as his fingers clutched her shoulders they encountered the warm stickiness of blood. He yanked her away from the edge of the door. The rusty latch jerked ruthlessly out of her flesh with a spurt of blood. Pearson didn't care. He shoved her back against the door panel, his hands groping at the waist-band of her trousers. His intentions were clear. The prospect filled Mimi with horror and made her even more nauseous than the searing pain in her shoulder. She was sure she would faint, or be sick, or both. She struggled valiantly to hold on to her senses. There was no one to come to her rescue even if she screamed. Her strength was puny compared with his lean, hard body and muscular arms. She sagged in despair.

Twenty-Three

Pearson had a young wife and family but he revelled in the feel of Mimi's small neat body. He fastened his mouth on hers with sickening force, taking away what little breath she had. Everything went black. Mimi felt his hard bony fingers groping at her stomach, trying to push away her trousers.

Through the mists she recalled a conversation between Alma and Libby. Her knee came up with all the strength she could muster. She was as surprised as Pearson. He recoiled with a furious gasp, clutching himself. Mimi was trembling violently, but she pulled open the door and slipped through. She sobbed in fear and frustration when the sleeve of her jacket caught in it. She pulled it free and shot the bolt on the outside. She didn't wait to fix the padlock they used at night. She made a limping sprint for her car. Her hands were shaking. She dropped the keys, half sobbing as she fumbled amongst the stones and soil. Her brain hadn't registered that Pearson was locked in the office until someone came to unbolt the door. Her only thought was to get away and never come back.

Her shoulder was throbbing and she could feel the sticky blood with the tips of her fingers. Her legs were trembling so much she had difficulty pressing the accelerator. As she came into Darlonachie she saw the lights on in the doctor's surgery. Better to ask one of the doctors to look at her shoulder rather than worry her father. He must never hear what had happened.

'The surgery doesn't start for another quarter of an hour,' the receptionist began, then she saw Mimi swaying and rushed out of her cubicle, yelling, 'Doctor, Doctor!' It was Doctor Ritchie who ushered Mimi into the consulting room.

'Put your head down, Mimi,' he said. 'You'll not feel so faint. However did this happen?'

'I-I caught it on the door latch.' He helped her ease her arm out of her cardigan but the material from her blouse was caught in the wound. 'I'm afraid this is going to hurt,' he warned. 'It is surprisingly deep. It's going to need stitches. What really happened, Mimi?'

She didn't want to think, even less to talk about it. She began to shiver but she didn't make a murmur as he stitched up the jagged cut and put a dressing on.

'I'll take you across to the house. June will make you a cup of tea. You're not fit to drive. Leave your car here for tonight.' Mimi tried to protest but she was feeling light-headed now. Mimi knew June through her friendship with Libby and their children. Steve had asked her to get at the truth but it was only when they reached Libby's that Mimi burst into tears and told them both what had happened.

'H-he will st-still be locked in the sh-shed . . .'

'He deserves to be locked in a prison cell!' Libby declared furiously.

'No, no!' Mimi stood up in alarm. 'I don't want Dad to know what happened. I'm not going back there, not ever.' She began to shake again. June frowned.

'You're suffering from shock, Mimi. I think you ought to get to bed. Didn't Steve tell you to take a hot drink and a couple of aspirins?'

'Y-yes, he did.'

'I'll take her home,' Libby said. 'We'll tell Uncle Willie you've had a bit of a fall.' She knew he would never let her out of the house if he heard about this, but the man deserved to be punished. 'Are you sure you don't want anyone to know about this, Mimi?'

'Yes, yes, I'm sure. I-I couldn't bear it. And he has a wife and two children. It would be awful.'

'Dear Mimi, always thinking of other people . . .' Libby sighed.

Later, Ian Blake returned to find Dick locked in the makeshift office and cursing profusely. He said Mimi had locked him in for a joke. Ian didn't believe him and his suspicions were confirmed when Doctor Ritchie telephoned him with a warning for Dick.

'Mimi needed stitches in her shoulder. She was in shock but she refuses to report the incident. Tell Mr Pearson I shall have no such scruples if I hear so much as a whisper of anything like this again.'

The following morning Ian Blake arrived at High Bowie. Willie had set off up the hill with his dogs when he arrived so Mimi made him a cup of tea but she was adamant about giving up her job.

'I'll sack him,' Ian promised.

'No. You've told me how good he is at his job and his wife and children would suffer. I only work two mornings a week so I'm resigning now.'

'Will you keep my accounts if I bring them to you here? Please, Mimi? You've made such a difference to my business. I could bring you all the invoices and accounts once a week.' Mimi agreed to this arrangement so long as he brought them himself.

It was Christmas Eve, a Saturday afternoon, when Ian Blake arrived at High Bowie with a gaily wrapped gift for Mimi. She was talking to Peter beside one of the hen houses so Willie invited the young builder into the kitchen while he shouted for Mimi. Willie quirked an eyebrow when he saw Peter frowning at the personable young man handing Mimi a Christmas present.

'All the employees get a Christmas cockerel,' Ian grinned, 'but that would be like bringing coal to Newcastle. Anyway my sister reckons all girls like a surprise so she chose this.' Peter seemed to relax at this explanation and he sat down beside Ian at the kitchen table.

'I shall put it beneath the tree and open it in the morning,' Mimi smiled, 'but please say thank you to Christine for me.'

'Christine?' Willie repeated, frowning. 'Christine Blake? She wouldn't be the wee bairn who used to come for holidays when Mr Blake was farm manager at Home Farm?'

'Yes, that's right. We both came. Chrissie can't remember much, but I do. Uncle Henry took me everywhere with him. There used to be a cart track just before we came to High Bowie land. He said the track had once been the boundary between the two farms, but two of the best fields from the bottom of High Bowie were put on to Home Farm.'

'Aye, I've heard that story before, now you mention it,' Willie nodded. 'It's a pity they took the fields away. We could have done with them now that I'm selling the hill for planting trees.'

'You've decided to sell then?' Peter asked.

'Aye, it seems the best thing to do for Mimi's future.'

'Och, you'll have no need to worry about Mimi's future, Mr Pringle,' Ian said, winking at Mimi and giving the cheeky grin which always showed a dimple in his cheek. 'I've already asked her to go out with me but this fellow beat me to it.' He looked at Peter with a twinkle in his eye. 'I'm just waiting for her to get tired of you then I shall be up here every day.'

'I hope Mimi will never get tired of me,' Peter said without any answering smile, 'so you'll have a long wait.'

'Aye, just my luck.' Ian gave an exaggerated sigh. 'I'd better be off before you throw me out, or give me a black eye.' He wished them all a happy Christmas and went off with a cheery whistle.

Willie seemed to be deep in thought for some time after Ian Blake had gone. He was beginning to think Josh and the rest of the family were right about Mimi being an attractive girl, in spite of her limp. Neither the young builder nor Peter was the kind to pursue a girl for a bit of extra cash.

After supper, when they were sitting before a blazing fire, he brought up the subject of the cart track again.

'I'd forgotten about that old track,' he said. 'It's rough and overgrown now but it could soon be opened up again with Billy's caterpillar tractor. It wouldn't do for a car, of course, but you'd be all right with the Land Rover, Peter.'

'I would? Where does it go to?' Peter asked, wondering what was on Willie's mind.

'It goes across to Darlonside, and it used to go on through the strip of woodland. It came out behind Darlonachie Castle.'

'I see . . .' Peter frowned, still at a loss as to what was in Willie's mind. Then he saw the twinkle in his eyes.

'I know you two have always been good friends, ever since you arrived in the glen, Peter. I'm wondering if it's a bit more than friendship these days.' Willie looked from one to the other and saw Mimi blushing, looking pink and pretty. Pride swelled in his breast. Her happiness meant more to him than anything on earth. 'Was young Blake right, then?'

Mimi chewed her lower lip but Peter knew he had to seize this opportunity; it had to be a moment for truth. He didn't want to make Willie unhappy but he loved Mimi. He would always love her, and it was becoming impossible to resist the temptation of making love with her.

'I know Mimi is not nineteen until March,' he said, 'but I've known for a long time that she's the girl I want to marry. I understand you will want the best for her, Willie, but so do I. My future depends on whether Mr McNay will renew my tenancy when the lease is up, and maybe you feel that's not enough security to—'

'Whisht, laddie!' Willie held up his hand, looking into Peter's earnest brown eyes. He had always liked the lad.

'Do any of us know how secure our future is? When we came to High Bowie we had a lot less than you have, but we were prepared to work hard to make it a success. I know you're not frightened of hard work either so I've no fear on that score. All I want is Mimi's happiness and you've always treated her kindly.' He turned to look at Mimi's flushed face and bright eyes. 'What about you, lassie? What do you want?'

'I love Peter, Dad,' she said.

'Well then I reckon it's time we changed places, lad. I shall have a bit of spare capital when they pay for the land that I'm selling for forestry. They'll not start on this side o' the glen until next August. If you wait until then I reckon we could swap houses. Do you think the factor at Croston would take me on as a tenant for your cottage when you move in here?'

'Oh, but I couldn't . . .' Mimi turned to Peter, her blue eyes wide and pleading. He squeezed her shoulder and she relaxed against him.

'It would distress Mimi too much if you were to move out of your home, Willie, and I should feel like a usurper. Couldn't we change bedrooms instead of houses? I could move upstairs and you could move down? Would you be happy with us all under the same roof?'

'Won't you young folks want a house to yourselves?'

'If you're willing to share then so are we,' Peter said. 'I know Mimi would be unhappy thinking of you on your own down at Fellow's Cottage. To be honest I wouldn't like it either.'

'Peter's right, Dad. You'd be miserable without your dogs and sheep to see every day. I know that bout of flu took a lot out of you but come the spring you'll be good as new.'

'We-ell . . .' Willie frowned. 'I've worked hard all my life. I can't say I'd enjoy having nothing to do except potter in the garden.'

'Besides if you're talking about combining High Bowie and Darlonside there'd be too much work for me on my own,' Peter said. 'Is that what you were thinking of when you talked about clearing the track?'

'That was the idea. You could run the two places together, I thought.'

'But you're not ready to retire yet, Dad.'

'And I don't want to give up the tenancy. If ever it is to sell I might have a chance to buy the land as a sitting tenant.'

Willie's smile widened as he looked from one young face to the other.

'I always knew you had ambition, laddie, but you have a kind heart to go with it, and that's a fine combination in a man. I think I'll open that bottle of malt whisky and we'll drink a toast to the future as well as to Christmas. What d'ye say?'

'Oh, Dad, I'm so happy!' Mimi flung herself into his arms and hugged him as she had done as a child. His face softened and he met Peter's eyes over her head.

'Welcome to the family, Peter,' he said. 'Will you manage to wait until next autumn for the wedding?'

They were more than happy now they could plan for a future together. Having Willie's blessing meant everything to them.

Mimi was nineteen in March and Peter took her to Edinburgh for the day to buy an engagement ring and to meet his sister, Cathy, for lunch. Already everyone knew they were to be married in September. Mimi didn't feel she should have a proper wedding without her mother but both her father and

Aunt Victoria insisted Mary would have wanted her to have a day to remember. Mimi had agreed but she insisted it should be family and close friends.

When Cathy joined them for lunch she inspected the new ring and rejoiced with them.

'I wondered whether you would be my chief bridesmaid, Cathy?' Mimi asked.

'Oh, Mimi, I'd love that. Are you sure?'

'Of course we're sure. You might wish you'd refused though when you hear Lucy and Kirsty are desperate to be bridesmaids. Molly says she has only agreed to dress up and be a bridesmaid because she is cousin to both of us but we think she feels quite special.' She grinned. 'She is a real tomboy, but she has already stated her choice for a dress the colour of primroses. How would you feel about that?'

'I think it would be lovely. Maybe we could have pale green sashes or something, though I believe it is the bride who decides these things.'

'I don't mind what anyone wears. I'm just so happy we're going to be married,' Mimi said and her eyes danced as she looked across at Peter.

She's lovely and so innocent, Cathy thought, *and she must have had courage to survive the effects of the polio*. She met Peter's eyes. He looked so happy and contented. 'I can't tell you how glad I am for both of you,' she said.

'We shall send Dinah and your father an invitation,' Peter said, 'though I don't expect either of them to accept. I'd rather they didn't, unless they can be happy for us.'

'We don't see much of each other. Whatever I do it never seems to be right. I've been thinking I might apply for a place in Dumfries to do my midwifery training. Dinah is very scathing about it. She reckons there'll be no need for midwives soon, with the contraceptive pill being made available in this country. She doesn't want babies herself.'

'The world would come to an end if nobody wanted babies,' Peter scoffed. 'Dinah always had some ridiculous opinions.'

'It would be splendid if you can come to Dumfries to train,' Mimi said with enthusiasm. 'You could come out to see us whenever you have time off.' Cathy surveyed her with her head on one side.

'You know, Mimi, I really think you mean that.'

'Of course I mean it. We would love to see more of you, wouldn't we, Peter? When he first came to Langmune to stay Peter used to tell me how much he missed you.'

'Did you, Peter?' Cathy asked. Her voice quivered as she looked at him.

'Yes, but you were the only one I missed.'

'You'll never know how bleak and empty the house seemed after you'd gone,' she said. Then she gathered up her handbag and pulled on her coat. 'It's time I was going. I'm on duty in three quarters of an hour, but at the first opportunity I shall make enquiries about the midwifery courses.'

'And you'll come down to stay and discuss the wedding and things whenever you get some time off?' Mimi prompted.

'I will.' Cathy bent and hugged her. 'I think you're so lucky, Peter. You both deserve to be happy.'

Towards the end of August Willie received the money for the sale of High Bowie's hill.

'They're expecting to put up a new boundary fence next week and then they'll be ready to start draining and planting.' He had mixed feelings about the hundreds of acres of land which were being planted with trees but there had been a scarcity of wood ever since the war and from his own point of view he knew it made sense to sell the hill, even if he did have some private regrets about changing the familiar landscape.

Peter understood how Willie must feel. He wanted to show Mimi the view from the top of High Bowie before it changed forever.

'I always wanted to go when I was younger,' she sighed when he mentioned it. 'Dad used to say I'd be tired before we got halfway up. I think he was afraid I might make my gammy leg worse than it is already, so I've never been.'

'He didn't have a Land Rover then though. If you would like to try we could drive up as far as it will go. If it's too hard going you must tell me, Mimi. The wedding is in a fortnight so I don't want you exhausting yourself.' He kissed her tenderly.

'I'd like to try it. We'll not mention it to Dad though. He'd worry. On Saturday afternoon he's going down to pay Billy for clearing the cart track with his caterpillar tractor, then he's going over to see Granny. If it's dry we could go then and take as much time as we like to get there.'

'All right. If you bring some of your home-made lemonade and some biscuits we'll have a picnic and a rest before we set off down again.'

'It's not the steepness that's so bad,' Mimi puffed when the day came as she struggled to keep up. 'It's all the rough humps and hollows.'

'We're nearly at the top though. You'll think it was worth the effort,' Peter encouraged. 'There's a bit of a dip just in front and it's boggy so I'll give you a piggy back like we used to do when I ferried you across the burn.'

'I'm a lot heavier now than I was then!' Mimi protested.

'And I'm a lot bigger and stronger,' he grinned. 'Trust me.'

As they stood together at the topmost point of High Bowie they turned to look back towards the south and the way they had come. Mimi gazed in wonder at the panorama of fields and farms and cottages, the wee clumps of woodland, the burn winding its way around bends and boulders.

'I can even see the glint of the Solway Firth in the distance,' she marvelled, 'and can that be Skiddaw and the Cumberland fells?'

'I believe so,' Peter smiled. 'Was it worth the effort?'

'Oh, a hundred times.'

'I'm glad you've seen it before everything changes. I suppose the trees will make a good shelter belt for the higher fields so there will be some advantages, but it will never look the same again. I wish I had a good camera.'

'We could ask Fraser to come up soon and take a picture. He was asking what we want for a wedding present. We could suggest a framed photograph of this view.'

'That's a splendid idea, Mimi. Come on, we'll find a shel-tered cranny to eat our picnic and rest a while.'

'All right. I love it when the heather is in bloom. It gives a warm glow to the hills. It will make a lovely picture at this time of year.'

'The first time your father brought me up here I felt as though something had tugged at my soul. I never want to leave this part of the country.'

'I'm very glad to hear that, because I don't want to leave it either.' Mimi smiled. They settled side by side in a grassy hollow, shaded from the heat of the sun. Just below them they could hear the tinkle and gurgle of a spring.

'I think this is where the burn begins,' Peter told her, 'but another one comes over from Langmune and they join together further down. That's why it gets so wide in the bottom of the glen.' Mimi had tied her jacket around her waist but she removed it now to make a pillow. She stretched out and closed her eyes, a smile of sheer happiness lifting the corners of her mouth. Peter looked down at her, his own eyes filled with love. He lowered himself beside her and for a while they lay quiet, filled with deep contentment. Mimi moved her head to Peter's chest and her fingers played imaginary tunes along his neck and jaw, up to his ear and then his lips, tracing their outline with the lightest of touches. He groaned then stroked her neck. Her muslin blouse was soft and thin and Peter pushed it aside, smiling when Mimi drew in her breath as she always did in response to his exploring fingers. He moved onto his side, cradling her head in the crook of his arm as he bent to kiss her mouth.

'Oh, Peter, I do love you so very much,' she breathed, her eyes closed. He kissed the delicately veined lids but as his hand moved lower her eyes opened and he saw the brilliant blue fire that burned in them. They had often teased and touched in tentative exploration, but they had been in the darkness of the car, or by the dim light of the fire, and conscious that Willie was asleep in the room above. Today, in the bright summer sunshine, on top of the world, they felt they were the only people who existed.

Peter removed her blouse and her bra and bent his dark head to kiss each small firm breast. He felt Mimi's fingers clutch his hair, drawing his head up until their lips met, hot with desire. She tugged at his shirt and he helped her remove it so that she could rub her cheek against the curly dark hair on his chest and down to his navel. It was Mimi's fingers that opened his trousers and moments later they were naked, revelling in the feel of the grass beneath them and the touch of each other.

'How can I wait two more weeks?' Peter groaned as his mouth explored every inch of her silken skin.

'We . . . can't. This is right . . . now . . . in this place. Our bit of heaven. Please, Peter.' Mimi's breath was coming in rapid little gusts as her desire grew and Peter knew she was right. This was their special place.

Afterwards they lay together, legs and arms entwined, belonging to each other completely.

In the front pew of Darlonachie kirk, Polly Pringle rose to her feet with the help of Victoria and her walking stick. She watched with love and pride as Mimi walked down the aisle on her father's arm; this was one of the most special and satisfying moments in all her seventy-eight years, she thought. Mimi had always had a happy nature but today she looked ethereal and her face had a serene radiance. Peter turned to take her hand, his smile warm, his dark eyes alight with love and tenderness.

Unknown to any of them Willie had swallowed two generous measures of whisky before he could set out to give away his precious bairn. In his heart he knew he had not given her away. She would always be a part of him and now he could welcome Peter as a son. He was proud of them both.

'If ever there was a marriage made in heaven, this is it,' Polly whispered to Victoria as Mimi and Peter made the vows which would bind their lives together.